A World Inv

'Suppose that magic was around, that it existed – just twists and flickers of it. Suppose it strayed in from somewhere and drifted around like smoke. Maybe it might find its way into men's brains here and there – drop an image, forge a link, ignite a spark. Men would start doing strange things – painting on cave walls, for example, or burying the dead with tools in case they were going someplace. Make up stories. Wonder.'

'Hold on.' Rebecca leaned forward. 'Magic from where?'

'From a place where there was so much magic that it could afford to lose some, not even realise it had gone.

'From some place next door.'

A World Invisible

JOANNA O'NEILL

Wooden Hill Press

Published by Wooden Hill Press

Second Edition 2010

Copyright © Joanna O'Neill 2008

First published in 2008 by YouWriteOn.com

ISBN: 978-0-9564432-0-5

Prologue

THE glass lid closed quietly on the wooden base and the key turned with a soft click and scrape.

The curator clipped the ring of keys onto his chatelaine. 'And that's the last.'

'Thank the Lord.'

'Indeed.'

The men spoke with satisfaction. Their work was done, the task completed, all made safe. It was evening, and tomorrow would be bright and fresh. A good feeling.

'Nightcap before you go?'

The younger of the curator's companions murmured his apologies – his wife, the carriage ride, the time – while the older clapped his hands together and accepted cheerfully.

But the woman lingered, staring down into the display cabinet, unable quite to separate herself from this last link with all she had lost. 'Whose fingers will next touch them? Who will reverse what we have done?'

The three men paused. 'No-one at all, for at least a century, my dear Emily. Perhaps longer.'

'But some day somebody will. What will it be like? What will he see?'

Where did my darling go? What will my little Gabriel be?

Her back still turned, the woman placed her palms against her thickening waist, reaching out with her senses to the baby she was convinced would be a boy.

'Our descendants, you mean?'

Our descendants, and hers. Will she produce a son, like my Gabriel, or a daughter? How could he leave me – leave us – for her?

'Of course! If only we could have... Don't you wish you could be there with them? Go through when they go through? Don't you wonder what it will be like?'

I want to see it and feel it and taste it. I want to part the vines and smell the breeze and understand what made Uriel.

The curator laid his hand on her arm. 'Emily, not one of us will be here in a hundred years' time. All we can do is pass on the instructions. Come along now and we'll find you a cab. Or you can travel with Foster here.'

Emily Seward walked with the three men, buttoned into their great-mantles, steady and reliable and so unlike her quicksilver lover. She glanced back at the cabinet.

Then the door opened; the curator turned down the gaslight and the cabinet was lost in darkness.

Boots scraped on stone steps and collars were turned up against the night air. Partings were said at the gate and footsteps receded.

Around the door, ivy crept, delicately probing for crevices, leaves unfolding, tendrils spreading, clothing the redbrick in softly whispering green.

Chapter One

THE pencil lightly held between index finger and thumb, resting on the curled middle finger; the hand relaxed, the wrist stable, only the arm in motion as the pencil point slides over the paper and the graphite trail is laid...

A single curving line, slow and sure, winding across the white field of the page and looping back upon itself twice, ending in a delicate curl... And where before there was only paper and graphite there is now the tendril of a vine, two-dimensional but unmistakable, a true representation of a living plant saved on the page for anyone to see. What magic there is in drawing. How immensely satisfying to identify the correct place for each element and then to put it there.

Rebecca lifted her hand from the sketchbook and looked at the vine she had drawn. Not perfect, but not bad. Perhaps each element had not been put in exactly the correct place, but the places were pretty good. With her artist's eye she judged the proportions of what she had made, measuring angles and spaces and relationships, and then checked against the casket in the cabinet in front of her and the vine that had been carved in the ivory over one thousand years before.

Close. She had emphasised the tendrils over the leaves because they attracted her the most – the spirals and the curls. They almost appeared to move, to tremble in some unseen breeze.

Actually, there was a light breeze in the gallery now – or rather a draught, of course. It was fresher than the museum draughts usually were, though, with a scent of something herbal. Someone must be wearing perfume.

She glanced along the gallery but it was quiet, as the Victoria and Albert Museum often was midweek – just a couple working their slow way along the cabinets, and somebody sketching at the display in the centre. He must have come after she had got started; it was surprising that she hadn't noticed him arrive, even if she had been immersed in drawing.

He was seated with his back to Rebecca, and all she could see of him was his hair hanging forward and that he was wearing a denim shirt and jeans. Then he moved his hand to hook the hair behind his ear and the curtain was lifted revealing the extreme edge of his brow and cheek and jaw, with its impression of age (twenties) and structure (sharp-boned) and colour (lightly tanned).

Rebecca sat forward a little. Now she could see his eyelashes and from them could gauge how his attention was split between the object he was drawing and the drawing he made. She observed him observing, looking steadily at the artefact in the cabinet for eight seconds? ten? and then down at the paper while he drew what he had memorised. The proper way, Rebecca noted approvingly, the artist's way, not flicking back and forth anxiously but looking, learning, and then reproducing with confidence.

Certainly confidence because he was drawing in ink. That was intimidating. Rebecca's finished work was often in ink, but produced with time and patience in her studio; her museum drawing was in pencil. With ink there was no possibility of removing an error of proportion or perspective, every decision there on the page for good. And he appeared to be using a sketchbook in a square format. That was intimidating too. Square sketchbooks are hard to find, and – Rebecca thought, glancing down at her commonplace rectangular book – suddenly strangely desirable.

The couple had reached the end of the gallery. There was almost complete quiet – just the occasional squeak of their shoes on the polished floor and the soft rasp as the artist's – the other artist's – hand moved across the paper. He lifted his head again to study his subject and some of the hair escaped from his ear and closed his face once more from view.

Rebecca thought, He is so intent on drawing that he has no notion of my being here, just as a minute ago I wasn't aware of him. And he certainly has no idea that I'm watching him.

For a long moment, as if of stretched time, she enjoyed the sensation of being hidden from him, observing him unimpeded by good manners. Then, as she saw him move his attention once more from subject to sketch, she remembered that she should be doing the same and turned her gaze back to the ivory casket.

She had only been able to see his back, anyway.

The casket sat on its plinth, eleven hundred years old. Eleven centuries of opening and closing and being picked up and set down and now resting in this sealed glass tomb. Vines crept about its ivory lid and sides, with grapes bunched and tendrils extending, reaching out to find and grip, a network of stems and roots growing denser and deeper, drawing in and thrusting away, both together, ancient and modern, antique as the millennium-old ivory and modern as the Virginia creeper in the garden at Manorfield Road, twisting and rustling and deeply, disturbingly green...

IT was not the first time Rebecca had been interrupted in her drawing by the museum closing. Once you get into drawing, really properly into it, you lose track of time. The five minutes announcement pierced her concentration and she leaned back, stretching her shoulders, and then felt about for her pencil case. On the floor, under her stool. She slipped her pencil in, and her eye fell on the sketchbook open on her lap.

'Whoa!'

The exclamation broke from her quite involuntarily, and in the quiet gallery sounded shockingly loud. The artist glanced up.

'You okay?'

Confused and embarrassed, Rebecca stared at him.

'No. Yes. Sorry. I'm fine.'

He looked doubtful. 'Sure?'

'Yes, yes, sure. Sorry.'

What an idiot. She felt herself flush and hoped it didn't show. She saw him drop his eyes to her page before turning away.

Rebecca looked again at her drawing.

The casket had disappeared. Or rather almost disappeared, for the outline of its chunky shape was just discernable at the top of the page through the tangle of foliage that had sprawled, coiling and trailing, outwards over the double spread, ignoring and over-running the spiral binding. Shockingly, the vine had gone mad, rejecting the subordinate role of decoration and seizing the limelight. As a representation of a ninth century casket it left a lot to be desired; as a study of rampant botanical growth it was rather wonderful.

But Rebecca had no memory of having drawn it.

AT home, after the obligatory five minutes with Aunty Edie, Rebecca opened the sketchbook and looked at her work again, trying to be objective. So what if she had been daydreaming? She had drawn this whether or not she remembered each line. How good was it, that was the question.

The balance wasn't always right – here and there the flow of the stems was interrupted and the page was a little top heavy – but the drawing was strong and dynamic, and she couldn't help but feel pleased. Too much concentration, or too little? Either way, imagination had got into the mix somehow. The vine held treasures.

There were grapes and flowers and leaf buds, and there were also small birds and insects, and spiders' webs stretched from stem to stem. There was a bird's nest lined with moss and with eggs inside. And then, bizarrely, there was an area where the stems sprouted thorns and became a dog rose, with open flowers and fat rosehips, and then, further on, scalloped oak leaves and acorns. There were five cockle shells held in the stems on the right hand page, and a fair stab at a mouse's skull, like the one which, strangely, lay on Aunty Edie's mantelpiece, and what looked like the pinion feather of a largish bird – a magpie or a pigeon or a seagull.

As the drawing developed across the page a handful of seemingly random objects began to appear – objects that had no business in any vine: a compass with spidery legend; the ornate hands – but no face – of a clock; a lit candle, its flame blown sideways by an invisible breeze; a scroll of paper with ragged, deckled edges; a spool of thread; and at the foot of the right hand page, surely almost the last thing she had drawn before being jerked from her trance, a key, with simple wards but a complex, decorated handle held tight in the coils of the vine.

Weird. Imagination in over-drive. Unsettling didn't come near.

Don't think about it. Aberrations happen. Forget it.

When she told herself not to think about something, Rebecca usually succeeded. Somewhere in her past, perhaps after her mother's accident, she had learned the power of distraction and now, determined to ignore the peculiar uncontrolled drawing, Rebecca closed the book and went to see what could be turned into supper.

Her flat – flatlet, really, or a flatling perhaps – had what was surely the tiniest kitchenette in London. Anything smaller would be just a cupboard.

There was a half-sized sink with a half-sized draining board, and a single cupboard with a counter over, on which could stand a sandwich maker, a toaster, or an electric casserole. They had to take turns, whichever was in use. There was a 'fridge, and the rest of the food – bread, rice, pasta – lived in a crate on top. There was absolutely no extra space at all, and Rebecca frequently opened a can or chopped vegetables at her desk.

Still, it was home and it was wonderful, because it was in the capital and everything, or everything she needed, was close by. Since cutting her ties with home and running away to art college, Rebecca had been living rent-free in this bedsit at the top of Aunty – Great-aunt really – Edie's Edwardian house, and she knew she was immensely fortunate.

Especially since dropping out.

Rebecca settled for a toasted sandwich, and plugged in the sandwich maker to start warming up while she sliced bread and cheese and tomatoes. Thank goodness summer was on its way and salad would be refreshing again instead of just cold.

Dropping out had been inevitable, she told herself with the unassailable conviction of the pig-headed. All the high-concept stuff, all the installation art, wasn't what she had wanted at all. She knew she had talent. She had been selling work for two years by the time she left school – designs for greetings cards, playbills for amateur dramatic societies; even a series of stitched silk wall hangings after being seduced by the sheen and jewel colours of silk fabrics, which she had exhibited in a gallery in nearby Southwold.

The college hadn't offered technical lessons in draughtsmanship, focusing instead on experimentation, and after two terms Rebecca was having no more. She had surrendered her student loan and put together a portfolio of illustrations suitable for children's books to tout round the publishers, and in the meantime had been admitted to a small craft co-operative in Wandsworth where she could exhibit her stitched hangings.

It was precarious and Rebecca knew she could not have survived without Aunty Edie, so the brief chats she endured every time she left the house or returned were, she supposed, a reasonable payment. Tiresome, but fair.

Washing up later, gazing out of the window over the rows of terraced houses, Rebecca wondered yet again what would happen if she didn't find work, proper work. She couldn't sponge off Aunty Edie forever and returning home to the farm was not enticing.

Something has to come. Soon.

Chapter Two

THE diary lay in a chest, the sort of trunk used by travellers in the nineteenth century to do the grand tour of Europe's cities of culture, or perhaps on the way out to India or South Africa. This one did not look particularly battered, just a knock or two and some scuffing at the corners, and the antiquarian didn't imagine it had travelled half that far. To and from school each term, perhaps – the trunk of a boarding school boy, packed with vests and books and mother's Dundee cake.

It was full of paper – letters; school reports; magazines of short stories and novels published in instalments; bits and pieces – an invitation to someone's wedding in 1869, a calendar for 1876, what appeared to be a list of household items: key, candle, reel of thread and so on; and photographs scattered throughout, some well preserved, most very faded.

At the bottom there were three books: a leather-bound stamp album with half its pages empty – probably a schoolboy's; and two diaries, one of which was that of Edmund aged thirteen, and one of which according to the flyleaf belonged to his father, James.

This was getting more interesting. Eighteen-fifties social documents were always of interest to historians both professional and amateur, and this one was in good condition, the binding whole and unscarred, the pages intact. It had probably lain in the chest for decades, perhaps over a century, and the chest had been stored in a dry, airy loft and had suffered no damp. Most promising.

The antiquarian set the stamp album and diaries to one side to be brought to the attention of the house's owner later. The stamps would have to be valued professionally, of course. The diaries might be offered to a local historian, if the owner did not wish to keep them.

The owner did not. 'What did he do?' the young man asked, flipping through the pages. 'Anything interesting?'

'I haven't read it all,' the antiquarian said. 'But he appears to have been an archivist of some sort – a librarian, perhaps. A quiet life, I should say.'

'A bit dry.' The new owner of the house cast the diary back onto the table. 'No, I don't want it. What do you do with stuff like this? Recycle it? Or do people want old diaries?'

'Well, you might offer it to a local history society. Most would be very pleased to add these to their libraries. Would you like me to ask around?'

No appreciation of the past, the antiquarian thought, as he stowed the unwanted odds and ends in his car boot.

There was indeed a local society that was very happy to receive the diaries, and one of their members, a retired school teacher, undertook to attempt to trace any surviving descendants of James and Edmund Foster. It took some time, but with a degree of luck added to her persistence she came up with a name and an entry in the London phone book, and when she telephoned, her enthusiasm was sufficient to persuade the sole direct descendent to agree to see her the following Saturday.

THE bell rang at two minutes to four: the irritating punctuality of the conscientious. Geoffrey Foster was watching the cricket but he switched off and went to answer the door, hoping the woman wouldn't take long.

Mrs Treadwell – it had to be her, wearing that bright smile of introduction – was in her early sixties, he guessed, and probably a bit of a blue-stocking: trousers and a trenchcoat, iron-grey hair and a firm handshake. 'Joyce Treadwell. Joyce. So good of you to see me, Mr Foster.'

'Geoffrey,' Geoffrey said, forced into Christian names. He stepped aside to invite her over the threshold, and glanced surreptitiously at his watch. Would she be gone by half past? Surely by five?

He didn't offer tea. They sat in the front room, which was rarely used and therefore tidy – the television was in the back, with the recliner and the hi-fi and the pc. Joyce Treadwell cut straight to the point, at least. She drew a leather book out of her bag and offered it to him across the coffee table.

'This is the diary of your great-great-great-grandfather,' she said, taking her time over the 'great's with relish, 'or so I believe. His name was James Josiah Charles Foster, and he lived from eighteen twelve until eighteen eighty-two, mostly in London. He just missed his seventieth birthday – he died ten days before. This diary covers eighteen fifty-two.'

Geoffrey took the book, mostly because it was expected of him. It smelled old, but not rank. The pages flipped easily, containing rather beautiful forward-sloping handwriting.

'He was a librarian for the Borough of Kensington,' the woman continued. 'I checked. He was essentially an archivist, I believe, working in the records department. Everything handwritten in those days, of course. No microfiches!'

A small joke. Geoffrey produced an appropriately small smile. 'And how can I help you, Joyce?'

'Oh no, no no, I haven't come asking for help. I should simply like your permission to keep the diary in our own records department,' she said, and Geoffrey recognised another small joke. 'It is quite rare for us to receive such a thorough account of a year of a Victorian's life. It would be well looked after. But of course, if you feel you would prefer to keep it ...'

Joyce Treadwell's hands were clasped in her lap, the left one covering the right. She's got her fingers crossed under there, Geoffrey thought. 'What's in it?' he asked. 'Any scandal?'

'Not scandal, no, but he was a bit of a fantasist,' the woman admitted, enthusiastic again. Geoffrey raised his eyebrows. 'No, no, not that kind of fantasy,' she added, unabashed.

Definitely a blue-stocking.

'No, he seems to have been involved with a group of people looking for an alternate universe. Most odd. Not what you associate with Victorians at all.'

'And did they find one?'

He expected her to laugh and demur, but instead she raised her voice another notch. 'Yes, indeed they did, or so they thought! Quite extraordinary. It's all in here. And it appears he was breaking the rules by writing it down, so I suppose that is a bit scandalous!'

'Really?' Geoffrey turned the pages. 'Alternate universe.' He was becoming interested despite himself. And this batty woman was asking his permission to take his own book away? 'Well, Joyce,' he said, smiling again. 'If you don't mind I would rather like to go through this myself.' He watched her face fall. 'I'm sure I'd be very happy to let your society have it afterwards. For posterity. But I'd like to read what old James Josiah has to say first.

'It was very good of you to bring it to me.'

Chapter Three

WROUGHT iron – stark, black lines mounted on white plaster walls. After the warm, stuffy gloom of the British Galleries the brighter light and cooler air of the Ironwork Gallery was a relief, and Rebecca paused.

I could draw this.

A visitor further along the gallery moved on and Rebecca saw that there was another artist already at work.

Ah… the same artist, in fact. She hesitated, reluctant to set up close to him after their exchange the previous week. But the iron grids and bars were very appealing and filled her mind's eye with images of Sleeping Beauty's castle and Rapunzel's tower.

For a moment Rebecca dithered, and then she registered that she was dithering and immediately stopped. She set down her stool. So what if she had looked an idiot last week?

As always when wrong-footed, Rebecca took the offensive. *I will not be diverted from my chosen course. What is it they say? – to think strangers are looking at you is a kind of big-headedness because in fact they haven't noticed you at all.*

Rebecca drew. She had chosen a gate from the nineteenth century – twisted vertical bars decorated with stylised foliage - and immersed herself in the business of producing freely drawn lines that were nevertheless reasonably straight and reasonably parallel.

She was interrupted by a visitor accidentally kicking her stool in passing. She came to with a jolt and glanced at her watch. Forty minutes had gone by. She looked at her sketchbook.

It had happened again – or had begun to. The decorative foliage wrought by the Victorian blacksmith had broken free in her drawing and was curling and diving away from the bars. The page was not full – forty minutes is not such a long time – but the intention seemed clear. The last tendril stretched towards the foot of the page, cut off by the visitor's accidental kick.

A little way back it had thrown a loop around a candle. The candle flame guttered.

Rebecca took a long, careful breath. Then she raised her eyes to the gate mounted on the wall in front of her. Three heavily stylised, very formal, very rigid iron leaves tipped the ends of three rigid iron bars. Just three, and all of them symmetrical and polite. She could see no reason – there was no reason – why the gate should have become the twisting, tumbling mess on her page.

Rebecca bit her lip and closed her eyes briefly. Alright, then. No leaves at all, not anywhere, just nice, straight, parallel lines. She swivelled her stool to face directly away from the first gate and began with determination to draw the nearest example on the opposite wall. It was stark – a simple rectangle of vertical bars with only a touch of decorative pattern at the top, where the bars divided and formed a narrow grid. No softness, no detail, and definitely no leaves…

This time Rebecca actually jerked backwards, recoiling, so that her stool scraped on the floor with a noise like nails on a blackboard. No doubt everyone in the gallery stared at her, but a cold grip had taken hold of Rebecca's stomach, and her head felt buzzy and strange. The sudden movement had caused her sketchbook to slide off her lap onto the floor and she had no immediate inclination to pick it up. But somebody else did.

'Hey. Here. You okay?'

The man, the artist, had left his place and come over, hunkering down to pick up the fallen book. He smoothed the page that had become bent and Rebecca saw him start. Then he looked at Rebecca. 'Good drawing.'

Rebecca started to reply, felt a croak, cleared her throat and began again. 'Um… thank you.' She realised the man was still squatting at her level, and hastily stood up, staggering slightly before she found her balance. She felt a bit sick.

The man rose too. 'It's interesting. What made you draw the vine?'

His voice sounded casual but careful. He thinks I'm unhinged, Rebecca thought. She dared another look at the book, open in the artist's hand. The gate was there, very correct, lines straighter and more parallel than she could reasonably have hoped for without the help of a ruler, and with the grid at the top well proportioned and regular. Oddly, she had drawn the gate several times in varying scales, becoming fainter as they retreated from the foreground. She didn't remember having decided to do this, but the illusion of depth was successful.

But behind all the gates a branch of ivy was growing forward, writhing, thrusting its way between the layers of vertical bars and spreading across the white paper, bearing larger and larger leaves as it advanced.

What made me draw the vine?

'I don't... I didn't... I mean, I'm not sure. I...it sort of ...'

Rebecca made an effort, breathing in and looking up. 'I'm drawing ivy a lot at the moment,' she said. (True.) 'I like ivy.' (Not true, not any more.)

The artist returned her gaze a moment longer, then gave her a small half-smile. 'Right.' He settled the sketchbook securely in her hands, and with a little stab of shock Rebecca saw the unexpected dark pattern of a tattoo on his wrist.

It was the spiralling tendril of a vine.

I NEED a break. And food.

Pencil touching paper was out of the question, and besides, it was already gone two and Rebecca needed lunch. Apart from simple hunger, eating would give her a chance to recharge her normality cells.

The café prices at the museum were too high for her pocket, and as usual Rebecca had made her own sandwiches. She bought an apple in order to legitimise her stake at a table, and slipped onto the bench at the far end of the café, hoping for a table by herself.

Not so. Rebecca wasn't surprised to find that someone wished to share the table. She was totally surprised to see who.

'Mind?'

Rebecca, mouth full, made some kind of muffled grunt and the artist set down his coffee and slid into the chair opposite her.

'Hi.'

'Mm.'

I will not be embarrassed just because someone chooses to sit down at the same table. Even if he has witnessed me making an ass of myself. Even if he is ridiculously goodlooking.

I'll ignore him.

'Are you at art college or university?'

A chat-up line if ever there was one. Rebecca said coolly, 'Neither.'

'So you're…?'

'Freelance,' Rebecca said. 'You?'

'Same. This is a great place for inspiration. You come here often?'

Do you come here often! Despite herself, Rebecca snorted, and the artist smiled, immediately looking younger and sweeter. 'Michael,' he said, offering his hand across the table.

Okay, so ignoring him wasn't an option.

'Rebecca,' said Rebecca, shaking it.

'So,' Michael-the-artist said, 'are you working on a particular project? You're chasing vines, I couldn't help noticing.'

Vines are chasing me more like, Rebecca thought grimly. 'Not intentionally,' she said, slightly to her own surprise. Her mood seemed to be lifting, possibly helped by the fresh air that was flowing through the café. 'I'm not sure where they're coming from, to be honest.'

Or to be more honest, I don't have a clue and it's getting to me.

'Just recently?'

'This week and last week.'

When you were here.

Rebecca said with careful nonchalance, sweeping crumbs with her finger into a little heap, 'You have a tattoo of a vine.' She glanced up and saw him nod, a small movement.

Then he said, changing direction abruptly, 'Are your parents artists?'

Surprised, Rebecca said, 'No. Farmers. Well, my father's a farmer.'

'And your mother?'

'Died.' Rebecca tidied the edges of her pile of crumbs. 'When I was seven. A pile of straw bales fell on her.' She still hated saying it. Why had she even been in the barn? Why hadn't somebody stacked the bales more carefully? Why on earth was her mother married to an East Anglian farmer anyway?

'What did she do?'

It was almost as if he had read her thoughts but he seemed innocent, looking down as he picked up his cup.

'She was a singer,' Rebecca said. 'Opera.'

'Was she good?'

That was an unusual response. Most people just said, Goodness, how terrible, and then shuffled a bit, looking embarrassed, which was unnecessary as it had been twelve years ago and she had very little recollection of her mother other than a vague presence of the exotic in the old farmhouse.

Rebecca said, 'Yes, actually. ENO, and all that. She was supposed to be the next great mezzo, but then she married a farmer's son and took a few years off. She was just getting going again when it happened.'

'The farmer's son being your father?'

Rebecca looked at him sharply. 'Actually no,' she said, her voice steely 'I'm an accident. What you get if you're careless on a one-night stand.' Grief, this was turning heavy. She leaned back in her chair. 'So that's my life story. What's yours?'

This is where I get the brush-off, she thought, brazenly allowing herself to meet his gaze. He was simply astonishingly goodlooking, beautiful even – smooth skin with no sign of shadow despite being very dark haired; unusually symmetrical features; and rather long hair, of course, which kept escaping from behind his ear and which from time to time he retrieved and put back. She wondered how old he was. It felt daring to be looking at him as if he were just a normal person.

But he smiled faintly again and said, 'As I said, freelance. At the moment I'm researching into some of the exhibits. Want to hear about it?' He looked down and took a sip of his coffee, and Rebecca thought, he's pretending to be cool but actually he wants to tell me.

Perhaps he fancies me.

No way. Too old. Although, how old is he? Twenty-six? Twenty-seven? Is twenty-seven too old?

She said, 'Yes, tell me,' and was careful to eat tidily while she listened. As she listened, her credulity was stretched to the limit.

*   *   *

'YOU need to let go. Try to zone out your surroundings. Empty your mind.'

It sounded a touch Zen. They were back in the Ironwork Gallery. The footfalls of visitors echoed from the entrance hall below; distorted strains of hushed conversations. Zone them out.

'Just think 'Candle'.'

It was going to be like one of those 'Magic Eye' pictures, perhaps – let your eyes lose focus and try to see behind the image until something appears floating in front.

A candle, perhaps? But where from?

Empty mind.

Was he English? Rebecca wondered. Probably, but there was something unexpected in his accent, or perhaps in his choice of vocabulary or phrase, that seemed a touch other. Irish, could he be?

No good – zone him out.

Think Candle.

How do you think Candle? What am I doing?

He had told her he was investigating whether or not certain items in the collection had an aura. An aura, for heaven's sake, like in a séance or something. She should have said goodbye there and then, yet for some reason hadn't. She hoped it was something to do with his ease of manner, his casual shrug as he broached the subject, the suggestion of cynicism shared with her. She hoped it wasn't just because he was gorgeous.

Candle.

The iron was dull black, beaten flat and then coiled round and up to form a hollow cylinder into which the candle had been put, a slender column, its flame holding steady. No guttering. The air must be very still.

Candle.

The wax around the wick formed a circle, the edge creeping outward. Soon, Rebecca thought, it would spill; a tear of molten wax would fall over the precipice, slide down the pillar, cooling as it descended and solidifying into a hard, rippling runnel.

Candlelight wavered about her as the pool of liquid wax

wavered around the wick. Shivering light fell on dark wood and gleaming brass. Someone in the far distance was humming quietly as if to himself... or perhaps he was closer, but behind the screen at the end of the choir stalls. Rebecca tried to catch the notes, identify the music, but it was too soft. The candle tipped in her hand and a drip of hot wax fell onto her wrist. She jumped.

'Ow!'

'What?'

The artist was watching her, his eyes narrowed and intent. Rebecca looked down at her empty, open hands and the complete absence of candle, and then up again at the iron candlestick the other side of the glass, locked inside the cabinet.

'There was...' She faltered.

'There was?'

Rebecca reached forward and touched the cold glass of the display case. It was hard and solid and most definitely there.

She swallowed. 'I think I just had a vision.'

Chapter Four

'So what did I see?' Rebecca asked. Demanded really. A cup of tea had worked wonders.

The artist had taken her down the stairs to the café with his hand under her elbow, for which she had been grateful. That she had managed the steps at all seemed remarkable. Tough, she had thought to herself, that's what I am. Hallucinatory, but tough.

She had drunk the tea he bought her and eaten the chocolate wafer – chocolate being good, restorative fare – and then they had climbed a staircase and passed under an arch into a narrow gallery, a corridor, really, where vast and faded sixteenth-century tapestries hung, their images of huntsmen and hounds, and ladies sitting sideways on their horses with hawks on their wrists, protected by the gloom. Michael had said this was a quiet corner, and he was right. Few visitors entered, and those that did passed straight through with barely a glance at the tapestries. Each time this happened, Rebecca noted, Michael stopped talking. She wondered whether the visitors noticed.

'What's going on, then?' she had asked. 'What just happened?'

The artist looked older now – perhaps twenty-seven had been an underestimate. He was frowning again, and from time to time ran his fingers through his hair like a man with a problem. It wasn't reassuring.

'Has anything like this happened to you before?'

Politician's trick, Rebecca thought: answer a question with another question. *Well, I can do that too.*

'What kind of thing?'

Michael opened his hands. 'Anything – unaccountable. A premonition, maybe, or an image of something you weren't looking at. Something that made you wonder.'

Rebecca hesitated. There was something... What was she trying to remember? It had been summer ...

Oh. She had stepped outside the farmhouse in the summer, in June, intending to collect some washing from the clothesline, and had been hi-jacked by an overwhelming sense of loss. She had nearly wept without the slightest idea why and had spent the remainder of the morning with a headache.

And lavender... There had been lavender lining the path through Nanna's garden, and the smell of it still pulled Rebecca back to holiday visits when she was small. Of course, lots of people had memories nudged into action by nostalgic scents, but lavender could make Rebecca hear her Nanna's voice calling from the kitchen window, make her skin feel warm as if in sunshine, and her feet a little sore where the leather of her sandals rubbed.

Now, in the tapestry gallery, she said, 'Possibly.'

Michael nodded slightly, still with that busy-mind frown.

Rebecca said suspiciously, 'Did you know that was going to happen?'

'No. No, I didn't expect you to – well – have a vision, exactly. I thought you might get something.'

'Get something?'

'Receive something. Have an idea suddenly, while you were thinking about the candle. Like an image in your head – a building, or some place.'

Rebecca stared at him. 'Why would you think that?'

'There are certain items in this collection – in this museum – which have...a certain quality to them. Something most of the items don't have.'

He sounded, Rebecca thought, both honest and shifty at the same time, which was actually rather interesting. He seemed to be feeling his way, choosing his words with great care.

He's trying not to scare me off.

In which case, am I being stalked?

'A quality?' she repeated.

'An atmosphere that kind of hangs about them still. As I said, an aura.' He smiled, although not warmly and not very certainly. 'How can I put this? It's like a memory, a whiff of their past caught up in them, in their actual, physical mass. '

Rebecca frowned. 'Are we talking ghosts?'

He backed away swiftly from that. 'Ghosts! Hell, no, not ghosts! Just – I don't know how else to put it. Just an aura.'

Just an aura. Rebecca sighed. 'So what did I see?'

'I don't know. From the way you described it, it sounds like a church, or a chapel.'

'You don't know?'

'Me? No. I didn't see anything.'

'Oh.' Nonplussed, Rebecca considered. 'Do you usually see something?'

'No.'

'I mean, other times. Or with the other things, the other items that have an aura?'

'No. Nothing. Never.'

'Oh.'

They looked at one another. At the far end of the gallery a woman with four children appeared. The children pulled faces at the gloom and the musty, old-fabric smell, and then giggled and made spook gestures at each other. Rebecca and Michael watched them herded along the passage.

Rebecca said, 'I thought you were the expert on this. I thought you were going to explain.'

The woman smiled briefly as she passed, and then they turned the corner and were gone.

'But you don't seem to know as much as I do.'

Michael said, 'I'd like to identify these things. Find out which items have this…aura.'

He walked away from her along the gallery. He had hooked his thumbs into the back pockets of his jeans and was looking down at the floor as he moved between the great, faded hunting scenes. The last dyes to lose their colour, Rebecca had once read, were the blues and greens. There were no warm colours left in the tapestries at all, no red or gold or purple; just a spread of pale hessian browns, like old sacks, and soft turquoise and dark forest-green. It was like being in an old wood, thick with undergrowth.

'Don't you know what they are?'

'No.'

'You were guessing about the candlestick?'

'I know that one. I don't know the others.'

He had reached the end of the gallery and now began his way back, his eyes running over the tapestries but idly, not really seeing them, Rebecca thought, his mind elsewhere.

She said, 'You want me to find them for you.'
'Yes.'
Rebecca thought of the flickering candlelight and the old-wood smell and the sound of an unseen person singing. Once again she felt the hairs standing up on her arms.
'Well, I don't want to. I'm not going to. Sorry,' she added, out of habit rather than because she really was. The more she recalled the vision she had had – had suffered – the more troubling it was. How long had it taken? For how many seconds, minutes even, had her body stood in the Ironwork Gallery while her mind was somewhere quite different? She had felt chilled and shaky immediately afterwards, and was a touch wobbly even now. No way was she undergoing that again... And how many times? Did he even know how much of the collection had an 'aura'? It was crazy.
Michael had reached her again and come to a halt, his hands still hooked into his pockets. His head was tipped back so that he looked down at her even more. Rebecca steeled herself to meet his stare.
I will not be coerced into doing something I don't choose to do.
His head relaxed and his eyes dropped. He gave her a small nod, and a rueful, upside-down smile. 'Okay. I understand. No reason why you should.'
'No.' Rebecca felt awkward now, having won so easily. 'It's just that – well, it wasn't very nice,' she said, conscious of sounding lame.
'No.'
'I mean, really not nice. Horrible, actually.'
'Yes.'
'So.'
Rebecca thought with longing of the cool entrance hall to the museum, and even more of coming out of the underground station at Tooting Bec a short walk from home. She jumped as the children tumbled into view again on their return journey. They hadn't found much to interest them in the Textile Study Rooms, then – hardly surprising. They'd be happier at the Natural History Museum, Rebecca thought, amongst the dinosaur skeletons. She

cleared her throat. 'I don't know why you thought I could help anyway.'

Michael looked at her steadily. 'You've been drawing vines even when none are there.'

'What?' Rebecca said, sharply and too loudly. She regulated her voice. 'What has that got to do with it?'

But Michael changed the subject yet again. 'Your hair is very black,' he said, looking at it.

Rebecca felt surrealism taking over. She put up one hand and touched her head. 'My hair?'

Michael grimaced, and then appeared to come to a decision. He glanced at his watch. 'Is four-thirty too early to eat?'

IT was too early, but Rebecca decided to manage. They walked along the Brompton Road towards the eateries, Rebecca aware that she was self-conscious.

I wonder if people think we're a couple?

She sort of, kind of, hoped people did.

They passed a mother and small child, and the child stared, twisting round to face them as they went by. A momentary May breeze lifted an abandoned newspaper from the pavement and blew it against the railings.

They found a pizza place serving all day and took a table near the window, where Michael leaned forward on folded arms and said, 'One thing. Listen to what I say and think about it. Give me a chance. Yes?'

'Okay.'

'Okay.' Michael began. 'Do you read science fiction? Fantasy? When you were a kid, did you read C S Lewis? Stumbling through the back of a wardrobe or jumping through a picture frame into another world... Where do you guess he got those ideas? Or Lewis Carroll? Or Jonathan Swift? Where did dragons come from, and unicorns, and mermaids? Narwhals! Oh sure, lumpy creatures with faces like pillows – how did they turn into maidens with golden hair? Where did Grendel come from? Or the Minotaur in the labyrinth? Or the Cyclops?'

Rebecca narrowed her eyes, but she had been asked to listen

so she listened.

'Imagination,' Michael said, 'sure. But fed by what? The daily grind of scraping together enough food to keep alive? The patch of land a man can patrol for game? The weather, the seasons, night and day? How did that add up to flying reptiles belching fire? Where did the magic come from?'

'Well, I –'

Michael raised a finger and Rebecca shut up.

'Suppose that magic was around, that it existed – just twists and flickers of it. Suppose it strayed in from somewhere and drifted around like smoke. Maybe it might find its way into men's brains here and there – drop an image, forge a link, ignite a spark. Men would start doing strange things – painting on cave walls, for example, or burying the dead with tools in case they were going someplace. Make up stories. Wonder.'

'Hold on.' Rebecca leaned forward. 'Magic from where?'

'From a place where there was so much magic that it could afford to lose some, not even realise it had gone. Some place next door.'

'Next door!'

'In a manner of speaking.'

Rebecca drew back and folded her arms.

Michael met her stare for a few seconds, then dropped his eyes. 'I know.' He raised them again. 'It has something to do with light.'

'Light.'

'Light from the two worlds getting mixed up, or exchanged maybe. I don't honestly know, it's just something I was told by someone who also didn't honestly know, but it helps to have it put on a scientific footing.'

He sighed, and Rebecca suspected her scepticism was showing, but he ploughed on.

'Maybe one crack got a little larger, large enough to be noticed. Maybe someone was curious, wanted to see where the magic was leaking to. Suppose he levered it apart, enough to suck in his belly and slip through? What would that person look like to our world? A god? A monster? An angel?

'And what if he fathered a child? How would that child be,

and how would his children be? And his children's children? Would they feel separate from others? Different? Alone...'

'Your pizza.'

The waiter's voice was a shock. Michael moved quickly back making room for the platter.

'Alone,' Rebecca echoed.

'Until they met each other.'

Rebecca stared. Then she said, 'Is that what you mean? You think we're – you think I'm – half, I don't know, half alien?'

Michael drew back his sleeve, revealing the tattooed vine leaf.

'That's ridiculous!' Rebecca felt flushed and annoyed, as if she had been taken for a ride. 'You're crazy. I'm out of here.' She reached for her bag.

'Wait!' Michael scribbled on a card and stretched across the table to push it into her jacket pocket as she stood. 'Don't throw that away. Think some more about this when you get home. Please.'

For an instant Rebecca hesitated, tempted to take it out and throw it down. But she didn't. She'd do it later, without making a scene. She swung her bag onto her shoulder and left the restaurant.

Chapter Five

THE sensation had been growing steadily and it was beginning to get to Connor. Really get to him. His skin felt hot and itchy, as if he had come too close to an electric fire. Like your ears feel when you've been wearing headphones for too long. As if you were blushing.

Connor wasn't blushing but he felt irritated and uneasy, and he wanted to be left alone to think, instead of which his attention was being hi-jacked by the guy in the corner. Connor knew he was watching him, but every time he sneaked a look the guy turned his eyes to the stone bust in front of him or down at the book on his lap.

So what's his game? What does he know? Ah, stuff him, what do I care?

But who wouldn't care if they were being spied on by some weirdo who smelled of herbs and had his own personal air-conditioning?

The atmosphere in the British Galleries was still and slightly stale as usual except for the area around the plinth and the bust and the artist. Connor had walked by twice to confirm it – definitely cooler and somehow outdoors-ish. And another thing: every woman who had come past while Connor had been there had had to kind of drag their eyes from him in order to walk on by. Connor had seen the effort.

It was spoiling his concentration. He turned back yet again to the Civil War paraphernalia, and then on impulse changed his mind.

He crossed the floor in four strides, already speaking. 'Do I know you?'

The guy looked up, all innocence, and took his time to answer. 'No. No, I don't think so.'

'Then why are you staring at me.'

The guy raised his eyebrows. 'Staring at you? I don't –'

'Every time I turn my back. I can feel it.'

Connor saw the change in the guy's expression and knew he

had hit home.

'I haven't been watching you.' The man angled his head a fraction. 'Do you think you know *me*?' he asked, turning Connor's question around, the different emphasis removing the aggression and turning it into a genuine enquiry.

And it might be genuine. Connor's temper had begun to cool. Facing the guy, and talking to him made him feel less under attack, less violated. Perhaps he'd got it wrong after all.

'No. At least …' The guy didn't look exactly familiar. If Connor had seen him before it would have been by chance – someone in the street, or on the bus, or queuing for fish and chips. And yet there was something … and that voice, with traces of what? – Irish? American? It reminded him of someone.

Now the guy was watching him alright, and Connor recoiled, put the fence back up. 'No, never seen you before in my life.'

And then, abruptly, he had changed the subject. 'You're interested in the Civil War?' He nodded towards the buffcoat and helmet across the room.

Wrong-footed, Connor looked too. 'Yeah. Well, in a way. I'm –' He stopped himself just in time. Christ! What the hell was going on?

'You're what? Researching?'

'Yeah, yeah that's right. Researching. For a project. For school. A school project.'

The guy nodded. 'Right. Well, good luck with it.'

Connor backed a step and then turned and walked across to the buffcoat, his mind jumbled with impressions of having had his anger adroitly defused, and of the guy's easy voice and searching eyes.

Had he seen him before? What buried memory was being stirred? Why was there a disturbance in the air, a silent crackle, like static electricity? Not to mention the bloody herbs.

After five minutes, endured to prove that he hadn't been chased away, Connor gave up and left. It was a relief to be out of the guy's presence; the air was easier to breathe, less electric, and his skin could cool down. In fact he felt so much better that he stopped in the middle of the Tudor exhibits, took his notebook out of his back pocket, and started to write…

*   *   *

THAT was bizarre.

Michael stared at the delicate stone lace of the collar he had been drawing and waggled his pen between finger and thumb. After a minute he clicked the cap back on and dropped it into his shirt pocket. He closed the sketchbook and stood up, folded the aluminium stool and slid it onto the rack across the room.

Wonder how far he's gone.

Michael turned the corner and almost tripped over himself as he recognised the boy standing, head bent, in the middle of the room. What was he doing? He eased himself back round the corner.

The boy was writing, scribbling quickly. Michael watched him shift the pad upwards in his right hand as his pencil neared the bottom of the page, then peel the paper upwards and flip it over and continue with barely a pause on the new sheet.

Interesting. He was left-handed, and he used his pad like a journalist or stenographer – one side of each page all through the book, then flip and back through the book again using the reverse sides. Not many people do that. For a start it implies you intend to keep whatever you write.

As the artist observed him, the boy shrugged one shoulder, and then glanced in Michael's direction. Michael withdrew a little further. The boy rolled his shoulder again, as if easing an itch or a sore muscle, wrote some more, and then suddenly looked right round just as Michael slipped back into the seventeenth century gallery. For a moment he stood flat against the wall, feeling stupidly like a movie private eye caught in a suspect's apartment. Then he heard floorboards creak and relaxed as the boy left.

Definitely interesting. Especially as he had most certainly not been watching him.

SITTING on a bench in the entrance hall, Connor read over what he had written. It was confusing, and disturbed him.

Writing wasn't usually like this. The words should come slower, with more consideration of line length and rhythm. He usually had an idea of the form of the poem at the outset, and chose words and phrases that fitted. This was more like – well, like a stream of consciousness, really. Words had waterfalled onto the paper, punctuation and syntax ignored. Undisciplined. Like brainstorming.

And yet they were more interesting than mere notes. There were areas – whole lines – where they had strung themselves together into chains that made sense and were beautiful in the mouth. Silently, in order not to draw attention, Connor said the lines over to himself, reading off the pad, and felt the play of the consonants over his tongue and teeth, heard in his mind how they would sound aloud. This was the hardest part normally, much more difficult than the meaning and emotion; yet today he hadn't thought about it at all.

Weird.

And what was all this stuff about a graveyard? What had that to do with anything?

Well, there was a spurious connection, of course – warfare-death-burial-graves. But he had been thinking about pre-battle mental conflict and fear, not the nitty-gritty of clearing up afterwards. And his intention had been concerned with premonitions and emotions, not with what things looked like and where they were. He read it again. This was practically a set of directions – go here, do this, see that… Mad!

Disgruntled, Connor closed his notebook and stood up, only to start backwards as he found himself confronted by the guy, the artist, now striding towards him with unmistakable intent. But there was no space to step backwards into. The bench caught him in the back of his knee and before he could help himself he had sat hard down again, still staring up at the artist, who had stuck out his hand at Connor and was smiling alarmingly.

'Michael.'

Connor reluctantly shook the hand. 'Er – Connor.'

The artist sat down. Connor shifted up a fraction. The artist ignored it.

'Hi, Connor. Listen, I think you can help me with a little research of my own. It'll take five minutes, no more. Would you just come up to the Ironwork Gallery a moment?'

Inexplicably, Connor found himself climbing the stairs, defeated by the bulldozing confidence of the guy, who hadn't stopped talking yet although Connor had ceased to listen.

'Bulldozing confidence'. His hand itched to pull out his notebook, but they had reached the top of the stairs and the guy – Michael? – was leading him down one side and stopping him in front of a case of candlesticks.

'Look at the spiralling one,' he was saying now, 'in the centre there.'

Feeling distinctly bulldozered, Connor looked. Each candlestick was designed differently, and this one was just a saucer with a coil of flat iron winding upwards from the middle. Simple, but it would work so long as your candle was slender enough to fit inside the coil. Most candles were, he supposed. Ordinary, household candles, that is, not scented things bought from gift shops. Household candles...or church candles – great columns of creamy wax, made to give hours and hours of light that wavered softly...flames flickering...smoke winding thinly upwards...the flame a blinding point of light in the dark...

WELL *that was plain enough.*

From the stairs, Michael watched the boy sitting up surrounded by a knot of people – first-aider, second first-aider (no doubt peeved not to have been first on the scene), two museum stewards and the inevitable onlookers.

Two of them, and within only a few days!

He had descended on the boy on impulse, hardly daring to believe it, afraid that he was going to run away, that he would lose him. The incident in the British Gallery alone had been enough to raise his hopes, but having read the boy's lips as he said over his poem – gravestones and dusk and networks of vines – he had known what he must do and had gone in quick, blind-siding the boy before he could think or argue.

And he hadn't needed to talk him through the candle at all – the boy, Connor, had taken one look and gone, just like that. It had been scary. His eyes had rolled up and Michael had instinctively grabbed him and broken his fall.

He had called for help and help had arrived within moments – just time enough to write on a card and slip it securely into the front pocket of Connor's sweatshirt before backing off.

Better if I'm not here when he comes round.

He watched until he was sure all was well before slipping away.

Chapter Six

REBECCA lifted down L-to-P and broke a nail. She yelped, but the Records Office was quiet and there was nobody else nearby. She bit off the ragged bit, tutted, and opened the book.

M – Mulligan. Rebecca hated her name. It sounded like an overweight cop in a New York patrol car. She had considered changing it, but reluctantly decided it might confuse her customers; few as they were, she didn't dare risk losing them.

She turned the pages, dense with lists of names. It was daunting to realise that every book on these shelves was the same, whether typewritten or manuscript - countless registrars over the decades copying down the details of countless births and marriages and deaths.

To test the system, she began by looking for her own birth; and there it was, including her dire middle name (*I'm not telling him that*) and her mother's name, and her father's...her true father's: Luc Francois de Maupassant – de Maupassant like the writer. His age was given as nineteen. Nineteen! He had been the age she was now.

Spooky.

But he was French so his birth would not be included in these records. Instead, Rebecca traced her mother's birth, and then the marriage of her mother's parents, and from there found her grandmother's maiden name and consequently her birth and her parents' names.

Eventually she hit the back wall – 1837, before which records were not collected centrally. Now for Michael Seward. R M Seward according to his card. Rebecca thought again of the scribbled note she had read before throwing the card in the bin – Raphael. Raphael. Could that really be what the R stood for? Could anyone really have named their son Raphael?

Rebecca reached for volume R-to-V, not expecting her search to bear fruit but going through the motions anyway.

See, Steph?

She was here today thanks mostly to her oldest, closest and

simply best friend. Steph was tall, willowy and blonde, and brainy enough to have breezed into Oxford. She was horribly accomplished, playing oboe in the county youth orchestra while at school as well as being a polyglot who took in foreign vocabulary as if by osmosis.

She had listened on her phone while Rebecca related the story of the strange drawings and the even stranger vision, and at no time told her to stop imagining things and get a grip. Rebecca rather wished she had. Instead she said, when Rebecca ran out of story to tell, 'What are you waiting for then? Go on down to the Family Records Centre and check.'

'What, Births, Marriages and Deaths?'

'Yes, of course! You've got to find out if he's right. Think of it – you might be cousins!'

Cousins! Holy smoke. But she had no choice – refusal would brand her a wimp. So Rebecca looked up the address and went along, armed with a pad of paper and a pencil.

And now here was Michael's name. She had been checking back through the years without noticing the dates and had found him – Raphael Michael Seward, born to Michael Gabriel Seward and Elizabeth Rose Seward, nee Ellis – in – heavens! Rebecca read the date and did the maths. He was forty-four! Forty-four!

Definitely too old, then.

Rebecca paused, recalling Michael's face. She made him frown, and then smile. No good, he wouldn't look forty-four.

Suppose we are related. That means at least a few shared genes. Any chance I'll look twenty years too young when I'm middle-aged? Not a bad prospect...

Raphael...

Hauling her attention back to the job in hand, Rebecca scribbled down the names and ages of his parents, and continued the search. Five minutes later she found the crucial entry, read the name, and dropped her pencil.

There, in ink: Michael Seward's grandmother was also a great-great-grandmother of Rebecca's. They were related. She had been drawing vines for the same reason that Michael had one tattooed on his skin; they were both obsessed with them.

But what was their significance? And how did Michael know

about it?

And would he tell her?

'CUP of tea, Aunty Edie?'

Rebecca cleared a space for the tray on the table next to the armchair. She was shameless, she knew, but having spent months escaping from socialising with her great-aunt she was now courting the old lady.

Who was bats, of course. She had been stubbornly independent all her life, and Rebecca liked to think she took after her, but she suspected that Edie would never have cut herself off from her father as Rebecca had done. Edie would have replied to the phone calls and letters.

Now in her eighties, arthritic and hard of hearing, she refused to sell what she called The Family Home, a great, rambling Edwardian terrace in grave need of rewiring and replumbing; and thank heavens, for otherwise Rebecca would have nowhere to live.

Aunty Edie was eccentric, loyal, unsentimental and actually very funny, especially on the subject of her childhood; Rebecca had felt twinges of guilt, scurrying past the drawing room each day, but conversations with Aunty Edie were apt to meander.

She sat on the sofa, poured the tea and said, 'Aunty Edie, tell me about your mother's family.'

'Oh they were a rackety lot,' Aunty Edie said. 'My grandfather married twice, you know, so there were a lot of them, although the terrible 'flu epidemic took too many.' She sipped some tea. 'Aunt Cicely was the worst of the bunch. Always off somewhere. She went all over the world, you know. She went to India, and America. That was in the Prohibition, you know, which always surprised me. I don't know how she would have managed...'

Prohibition – mobsters and violin cases and cars with running boards and white tyres. Or was that just in the movies?

'Do you remember meeting her?'

'Oh yes, family weddings and things like that. She was a stunner. Lovely figure. Jet black hair. Just like your dear mother.'

'Did she look young for her age?' Rebecca couldn't stop herself from asking.

'I don't know. I was a child, children don't notice things like that. She had a chap younger than herself though, I do remember that. It was such a scandal. A paramour. I don't know what became of him. She never married.'

'Did you like her?' Rebecca wasn't sure where that came from, but it seemed to matter.

'Oh yes,' Aunty Edie said with conviction. 'Such fun. And so generous. She made you feel like you could touch something special just by being with her. And look.' Aunty Edie fished from the neck of her blouse a fine gold chain. 'She gave me this when I was sixteen.'

Rebecca leaned forward, expecting to see a St Christopher or a crucifix.

But it was neither. Rebecca stared at the delicate gold ornament shimmering on the chain. Exquisitely patterned, the veins delicately engraved on its surface, the gold vine leaf gleamed softly.

'THAT'S pathetic,' Steph told her. 'Come on, 'Becca, you've got to call him!'

'Easy to say. He could be anyone. A con-man. A charlatan. He might have got my details and gone back through the records and then just borrowed the name of the real Raphael Michael Seward to haul me in.' It sounded paranoid even to herself, but it was difficult to explain the unsettling effect Michael had had on her. To tell her friend, 'He might be dangerous' was perhaps a step too far, but only a small step.

Steph hiccupped on the end of the line. 'Raphael?'

'Ah...Yes. He doesn't call himself that, though.'

Steph snorted. 'I should think not! Can you imagine!'

Rebecca imagined, and smirked. It was pretty preposterous. On the other hand Steph hadn't seen him. She decided to keep quiet about that. 'Anyway, Michael Seward is forty-four and this guy looks twenty-six. Thirty tops.'

'I still think you should ring him. Don't meet anywhere

private, obviously, but there'd be no harm in speaking over the phone.'

'And how precisely do I ring him if I don't have his number?'

'You have got his number. You said he gave you his card.'

'Ah.'

Yes, yes, good point. Rebecca said cagily, 'The thing is, I sort of threw it away.' She expected a telling off, but her admission was met by silence. 'Well, I was annoyed,' she said into the void. 'I didn't think I'd want it any more.'

'So what are you going to do?'

Thinking aloud, Rebecca said, 'I suppose I'll do some background checking. See if he exists in the real world.'

'How?'

How indeed!

'I'll let you know when I know!'

Rebecca ended the call and thought. It wasn't going to be easy. There was no place of work to try because he had told her he was freelance. Equally, no point contacting art colleges or schools.

She Googled 'Michael Seward' and came up with a research Fellow from Cambridge working in microbiology, a Baptist minister from Ohio, and a rock guitarist in California.

She bought a copy of Artists' and Illustrators' Magazine but there were no advertisements for a Seward.

She visited the library and went through all the lists in the current Writers' and Artists' Yearbook and found one Seward, based in Cornwall, and he wasn't a Michael anyway.

She trawled the London telephone directory and rang every M and R M Seward, and talked to lots of people, all of whom were not Michael.

'Maybe he's disappeared. Maybe I imagined him. Maybe I'm mad.'

Steph, on the phone once again, weighed up the options, giving each its due consideration. 'Could be, could be. What about asking at the V and A?'

'You mean, again?'

Rebecca had already asked: 'Have you noticed an artist drawing here? Dark hair, quite long, and jeans.' It wasn't much to go on, but she felt shy about adding, 'and he's dead gorgeous'.

'Well you can't have asked everyone, not possibly.'

Rebecca sighed and went back, asking the same question, fingers crossed that she wasn't asking it of the same people. Judging from the looks she got, some of them were.

And then the breakthrough, proving once again that Steph was not only attractive and brainy but had an annoying degree of commonsense. One of the stewards – an old guy who seemed pleased to chat, said, 'I think I know who you mean. Michael. Draws with a pen, doesn't he?'

'That's right,' Rebecca said, hope rising.

'I like to look at what folk are drawing. He's very good, isn't he? Hair down to here?' He indicated just above his shoulder.

'Yes, that's right.'

'Good looking chap.'

'Yes.'

'Handsome.'

'Mm.'

'One for the ladies, I should say.'

'Yes,' Rebecca agreed, trying to be patient.

Maybe I should have been saying that all along.

'Cabinetmaker.'

'Pardon?'

'He's a cabinetmaker, isn't he? Michael?'

'Is he?' So not purely an artist, then. A craftsman, a designer-maker.

'I like to make the odd thing, you know – shelves and so on. I use screws though, of course. No dovetails for me!'

Rebecca said, 'Do you know where he lives? Or where he works?'

'No, lass. No, he's never said.'

Well, it was a start. Rebecca went home via Islington, where the Crafts Council offices held their register of makers, and at one of the computer terminals she selected 'Furniture' and went to S.

And there he was. Michael Seward's entry consisted, as did everyone's, of a brief cv, a statement about his inspiration, several images of his work, and a photograph.

You can take more time looking at someone's picture than

you could ever do looking at the person in real life. Rebecca spent a long moment looking at this one. His hair was even longer, pulled back in a pony tail, but it was unmistakably the same man. The entry was eleven years old.

So he had been using the name for at least eleven years. So he probably did exist.

His work was mostly boxes – exquisite, strange, complicated boxes using wood with wild patterns of grain. Some of them made a feature of their hinges and lids, some had their working parts concealed in some cunning way; all of them looked peculiarly alive, somehow.

And the entry gave the address of his studio.

Chapter Seven

THE farther up the road she walked, the less Rebecca wanted to reach the end. By the time she stood at the gates to the yard she was pretty certain what she most wanted was to turn round and go home.

She gazed through the open iron gates into the mews – eighteenth-century stables facing each other across a cobbled yard. Now the buildings were rented to craftsmen. There was a signboard on the gate listing the occupants: Paul Richmond – Ceramics; A J Hall-Johnson – Silversmith; Paula Mackintosh – Spinning and Weaving; R M Seward – Cabinetmaker.

Reading his initials on the sign, Rebecca realised that they were the same as hers – R M Mulligan. But in her case it was her second name that she chose to hide, not her first.

How was she going to do this? What had she been thinking of? She wanted it to be this evening, with all this behind her.

Right, that's it then.

For as long as she could remember, Rebecca had accepted that the best means of defence was attack. When faced with something she didn't want to do, she did it directly, quickly, and determinedly. Now she pressed her lips together, crossed the yard and pushed open Michael's door.

There was an immediate sense of wood – the smell of it, resinous and foresty, and stray curls of shavings under her feet. There was also a beautiful scent like honey with the sweetness taken out. Rebecca searched her memory. Beeswax?

The shallow room ran the width of the studio unit. On the facing wall a glazed cabinet contained a row of wooden boxes, from rich chestnut through glowing amber to the silver-grey of bleached driftwood. It was impossible not to stop to look at them. Each one was individual and completely beautiful; each one was so desirable it hurt not to break the glass, grab it and run away.

From the next room came the noise of serious machinery – an electric-motor roar interspersed with the whine of something having something very nasty done to it.

Rebecca dragged her eyes away from the boxes and moved to the open doorway. The workshop was much bigger, probably thirty foot deep, and housed machinery that might have escaped from a nineteen-sixties Bond film – circular saws and perpendicular saws and drills. Stacks of timber leaned against one wall, and there was a rack holding hand tools above a massive workbench. In here the foresty smell was considerably stronger.

Michael Seward finished feeding a plank through a saw, and then put down the two halves and flicked a switch. The noise died, and he took off the ear defenders and visor he had been wearing and dropped them onto the workbench.

'You checked.'

THERE was one more room, a corner partitioned off from the workshop, with a sink and a kettle, and a desk with pc, printer and scanner, stacking trays (full but tidy) and angle-poise lamp. There was another lamp on the drawing board; the window was high and let in little natural light.

Michael Seward made tea – tea in a pot, Rebecca noted with interest – and untwisted the wrapper of a pack of biscuits. Then he perched on the drawing stool, hooking his feet over the bar, and Rebecca sat in the swivel chair at the desk.

'So, do you want me to tell you a story?'

'I'd like you to tell me the truth,' Rebecca said, the words sounding more tart than she had probably intended.

She saw the side of his mouth twist. 'Okay. But hear me out and don't interrupt.'

'ONCE upon a time,' Michael said, 'there were seven Londoners, six men and one woman. They were honest and intelligent and decent. But each of them had a secret, and that secret had brought them together in the late eighteen-forties to discuss what they realised was a connection between them. Each of these people had become aware of a rift between our world and the world next door, and they were afraid that the cracks would be discovered.

'The Royal Society has a lot to answer for. The sort of people who were struggling to understand steam power and electricity and anaesthesia were also trying to discover the links they guessed must exist to allow the exchange of ideas between our world and the other. It would only be a matter of time, our particular Victorians were sure, before the largest breach would be tracked down and identified, and they feared that this would be a disaster.

'Most people were not ready for that kind of knowledge. It could be destructive, and so they sought to make the breach secure. Easier said than done, but they were helped by the intervention of someone from the other side who – well, shared their concern, unlike most of his race. He could do nothing by himself, from the other side, but with his advice they devised a way of sealing the crack, leaving only the finer, less traceable fissures. A lock was conceived which would hold for a century.'

'A century?'

Michael smiled ironically. 'Sure – one hundred years. Isn't it traditional?

'They were Victorians, don't forget. The British Empire had touched people all over the globe. It was the fount of knowledge, the seat of learning. It had the oldest and best universities anywhere on earth. It had the most trusted justice system, borrowed and copied by younger nations on every continent, and the most advanced social welfare system for its time. It was astonishing the world by moving towards abolishing slavery. English was the richest, most diverse and most adaptable language in existence, and was already spoken by more people in the west than any other.

'They thought that even the British were not yet ready for intercourse between the two worlds, but they had every confidence that in one century we would be. They were convinced that at the rate at which the world was changing, men would be secure and care-free by nineteen fifty.'

'Ha!'

'Yeah. Well. It isn't so surprising. Look at the science fiction that was written even as late as the nineteen twenties and thirties. Poverty eradicated, universal peace, no famine or natural disasters or crime. Smiling people gliding to work in silver flying machines. Utopia. How could they know it wasn't going to happen? That instead we got two world wars and countless other conflicts, terrorism, third world debt, cancer and Aids, the energy crisis and global warming?

'So they put a lock on the way between the worlds that would last for a century. They did that in eighteen fifty-two. What's one hundred years from eighteen fifty-two, Rebecca?'

Rebecca answered obediently, 'Nineteen fifty-two.'

'Right.'

Rebecca narrowed her eyes. 'So the crack is open again?'

Michael opened his hands. 'Not exactly. The lock has never been taken off. But it wasn't designed to last this long. It's over one hundred and fifty years old now, and it's beginning to fail. There are leaks, and soon, I think, it's going to shatter.' He paused, then said, 'You've heard about this expedition to Alaska?'

Puzzled by the change of subject, Rebecca said, 'The Geographical Society thing? About the Northern Lights anomaly?'

Michael nodded. 'It's another crack, I'm sure. Something peculiar is happening in Kashmir as well, according to a couple of websites, but no-one has made the link yet. Magic, or whatever you choose to call it, is leaking through because the lock here is beginning to fail.'

'And then?'

'I don't know, but it won't be good. We're not ready, maybe we never will be. What do you think people will do when they realise there's another world they can reach, one full of wonders. Energy crisis? We'll just drop by and extract everything we can, they won't notice. Rogue states got nukes? Well, hell, the neighbours'll have something better than that, stop 'em in their tracks. Terrorists got there first? Then we'll obliterate their side of the globe, that'll teach 'em, huh?'

His sarcasm was bitter. Rebecca stared at the floor. Did she believe this?

'How do you know all this? About the Victorians and the lock and everything?'

'My great-grandmother was one of them.'

'Your great-grandmother!' Rebecca was oddly shocked.

Michael's voice was matter-of-fact. 'Each of them undertook to pass the knowledge of the key to their children, and then grandchildren, and so on. It was to be done orally, with nothing written down in case the information fell into the wrong hands. My great-grandmother taught my grandfather, who taught my father. My father taught me.'

'Oh.' Rebecca was still wrestling. 'But in that case, why do you want me to help? Can't you just – well, go on and do whatever you have to do?'

Michael grimaced. 'I don't have all the information. As a safeguard – ha! – each passed on the information about one – only one – pointer. It seems it didn't occur to anyone that the lines might die out. The soaring self-confidence of the Victorian middle class. But whether they died out or whether they just stopped believing, as far as I'm aware I'm working alone. What I told you before is true. I need to identify these seven items from the collection and I think you can help.'

'Seven.' Rebecca said.

'Seven. Magic number seven.'

Rebecca thought some more. 'And they're all in the V and A, these pointers?'

'Sure, that was the whole idea.' He read the question in her face and elaborated casually. 'They founded the museum to house the pointers. Like hiding a book in a library.'

'Or a needle in a haystack!'

He smiled ruefully.

'But you mean to say – you're actually telling me the Victoria and Albert Museum only exists because seven guys needed to hide a handful of objects for a hundred years? That's wild!'

'They founded a museum. Victoria jumped in on the act later and renamed it. It moved home a couple of times, but the collection remained intact. They started by taking most of the Great Exhibition. Quite a neat idea, really.'

Some understatement, Rebecca thought. Her mind was on the verge of buckling. She ran over it again, the story and the ideas, trying to see if it held together.

'What about the others? You said the descendents of the other people, the other Victorians, might have stopped believing. Why?'

'Mundus Caecus was what they called themselves. It means Invisible World, wherein lies the problem. With the crack closed completely for the first time in thousands of years, most of the flow of the magic to this side just – dissipated. Evaporated. Whatever. It wasn't there any more.

'People became hard-nosed and pragmatic. Science and technology, you know? The dreamers were gone. Sure, there were people who kind of remembered and tried to write stuff down, tried to pass it on, but the fresh people being born were having none of it. Why would they? They'd never been touched. It's quite likely that in two generations even the descendents of the Mundus Caecus Society didn't give any credence to what they were being told, and what you don't believe you don't remember. So that was that. Gone in three generations.'

'Not quite,' Rebecca said.

Michael looked at her.

'You believe it,' she said. 'Why?'

'I told you before. Same reason that you're here now.'

Rebecca's mouth was dry. 'You want me to believe that you – that we are both descended from some – alien being – that came here from another world in eighteen fifty?'

'And fathered Emily Seward's child, from whom both you and I are descended.'

He's serious, Rebecca thought. He really does believe it.

Do I?

She looked up at the patch of sky through the window. 'Isn't it a bit of a coincidence that we met? How many people pass through the V and A in any one week?'

'You forget how we met. If you hadn't had a psychic experience and jumped out of your skin I'd never have noticed you.'

Rebecca felt herself flush. 'But if we've both got – oh Lord, alien blood – why is it only me that can detect these things? Why don't you have visions?'

Michael shrugged. 'I don't know. My father told me that the traveller, the alien if you like, ensured that each of the pointers contained a small amount of matter from the other world. In those days most people were sensitive to its influence. Think of all the recorded ghost sightings and the interest in spiritualism. Almost anyone could have picked up the message contained in the pointers. But now...' Michael pulled a face. 'My guess is that this sensitivity is just one aspect of our mixed race. You still have it, I don't. There are probably other things I do better than you, but not this one. And unfortunately this one is crucial.'

'It still seems like a long shot, that we were both in the same gallery, drawing from the same collection on the same day.'

Michael shook his head. 'No, not a long shot. It can't be, because you're right – too many people come through for it to be chance. My guess is that we're being drawn to it, this stuff, this matter that they included in the artefacts. Don't ask me how. And I agree it sounds lunatic, but it's what I keep coming back to. The pointer, the key, was calling us.'

'Calling us!' Rebecca almost snorted.

'Okay, call it some kind of force we don't understand. But we do share the same blood – or genes, if you prefer. We are connected to each other, and we're connected to the key, and the key needs us.' He paused. 'Look, you found me easily enough, didn't you?'

'What do you mean?'

'I mean despite having thrown my card away.'

He was watching her steadily. Rebecca's mug of tea had grown cold between her hands.

Magic keys and changeling cousins.

She sighed, put down the mug and stood up. 'I'm sorry,' she said. 'Maybe it's true and maybe it isn't. I accept that we are related, distantly. But this isn't my problem. I don't have time for this.' She watched him lower his eyes, saw the planes of his face subtly change. 'I'm sorry,' she said for the second time, 'but I can't help you.'

Chapter Eight

HE had always been a hoarder.

It took Geoffrey Foster nearly two hours to find the book he was looking for, grovelling about in the loft, bent double beneath the rafters, at risk of slipping a disk as he moved crates of books and papers containing the debris of his past – the years at the city bank before he lost his place, the early days building the estate agency. But eventually he found the box he wanted, the one containing the junk from his father's house after the clearers had finished. He had barely looked at the stuff, just casting a swift eye over it in case there was anything of value. At the time he had assumed not; perhaps now he needed to reconsider.

And there it was; his memory had not played him false.

A diary, leather-bound like the one the Treadwell woman had brought him, but dated one year earlier. And in equally good condition. Well done, James Josiah – you knew how to look after your stuff.

Now perhaps he could begin to make sense of the story.

'DAD'S looking for you,' Shauna said as Connor squeezed past her on the narrow stairs. 'The car?'

'Sod.'

He had been supposed to change the wheel on the twenty-year-old wreck parked out the front, not because his father couldn't do it, but because his father believed it to be the duty of his only male offspring to keep the household machines running. On the whole Connor didn't mind – there was a certain satisfaction to fixing things – but tonight he had plans.

'Where is he?' he asked his sister.

'Where do you think?' She turned into the back room where her sewing machine was set up.

Pub, then. That gave him a couple of hours at least.

Connor went into his bedroom, just a cupboard really, more than half of the floor taken up by the mattress. Clothes, books and everything else were piled into a stack of cardboard boxes. But as the only boy he at least didn't have to share. Now he began hefting boxes and burrowing through strata of old notebooks, bootlegged videos, dead batteries and worn playing cards until he reached the shortbread tin.

Red tartan, with a bloke wearing a kilt and playing bagpipes. Connor took off the lid and sat back on his heels.

The shortbread tin was his treasure chest, but it was not full; Connor didn't possess much treasure. There were two or three photographs, a note to his mother from a primary school teacher praising his story, and a printed certificate for a poetry competition run by the local newspaper, which he had needed to fold in half in order to make it fit. Stuff like that. And at the bottom, a soft-edged, sepia photograph from another era of a girl in a smock smiling shyly at the camera, faded out to an oval and framed by a pen-and-ink drawing of ivy. His grandmother as a child. She had given it to him before she died, even though he'd been only four.

The vines looped and curled around the Edwardian child. Gran had been one hundred and two when she died. Connor stared into the eyes of the photograph, meeting their long ago gaze. Then he slipped it into his hip pocket and hid the tin box back in its carton at the bottom of the stack.

He had four, maybe five hours. His father wasn't likely to be home before eleven. He'd skip supper.

Connor had already memorised the address on the card he had found in his pocket and the handwritten message on the back: '*I can tell you why you saw what you saw. I believe we are cousins. Michael*'.

EXTRAORDINARY. Or perhaps he should say, curiouser and curiouser.

Geoffrey Foster had read the diaries in spare moments. After a few days he made more spare moments available. Then he skimmed through a second time, marking the most interesting pages. Then a third time, carefully, making notes as he read.

The question, of course, was this: was James Josiah Charles

sane or off his rocker? A pioneer of metaphysical science or a screwball? Either seemed possible. On balance, perhaps the screwball...

But suppose not? It was, after all, an hypothesis that several reputable theoretical scientists had given credence to, although confined to science fiction during his own undergrad years at Oxford. A parallel universe, running concurrently with this one – not far away in measurable distance, but unreachable.

What if it wasn't unreachable? What might such a universe hold? If there was truly a way between the worlds, as James Josiah believed, then theories of mutual destruction through implosion or neutralisation could be discounted as they clearly hadn't happened. If the only thing that stopped intercourse between the two universes – states of being, worlds, whatever you chose to call them – was will, then why not alter that will and choose to go between?

What wonders awaited on the other side?

What riches?

Chapter Nine

REBECCA wanted to inflict damage on something; stabbing a kitchen knife into a pillow would have been good. From having had a grip on her life – perhaps none too secure a grip, but a grip nevertheless – she now felt control sliding through her fingers, and keeping hold was like trying to catch water in her hand. Everything was going wrong.

To begin with she wasn't sleeping well, and for a lifelong eight-hours-a-night girl this was a problem. She went to bed with her brain buzzing and woke with a thick head and a bad mood which lasted most of the day. Working alone from home didn't help, although she usually took a thirty-minute walk in the fresh – well, fresh for Tooting – air after breakfast. After that she climbed the three flights of stairs to her tiny flat, sat at her desk and miserably failed to work.

All she could draw were vines. Vines over everything, spreading and proliferating as if some witch had got into her fingers and bent them to her own wilful aims. She should have asked Michael about this, demanded a reason for the botanic invasion. It was no joke. Rebecca had her portfolio to build, and needed to work on a range of illustration styles – pen-and-ink, watercolour wash, silhouettes – for presentation to commissioning agents in the competitive field of children's publishing, and instead of a pea and a princess and a pile of mattresses she was drawing vines.

Embroidery was as bad. The guild had an exhibition shortly and Rebecca had intended to show a series of six small panels in her usual style – jewel-coloured silks, with the images drawn in stitch using her sewing machine. Each was to represent a fairy tale or nursery rhyme, but clearly it wasn't going to happen.

Vines.

In desperation Rebecca caved in, stitched swirling, spiralling foliage across the silk, and actually enjoyed herself, placing the veins of the leaves and the reflective highlights on each grape in the heavy bunches, coiling the tips of tendrils. It seemed she was permitted to widen her horizons botanically at least, and some of the panels involved wavy-edged oak leaves, the acorns neatly cupped, or five-fingered chestnuts with spiny green nutshells, or flying sycamore wings. The borders became all, with only a tiny central area which Rebecca filled with a single flower – a rose, a daisy, a pansy.

But they weren't as she had meant them to be, and Rebecca knew she was not in control.

Nothing helped her. In the garden below her window thick green ivy covered the dividing wall. In the hall Rebecca saw her harassed face reflected in the mirror with its bevelled, rainbow edge that had always hung there but whose engraved vine leaves in the mahogany frame Rebecca had never noticed before.

And Steph was no use. 'You should have helped,' she told Rebecca over the phone. 'It's your guilty conscience that's hamstringing you.'

'I'm too busy,' Rebecca had countered. 'I've got a living to earn.'

'Like you are now?'

And in the meantime Aunty Edie was re-reading Hemingway's 'For Whom the Bell Tolls' with its theme of self-sacrifice, and the independent cinema in the high street was advertising a season it called 'David and Goliath', including 'The Seven Samurai', 'Twelve Angry Men' and 'Norma Rae'.

Then she overheard the milkman telling Aunty Edie at the doorstep that he would be taking a month off in order to go to the lake district and try to help his father reclaim his cottage after flood damage. 'It's not going to help my business down here,' he said, 'And I doubt I'll be able to do much but you've got to show willing, haven't you? Blood ties, and all that.'

Blood ties.

Rebecca flipped. She ran back up to her flat and grabbed her shoulder bag, and then down the stairs again, past Aunty Edie in the hall and the milkman still on the step, and along the road towards the underground.

This was going to get sorted out.

Simply having made the decision seemed to lift some of the weight off her; she felt more cheerful on the tube than she had done for a week.

Perhaps she wouldn't need to spend much time. After all, how long could it take to identify seven objects on display at the museum? No, six, because the candlestick was already known. It would probably be a case of walking slowly along each display with her mind open and receptive. Well, that would take a while, of course – it's a big building – but not forever. It was a finite task, that was the thing, and at the end of it her duty would be done and she could enjoy a warm glow.

She walked briskly to the mews where Michael had his workshop, looking forward to getting it all settled, and it therefore came as a shock to find that, annoyingly, Michael had company.

A tall man in a dark suit was talking to him, forcing Rebecca to hang around pretending to examine the beautiful boxes while she waited. She sneaked surreptitious glances his way from time to time, hoping to see the stranger writing a cheque or shaking hands or giving some other sign that business was being concluded, but no such luck. They seemed to be talking about something quite unconnected with furniture – Rebecca caught the words 'resource' and 'reward' and vaguely wondered whether he was in the timber trade before Michael was suddenly at her elbow. He had his back to the visitor.

'Excuse me,' he said, rather formally. 'I'm afraid I'm going to be tied up for a while. It might be better if you came back later.'

Rebecca started to speak but was cut off by Michael's taking her arm and walking her firmly past the visitor and out of the door, and she found herself in the mews yard, her mouth still open and Michael's parting words in her ears: 'Two three two Trentham Road, seven o'clock.'

She stared as he closed the workshop door on her, and then – for want of an alternative – went home. It was thoroughly annoying and Rebecca travelled back to Tooting with her mind in a muddle, hoping she would be able somehow to deduce which of the Trentham Roads listed in the London A-Z was Michael's.

Fortunately – and no doubt Michael knew this – there was only one.

Instead of attempting to draw, she spent the day mounting the stitched panels and photographing them ready to be catalogued on her laptop. After that she filled out the exhibitor's form for the show and packed the hangings into a plastic crate ready to be taken to the gallery, and by then it was mid-afternoon and she still dared not pick up a pencil.

So she filled in time by planning in her head and writing in words how she might illustrate certain of Hans Anderson's tales – that much she could do – until eventually it was late enough to fix some supper, leaving plenty of time to catch the tube to Michael's home.

She walked along the pavement, counting the houses and trying to guess ahead which one was Michael's.

She was becoming envious. The houses were Victorian terraces, three storeys high with spectacular, floor-to-ceiling windows at the top, arched and projecting out from the walls and roof with curved, glazed ceilings. To sit in one of those would be like sitting in a conservatory; the light coming in would be fantastic. They had to have been built as artists' studios, surely?

Two three two. There were names alongside the three bell pushes in the open porch, 'R M Seward' at the top. Rebecca pressed the button and heard Michael's voice, distorted through the system, before the door unlocked and let her in.

Michael had the whole top floor. He opened the door to her and Rebecca followed him into a room at the back – *blast, I wanted to see that window* – and found herself in a small space lined with bookshelves. There were two upholstered armchairs and three wooden ones, no two of which were alike. A wooden chest acted as a coffee table, and there was a woven rug in all the reds from terracotta through scarlet to burgundy.

It was a room Rebecca immediately felt comfortable in – neither a showroom nor a pit, and quirky; she would have loved half an hour to read the titles of the books.

But there was business to be done, and she got straight to it. 'I've changed my mind,' she said baldly. ' I think I should help. I want to help. How do we start?'

Michael gave her that half-side-of-his-face smile. 'Coffee or tea?'

'Oh, thank you, coffee please.' She trailed after him to stand in the open kitchen doorway off the tiny landing and watched him.

The beautiful aroma of fresh coffee filled the kitchen. When he switched off the grinder, she said, 'That's what I wanted to say this morning.'

'I know. That's why I wanted you to go away this morning.' Michael turned round, leaning on the edge of the kitchen counter while he waited for the kettle to boil. 'This isn't something to spread around. We have to keep it to ourselves or there could be interference.'

'Who would interfere?' Rebecca asked, thinking of the quiet museum and how innocuous it would be, gazing at exhibits which after all were there in order to be gazed at.

Michael shrugged. 'Anyone who wants the gap left open. Anyone who wants to go through. Disaster, remember?'

Fire, famine and flood. 'Oh. Yes. I suppose so. Thanks.'

She took the mug and they returned to the back room.

'You're certain about this? What made you change your mind?'

'I'm certain,' Rebecca said, and felt it was the truth. 'To be honest, I've been all over the place since we spoke. For a start I can't draw anything except these wretched vines – I haven't been able to work at all. And I can hardly think about anything else either, it's driving me crazy. What are they about? Where do they come from?'

Michael shrugged. 'I can only guess. They've haunted me for as long as I can remember. I used to think they were reaching out, trying to pull me in.'

It was a disturbing image. What had his childhood been like, taught to believe in a fantastical secret he could never share? Despite what she had said, Rebecca knew the vines weren't really driving her crazy, but what if they had been insinuating themselves into her thoughts all her life?

Is he really as sane as he seems? Or am I drinking coffee at night in the house of a psychotic?

She glanced sideways, trying to gauge the distance to the door, but Michael didn't give the impression he was about to leap on her and lock her in the basement. He had leaned back in his chair and was looking out of the window over the backs of the houses.

He said, 'It might not be so easy as you think. It might not even be particularly safe.'

'Not safe? Why?'

Michael sighed. 'The guy at the workshop this morning. He guesses something. Quite a lot, actually. He's managed to get his hands on some diaries that contain a whole load of stuff that should never have been written down. They all agreed not to but it seems someone did.'

'So you bundled me out the way. You didn't want him to know I was involved.'

'Yes.'

Had that been chivalry, Rebecca wondered, or hard-nosed pragmatism? She jumped as the intercom buzzed. Michael showed no sign of surprise, merely setting down his mug and leaving the room.

Rebecca tried to recall the appearance of the man in the workshop, but could only come up with an impression of business clothes and that he had been tall – taller than Michael – with curling dark hair

Her attention was brought back to the present by the arrival of a stranger, and she instinctively stood up, her customary defence against being looked down upon.

It was a boy, and a scruffy one. His uncut black hair was dishevelled and he was wearing astonishingly rough clothes. He looked as taken aback to see Rebecca as she felt seeing him.

Michael, though, was unfazed. 'Coffee or tea?' he asked again.

As if, Rebecca thought.

'Coffee. Thanks.'

Oh.

Michael vanished to the kitchen and Rebecca and the boy looked at one another.

Bother this.

'Hi,' Rebecca said breezily, projecting the impression that she was the senior guest in rank as well as in age. 'I'm Rebecca.'

'Just a sec. I need to pee.' The boy shot out and Rebecca heard his footsteps cross the landing and a door slam.

He knew where the loo was.

Blast.

Michael returned with tea and this time took one of the wooden chairs. It had smooth spheres about the size of tennis balls mounted on the ends of the arms and Michael rested his hands on them, curving his fingers over their polished surface. 'That's Connor,' he explained. 'He's going to help as well.'

Wonderful, Rebecca thought. 'Yes?' she said politely.

'I know, I know. But he was extremely sensitive to the candlestick, and he's keen. And there's enough to do even with three of us. Or two of you, rather.'

'Two?'

The loo flushed and Connor came in, plonking himself down in another of the wooden chairs as though an upholstered one would be too girly for him. Now everyone was on a higher level than Rebecca.

Hmm.

Michael said, 'Connor, meet Rebecca. Rebecca, Connor. We are a team, and we need to work together as a team.

'And we need to get on with it immediately, because time is against us.'

Chapter Ten

CONNOR was having difficulty paying attention. He had been shocked and hurt to find this girl here; he had thought he was special. Now it seemed this girl had visions too, although he suspected from one or two things Michael said that she wasn't as good as he was... if you could call it being good at something if you passed out afterwards. She sat amongst the cushions as if she were a princess holding court and he and Michael, perched on hard chairs, her attendants.

It didn't help that she was stunning. Her hair was as black as his own – probably another mongrel, then. It was cut very short and boyish, but it didn't stop her looks coming across. Connor found it easier not to look at her, but even in his peripheral vision she seemed to – shine, somehow.

And so bloody superior. It hadn't escaped him that she was surprised he drank coffee, and surprised all over again when he drank it black and without sugar. Though she hid it well.

With an effort, Connor wrenched his attention back to what Michael was saying. Or reiterating, rather, for Connor had heard this before – the gap and the key and the way the aura around these objects would send you in the right direction to find what you needed; and about having to act now, before the lock broke and the rift widened. But not about this guy with the diaries – that was new and scary.

'How did you find him?' he asked.

'I didn't. He found me.' Michael shook his head. 'It isn't easy tracking genealogy forward or I'd have done it myself. He has to have invested a lot of time in this, which is worrying. He isn't just dabbling, he's serious.'

'But what did he say?' Rebecca asked.

'Just that. That he has these diaries and knows about the gap and the lock, just doesn't know where it is or how to access it. He's no idiot, he has a degree in theoretical physics from Oxford, although he's in the property business now. He wants to recruit me, use what I know, but I got a strong impression of greed from him. He's in it for what he can make.' Michael sighed. 'Just as I said, Rebecca. Exploitation and profit, and who cares about the danger?'

'Pandora's box,' Connor said.

Pandora's box?

Rebecca glanced sharply at him – classical references were unexpected. It was Pandora who had disobeyed her husband and taken the lid off the box of horrors, releasing pestilence, famine and warfare into the world, not to mention leaves on railway lines and finding the customer in front of you has bought the last one of the thing you wanted to buy. And broken fingernails. And spots.

At least Connor didn't suffer from those, despite being fifteen or whatever he was. Instead, his skin was clear and lightly tanned; very symmetrical, well set off actually by the uncombed hair... The influence of Faerie blood, Rebecca thought ironically, and then caught herself and turned her attention back to Michael, who was telling them where he intended to go in order to take the stranger off their trail.

'Scotland!' Rebecca repeated, shocked. 'Does it have to be so far?'

'It gives us an advantage if it is.' Michael cupped his hands around his mug and leaned forward. 'Think. I'm betting he's the sort that drives everywhere. He's probably got a BMW or a Mercedes, something expensive that makes him feel good. I'll take the train but he'll drive. Then if I want to get back quickly, I can fly and he'll still have to drive, which will give us a whole day in hand. I hope we won't need it, but if we do...' Michael leaned back in his chair again.

'How do we contact you?'

Rebecca shifted. *Good question; I should have asked it.*

'I'll set up a new email account. Don't use any of the contacts you already have – he's got them too. I'll send you the address.'

'I haven't got email.'

Rebecca was astonished. 'Well get one,' she said shortly.

Connor shot her a poisonous look.

Michael said swiftly, 'That doesn't matter, provided you two keep in touch. Foster doesn't know anything about either of you so he won't be watching you. Do you have a mobile?'

Connor made a small movement. 'No.'

'Okay, I'll fix one up for you. Don't argue, it's important, I need you to have one. I'll do it tomorrow.' Michael stretched his legs. 'Any questions?'

Any questions? Only a thousand. But oddly Rebecca didn't feel resentful or worried about being dragged away from her career. In fact she felt invigorated at the prospect of a bit of cloak-and-dagger, and even reasonably positive about having to take Connor on. *Pandora's box, eh? More than meets the eye there.*

Connor watched as Michael opened the door for Rebecca. They made a perfect pair – the right height for each other, her chin about the level of his shoulder, and with the same colouring and same slim lines. Slim but not skinny. Goodlooking without seeming to try. Golden people, people for whom life without a mobile phone or email was inconceivable.

He could barely begin to imagine what it would be like to be them...

GEOFFREY Foster finished the final call and closed his diary. That cleared all his appointments for seven days; he'd deal with next week later. The Ferguson-Halls had been unhappy and he wouldn't be surprised to learn in time they'd taken their property to another agency – Kent Walker, more than likely.

Well, sometimes you had to take risks in order to stay in the bigger game. Estate agency, even at the high end of the market, had never been intended to be more than temporary anyway.

Not that he hadn't done well, within the limits. He could talk the talk, dress well and make the right jokes. He knew how to mix with the people on both sides – sellers, moving up the ladder, or cashing in their London house in exchange for a pied-a-terre in the Barbican and a small mansion in the Cotswolds; and buyers, wanting dockside conversions while starting out, or one of the three-storey Edwardian jobs in Chelsea or Kensington because they'd got married.

Oh, he knew how to mix with them alright, but they never wanted to mix with him – the agent, the servant, the man in the suit whose name they couldn't remember despite the fact that he'd been one of them once, or on his way to it.

Two years, that was all he'd had. Two years in city banking with one of the biggest names in commercial finance, his own bank balance growing, a few investments showing potential, not a bad apartment along the embankment. And then his department head had screwed up and everything had evaporated, the whole section dismissed through no fault of their own and about as enticing to any other employer as a dead dog on a warm day.

No chance of another crack at it. Two paltry years and he was flat on his face.

The apartment had had to go, of course, couldn't afford the monthly payments. He'd liquidated some investments and bought a flat in Wandsworth, two streets away from the Common, in a road full of families with school kids that slouched past in green or navy uniforms. As a bachelor, he was left alone and didn't need to expend energy and imagination ducking invitations to breast cancer coffee mornings or feed Africa jumble sales, thank heaven.

Estate agency had seemed as good a stop gap as any. You didn't need training to sell smart houses to people who wanted to buy them. After a couple of years with Kent Walker he had broken away and set up independently, and his manners and awareness of the market had drawn a steady supply of clients to him.

But he hated it; he hated giving tours of penthouse apartments and regency town houses that were far beyond his pocket now but should have been his – would have been his, if life had followed its proper course. He hated the owners, leaving him to conduct the tours while they buggered off to their cottages for the weekend, and he hated the buyers with their fat little wives and their fat little accounts. Bastards, the lot of them.

Or there were the Michael Sewards, the drop-outs, the ones who pretended they wanted none of it because they had as much prospect of scraping serious money together as of winning a Nobel prize. Surrounded by sawdust, living in jeans, making things, and behaving as if there were some sort of inherent virtue in the choices they had made.

No respect at all. Seward had spoken to him as if he were a salesman, a cold-caller impinging on his time, rather than someone making him the biggest offer of his life.

Well, the offer wouldn't be repeated. Unfortunately Seward knew something, Geoffrey was sure of that. Probably not much, but Geoffrey had seen the flicker in his eyes. And if Seward didn't intend to join forces, help Geoffrey along in return for a piece of the returns, then he might well be alarmed into doing something by himself right away.

And sure enough he had booked onto the train leaving for Edinburgh tomorrow evening. What an amateur. He could have no conception of how easy it was to get information if you looked the part, as Geoffrey took care to. Being tall and reasonably presentable helped, of course, and these days he allowed his hair to grow just a fraction longer, knowing that it made him look more approachable. The woman in the ticket office didn't even hesitate before she answered his oh-so-casual question about the previous customer.

Edinburgh, then Aberfeldy. Geoffrey checked. Aberfeldy was a small market town close to Loch Leven. It had two hostelries – an inn and a hotel. Geoffrey picked the hotel as being the more impersonal and booked himself a double room.

Chapter Eleven

'ALRIGHT, I'll do it.'

The jitters in Rebecca's stomach immediately went into overdrive.

She'd felt annoyingly fluttery since arriving at the museum, making quick scribbly sketches of people coming and going while she waited for Connor, and then she had thought Connor was to be the bloodhound.

Wrong, apparently. 'I'm not doing it. You can,' he had said, and even as she opened her mouth to protest ('But you're the star, you're the expert!') she had seen his eyes and found her mind changed for her.

Oh well… She had expected to be doing this before Connor had arrived on the scene anyway.

Now Rebecca positioned herself in front of the glass and concentrated on the spiralling candlestick.

Here we go again. Think Candle.

She thought. Candles – candle wax – candle flames – candles in church, candles during a power cut, scented candles around the bathroom (*yes, yes, I know*), stripy candles on a birthday cake, the joke sort that keep relighting themselves …

'Don't forget your bag, will you, love?' The steward pointed at Rebecca's feet.

'Oh. No. Thank you!'

Nothing. No zoning out of anything – just a normal museum morning. At the far end a couple of stewards were discussing holidays, and a group of teenagers with sketchbooks were being giggly in the hall below. Rebecca found herself wondering which school Connor was truanting from, and realised she was getting distracted.

'I can't do it. I can't get anything. It's not like last time.' She frowned. 'Perhaps it only works when Michael's here.'

She looked at Connor, who looked back. He appeared to have relaxed somewhat. If it was only going to work in Michael's presence, they were scuppered. 'You try,' she said, for the sake of completeness.

Connor stepped up to the case. He looked as if he were nerving himself for it. Whatever had it been like for him last time? Well, if he had really fainted... She watched him shove his hands into his pockets, and then quickly take them out again and hold them away from his sides just a little – a defensive measure should he collapse, she supposed. He stared at the candlestick, the concentration on his face clearly visible. And suddenly he was talking.

'Dark wood. Brass – polished, shiny. Stone floor – big slabs. Coloured organ pipes – pink and blue and brown. Nicer than it sounds, though. Stained –'

'Hang on, hang on!' Rebecca jerked into action, scrabbling to open her sketchbook. 'Okay, go on.'

He was speaking perfectly calmly, as if describing a scene in front of him. 'Stained glass windows – biblical scenes. A tree, the crucifixion. Blue curtain –'

'Slow down!' Rebecca's pencil was flying. 'Did you say organ pipes? Painted organ pipes?'

'Yes, very ornate. Then a stone font with steps up to it, and a dark blue curtain to one side – the right side if you're facing the alter. And it's behind the curtain, in a cupboard.'

Connor came to a stop and met her gaze.

'What?' he asked. He sounded defensive.

'Astonishing!' Rebecca couldn't help smiling. 'It was as if you were watching a film, or looking out of a window. All that detail! I didn't get that – just a vague atmosphere, really – choristers and candlelight, that kind of thing. But you...' She shook her head. 'You were in control!'

She watched Connor think about this, his black eyebrows drawn together. 'It was much easier than last time. Last time was like – a steamroller. What have you got?'

Rebecca glanced at her notes. 'I have no idea. A church, obviously, but heaven knows – ha! – how we find out which one. I suppose the window and the organ will narrow it down a bit.' She looked back up as reality struck her. 'But it could be anywhere in the country. This is going to take forever!'

*   *   *

THEY had coffee in the museum café, Rebecca treating Connor and throwing in a chocolate brownie as well. For all her worry about her bank balance, it was plain that compared with Connor she was doing very nicely, thank you. His accent did not match his vocabulary. He also swore much less than Rebecca expected, despite his wary eyes and the holes in his jeans. He didn't quite fit in his pigeonhole.

Oh well, neither did she. Anyone seeing her, Rebecca knew, would assume that she was a student, probably at one of the better, longer-established universities, instead of which she had dropped out, run away from home, and was unemployed.

'I think,' she said, lassoing her thoughts back to the matter in hand, 'that Michael was a catalyst. No, not a catalyst – an amplifier.'

'Amplifier?'

'Yes.' She checked out the theory in her head and liked it. 'He can't get anything from these auras, can he? He told us that. But I only got my vision – a wobbly one – when he was right there next to me, probably concentrating on it as well. Without him I get nothing. But you, ' Rebecca leaned forward and tapped her finger on the table. 'Without him you were able to see something – well, a lot – and stay in control, but when he was beside you, you were deafened. It overwhelmed you. Like the volume turned up too high.'

She saw the boy consider. 'I suppose so. You might be right.'

'I am right.' Naturally, Rebecca thought, I usually am. 'This is going to be a doddle. You tell me what you see and I'll write it down. I suppose the vision didn't take you out of the church as well? It would be really helpful to see what it looks like from the outside.'

Connor shook his head.

'Oh well. Think about it later.' Rebecca closed her sketchbook. 'Right. Next.'

They had each committed Michael's list of objects to memory, having been convinced by him that nothing should be written down. Candlestick; clock; key; page; telescope; and thread. Learn them alphabetically so that you both have them in the same order, he had told them. Strangely, the list made a kind of sense to Rebecca, although she couldn't imagine why. The items seemed to have been chosen quite at random, yet by the time Michael had reached 'telescope' an image of a spool of thread had popped into her mind in anticipation.

Telepathy, perhaps. Another result of these shared genes? Whatever.

A clock could be almost anywhere in the museum, made out of silver or porcelain or plastic. But there was a display on the wall near the centre of the Ironwork Gallery of keys which seemed likely to hold the one they needed. Having finished their coffee they returned upstairs and stood in front of the cases.

They were strange-looking things, not much like modern keys. Some of them dated from the thirteenth century. *Someone locked and unlocked a door with this eight hundred years ago.*

The wards were more interesting than the handles; one consisted of a rectangle full of holes, another a single horizontal rod with one small kink in the end. On the wall between the two cases were three gigantic examples, half the length of a man's arm and as thick round as his wrist. They surely had to be for display, there surely could not have been a lock for these?

'Which one, then?' Rebecca asked.

Connor ran his eyes over the cases, presumably listening for something. Rebecca waited, this time with a notebook in her hand and pencil poised. She hadn't intended to use up a page of her sketchbook last time, but had grabbed the first paper that came to hand.

She watched Connor closely as he peered at each key in turn, and saw the moment his head tipped back and his expression changed.

'This one,' he said, nodding at the case.

'Which one?'

'Third from the right, top row. With the leaves on the handle.'

That figured. Rebecca said, 'Are you okay? Alright to do this?'

Connor nodded briefly, and Rebecca saw him splay his fingers again, preparing himself for the worst. She glanced around. If he did fall at least there wasn't anything to hit his head against on the way down. She would have to try to catch him, of course, stop him crashing onto the wooden floor, but she ought to manage so long as she was paying attention.

I wonder how much he weighs.

'Okay, fire,' she said.

Once again there was no suggestion of anything spooky, no trance. Good thing too, as they didn't want to draw attention to themselves. Connor simply focused intently on the case, staring at it, staring through it, as if seeing something beyond the mount, and then spoke.

'There's a yellow stone wall with a wooden door in it. Old wooden door, huge, with another door, a little door, set into it. Like a castle. Ahead there's open air, and grass – neat, mown grass with a path straight across. There's a sundial in the middle – like a stone bird table but with the metal thing, the dial thing, sticking up. Then further ahead, more yellow stone buildings. On the left is this little room, wooden walls with glass windows. Like a cubby hole, you know? It's very old. Lots of pigeonholes behind. Cupboards below. The key's in one of the cupboards.' He straightened up. 'That's it.'

Rebecca was still writing furiously. 'Pigeonholes and cupboards. Got it.' She looked up at him, still annoyed at being shorter than someone younger than herself. 'I think I know this one, or where to start looking anyway. This sounds like one of the Oxford colleges. Or Cambridge.'

Connor looked suspicious. 'How do you know?'

'I have a friend at Oxford. I'll ring her tonight, see what she thinks. Don't worry,' she added, correctly interpreting Connor's expression. 'I won't tell her what we're doing. I'll just find out whether this is somewhere in Oxford, that's all. Then we can go and get the key. It'll be easy.

'Now for the clock.'

Chapter Twelve

BUT they couldn't find the clock, and Rebecca went to Oxford alone.

She hadn't set out to leave the boy behind, but when Steph, with no prompting, invited her to come for the weekend it made perfect sense. After all, there was nowhere for Connor to stay.

And she had lied about not telling Steph what they were doing, because as soon as she was speaking on the phone it had all poured out. Well, she had to give some reason for the peculiar questions, and it was hardly likely that Steph's being in on it would cause any problems.

So now she was on her way to Oxford and in a bit of a jumble, one way and another. She had visited Steph once before, when she herself had been safely and smugly at her own first choice of art college and envied her friend nothing. A bit different now, having dropped out and living a solitary life at the top of a maiden great-aunt's house with her nose to the grindstone and money a constant worry.

It had been her choice, and most of the time she knew it to be right for her, but riding the train through the Oxfordshire countryside in the early morning sunlight made her wish she could be a student again, with only essays and exams to be worried about, instead of contracts and bills and bank statements.

And finding keys, and solving riddles, and preventing a breach with another world, if that was indeed what she believed.

Do I?

There it was again, the perpetual, nagging question: Do I believe this stuff? Was 'A Midsummer Night's Dream' real? Why honestly am I doing this – to save the world, or to exorcise this compulsion to draw vegetation?

Steph met her at the station and they bought lunch in the covered market, and a big box of tissues because Steph had a cold.

'Don't give it to me,' Rebecca warned, eyeing her as she wiped her nose.

'Some chance. You're never ill.'

'I had 'flu when I was ten.'

Steph snorted.

They walked up the High, past the shops and restaurants, to the plain stone wall of Gloucester College. The grey oak door was propped wide open and they stepped inside.

Feeling like a bank robber, Rebecca cast her eye around the quad. The porter's lodge inside the doorway looked encouragingly like Connor's description, but it was on the right, not the left.

Steph had a room up two flights of stairs in a nineteen sixties block behind the main quad. 'Next year I get one of those,' she told Rebecca as they crossed the neat rectangle of grass looked down upon by ancient leaded windows. 'Second-years get a room on Main Quad, and then in the third year we're on our own, out in the real world.'

Still won't be as real as my real world, Rebecca couldn't help thinking. Steph led the way to her room, and after digging out plates and unwrapping the bread and cheese they had bought, Steph blew her nose yet again and said, 'Right, what have you got?'

Rebecca delved in her rucksack and withdrew the notepad. 'I don't know that this is Oxford, but it made me think of it. Listen.' She read aloud the notes she had taken while Connor had been 'reading' the key. He had been so fluent, reading seemed the best term to use.

'See?' she asked when she had finished. 'The little door set into the big door, that sounds like a college, don't you think? It sounds like here!'

'There's a couple of others too. Mary's, for a start, and Cardinal's. Maybe Teddy Hall.'

Rebecca noted the casual shortening of the historic college names and decided not to let it irritate her. Steph swallowed and went on, 'The problem is that most of the limestone colleges have that sort of porter's lodge by the main entrance. Necessary really. The trick's going to be how to work out which one you want.'

Rebecca re-read the relevant notes. 'Wood and glass, on the left as you enter, with pigeonholes along the back wall.'

'Yup,' Steph said, 'That's the standard.'

Hmm.

'It has to have open air ahead. And grass.'

'They've all got grass.' Steph said. 'Come on, eat up and we'll get started.'

They tried St Mary's first, walking through the quad and turning to look back. It looked like a match. Casually, they drifted back until they could see through the glass. Wooden cupboards from floor to shoulder height faced them; the pigeonholes were on the end walls, left and right.

So it couldn't be this one, could it?

'No good,' Rebecca said.

'No.'

They peered through the window, willing the pigeonholes to be on the back wall instead.

'I suppose they couldn't have been moved?'

'Unlikely. Why would they be?'

Rebecca sighed. 'How many limestone colleges are there?'

'Fifteen? Eighteen? A lot.'

Rebecca turned and looked round the quad. It was not very helpful of the key – the key in the museum – to give so wide a description. She had expected more than just a porter's lodge in a college. Perhaps the Victorians had known all the colleges so well they had the information at their fingertips. Lucky them.

The old colleges were so beautiful. Rebecca feasted her eyes on the golden buildings, and the chestnut tree in the centre of the grass, and the paved paths running diagonally across from corner to corner.

'Oh! Oh!'

'What?'

Rebecca almost shook as she fumbled in her bag for her notebook. 'The tree! The tree! It shouldn't be there!'

'What on earth –'

Rebecca flipped the pages. 'No, listen, it should be a sundial. And the paths don't run diagonally, there's just one straight down the centre. That's the clincher – that's the sign! That's how we identify the college!'

Steph smiled slowly. 'Oh yes! Clever you! Clever old Victorians! Okay, so we need a sundial.'

Cardinal's College had a sundial. Actually so did several

others, but Cardinal's had the right shape of lawn and the right kind of path and a sundial like a bird-table in the middle. When they arrived they found a porter's lodge split on either side of the main entrance, the porter's own little room, with television and armchair and dog bed (dog bed?) on the right and the mailroom – half-height cupboards on the back wall and pigeonholes above – on the left.

Spot on.

'But how do I get the key?' Rebecca asked.

They went to a coffee shop to think about it, and took their cappuccinos to a table near the window. Rebecca stirred her creamy froth around.

'All the porters must follow pretty much the same routine, surely,' she said, thinking aloud. 'They all have gates to lock up at dusk or whenever. They must take time away to do that.'

Now that it came to the crunch – this was robbery she was contemplating – she found her feet growing chilly.

'Not necessarily. Some of the colleges have electronic locks now. They do them centrally with a flick of a switch.'

Modern technology didn't fit here, Rebecca thought moodily, and it certainly wasn't going to help her cause. 'Is Cardinal's one of those?'

Steph shrugged.

No. It wasn't as if they could ask one of Steph's Cardinal's friends, When is your porter's lodge left empty and unlocked, because I want to get in and pinch something?

A new thought struck Rebecca. 'Do they all have a dog?'

Steph snorted. 'Hardly! They're not standard issue.'

'So you don't know whether the porter will go off and walk the dog at some point?'

''Fraid not.'

Rebecca spooned some of the froth into her mouth. 'What about,' she said slowly, 'food?'

'Food?'

'How and when do they eat when they're on duty?'

She looked at Steph and Steph looked back.

*   *   *

'I HOPE this guy doesn't bring sandwiches,' Steph said, 'or eat late. I'm starving.'

Her cold had made her grouchy. She wasn't taking this seriously, which was understandable. Steph hadn't been plagued by psychological vines, or suffered visions, or met a weird teenage boy who shambled about spouting poetry.

Or an ageless man called Raphael who had a tattoo and haunted, haunting eyes.

Rebecca said, 'I'll treat you to dessert.'

The main problem was how boring it was to sit on the bench in Cardinal's main quad pretending to read while actually keeping the porter under surveillance. Steph had said that the Gloucester porter, who was on duty alone after five o'clock, had his supper on a tray, for which he had to leave his station and cross the quad to the buttery. It only took five minutes and he didn't bother to lock up while he was gone. 'At least, not always,' she had asserted. 'I know I've gone to collect stuff from my pidge when he's not there.'

It had seemed as promising an opening as anything. If one college had that system, others might too, and at least it would cost them nothing to see.

'I've got a numb bum,' Steph complained. 'Bumlago,' she added, reviving a very old joke.

'Run around then. I'll keep watching.'

She reviewed her sketchbook. She had been filling the time drawing the different faces of the buildings around the quad, most of which had some kind of creeper clinging to the stone. She hadn't been able to concentrate properly, allow her drawing-brain to take over, because she had needed to remain conscious of the porter's activities across the grass, but it was practice of a sort and an opportunity to collect visual information. The vines were not brilliantly drawn, but at least they had stayed in their place instead of rampaging about strangling things.

Is that because they've got me where they want me?

She closed the book and stood up too, shaking out her legs. 'Oh come on, Mr Porter, go and get your supper!'

Immediately the door opened and the porter emerged followed by a brown and white spaniel, and the two of them sauntered along the path round the farther side of the quad.

Magic!

She and Steph gathered up their bags and made off the other way, trying to look innocent.

'What are you actually going to do?' Steph asked out of the corner of her mouth.

'Shut up.'

Open the door and walk in, presumably, although the prospect made the hairs on her arms stand up. The key was in a cupboard, Connor had said.

Which cupboard?

It had sounded so easy, so complete in the museum; now Rebecca's head was bursting with questions she should have asked: Which cupboard? Where in the cupboard? A key was a pretty small thing – would it be inside something else? What? How would she recognise this particular key? How on earth could it still be there more than one hundred and fifty years after it was hidden?

This is madness.

'I'll wait outside,' Steph announced, treacherously.

Devoid of moral support, Rebecca gritted her teeth, pushed open the door and stepped into the illicit territory of the porter's lodge.

Before her were pigeonholes and below them the cupboards, plain faced and anonymous. She began opening doors.

Shelves, packed with a jumble of stuff that was no help at all – box files and pencil tins and sticky tape and envelopes, and mugs and dominoes (dominoes!) and an old telephone handset. No good, no good!

Next cupboard. A stack of magazines, a torch, spare cable for something electrical, a cash box.

Hissing, she opened the last cupboard. On the inside of the right hand door was taped a tattered sheet of paper listing extension numbers and codes. The inside of the left hand door had rows of hooks on which were hung keys, mostly the Yale type with plastic fobs but also some older, traditionally styled keys and one or two that looked really ancient. And at the bottom, near the hinge, a key with an elaborately wrought handle and simple wards that made Rebecca catch her breath.

She reached for it, unhooked it, held it in her palm. It was cold, and heavy for its size. A length of narrow, faded ribbon was tied through the handle and there was something written on it.

Rebecca peered.

In tiny, stitched thread were the figures 1 8 5 2.

Heart thumping, she shoved the key in her jeans pocket and slammed all the cupboard doors shut. Then she shot out of the lodge, slammed that door shut as well, and ran down the stone steps under the archway and into the street.

'I've got it!' She closed her hand over the hard shape of it in her pocket. 'I've got the first one!'

Chapter Thirteen

AUNTY Edie was napping in the parlour with her feet up. Thankfully, Rebecca climbed the stairs and let herself into her flat. She hung up her coat, dumped her rucksack in the corner and dropped into her chair. Then she withdrew the key from her jeans pocket and held it on her palm.

It looked very old. The iron was dark, although not as black as the medieval keys in the museum. It was warm now from having been in her pocket, and felt smooth to the touch.

She turned the ribbon over with her finger, peering at the tiny stitches that marked the date. The knot was tight and probably impossible to undo. It had been tied more than one hundred and fifty years ago. Who tied it? Someone wearing a crinoline? Or a stove hat and tail coat? It had been tied while Charles Dickens was campaigning against the Yorkshire schools; while Trollope was still a postmaster, scribbling away every evening; before Atlanta burned in the American Civil War; before Albert died and when Victoria was still wearing coloured gowns. It had been dangling from that hook on that cupboard door in that porter's lodge for one and a half centuries, waiting.

And now she had it in her hand.

But she couldn't keep it in her hand forever. Where should she put it for safekeeping? Not that she was likely to be burgled – not that a burglar would be likely to steal this even if she were – but it was irreplaceable and needed a secure home.

Not her underwear drawer, reputedly the first place burglars look for hidden jewellery. After some thought, Rebecca sealed the key inside one of the small plastic bags she used for beads and dropped it into her biscuit tin. That way she wouldn't have a chance to forget where it was.

She woke up her Mac, accessed email and called up a new document to let Michael know the first element was retrieved.

*   *   *

WHY now, Celia wondered, why should this business especially preoccupy her now?

Not for any obvious reason that she could see. The first anniversary of the old man's death had passed without disturbance. The bizarre arrangements he had left had not been commented on recently, even by the appalling Olwen – who persisted in the belief that they were friends with an astonishing imperviousness to rudeness – and she was not aware of having had her attention drawn to the cottage beyond what was usual and inevitable. Yet for several days it had possessed her, squatting in her mind all her waking hours and looming through her sleep.

Why now?

Usually there was some event, some recollection, that was the trigger – an item in the news, perhaps, or a notice in the obituaries of the death of an acquaintance – ever more frequent now, her age being what it was. Not that she allowed anyone she met these days to know it, of course. She took great care with her grooming and wardrobe, just as she always had, and they would never have believed her.

But nothing of this sort had occurred recently. The curtains remained drawn behind the cottage's low windows and the day-trippers tramped their careless way through the house and gardens. She continued to report for duty on her scheduled afternoons, taking up station beside the abandoned toys or costumes or musical instruments, trotting out the same trite replies to the same trite questions and doing her best not to allow her distaste to become apparent. It was all she could do, and so she did it, while her expectations dwindled and the bitterness grew.

But what had recently happened? What had changed? What was pressing this business to the forefront now?

She must watch and listen. And think.

REBECCA woke feeling groggy, her mind a jumble of thoughts and visions and emotions. She hadn't slept well, which was unusual, and felt unsettled.

Hardly surprising, all said and done.

Until today – or rather yesterday – she had not really believed in what she was doing. Not truly. She thought she had, obviously, or she would never have been induced to take precious time away from her work to indulge in petty (*I hope it's petty*) larceny.

But it was different now, and from this new place she had arrived at, this new Rebecca could see that she had been going through the motions before – doing what was expected, what she had agreed to do, as if in honour of a contract.

All that had changed. The moment she had seen the key on the hook, the instant she had read the date stitched into the ribbon, she had entered a new state of being, as if through a door. Like the paternoster machine she had seen in Yorkshire at one of those 'hands on' museums, she had stepped onto a platform and it had lifted her away from her everyday life, transporting her to somewhere close by but entirely new.

It was tremendously exciting, so exciting that it left her no room to think about anything else. There were only the trails she had to follow, and the elements of the key she had to collect, and Michael whom she would tell.

Michael.

If this was real, if all he had told her was true, then it followed that he had told the truth about his pedigree also – and hers. 'A fairy?' she had said, a little too loudly, too aggressively. 'Are we talking about fairy blood?'

Michael had raised his eyebrows. 'No. Absolutely not. Let's just say he was someone not human, from another place not this one. And he brought with him – left behind him – qualities unlike ours.'

In other words, a fairy bearing magic. Holy cow.

And if Michael bore Faerie blood, then so did she.

And so did Aunty Edie.

Rebecca ate two bowls of cornflakes, being out of bread even half-way fresh, and descended to the ground floor. Her aunt was in the back room clearing the table after her own breakfast.

'Aunty Edie? Have you got a minute?'

Aunty Edie put the kettle on and made them a pot of tea, despite having only just finished one, and they drank it looking out over the back garden with its tubs of red and white geraniums.

Rebecca said, 'I thought I'd better warn you that I might be away from time to time for a few weeks. I'm doing some research' (true) 'and will probably have to go up to Oxford again. Or somewhere else. I'll let you know, of course.'

'How lovely. What are you researching? Art history?'

With her grammar school background her aunt had never really got to grips with the non-academic nature of Rebecca's chosen career. She seemed sure that some good, sound essay writing must come into it somewhere.

Rebecca said, 'Sort of,' and quickly moved on. 'Aunty Edie, you were telling me about your Aunt Cicely. Do you remember anything about the rest of the family?'

'Oh, you're doing genealogy!' Edie said, understandably getting the wrong idea.

Although, perhaps not.

'Um, well, I have been to the Family Records Office,' Rebecca admitted.

Aunty Edie got to her feet. 'Just a minute. Now where is it? '

She delved into the bottom cupboard of the sideboard and then straightened up holding an old Woolworths exercise book. 'Look. I did what I could before Mother died. I didn't have much time to spend on it, but I got this far.'

She handed the book to Rebecca.

'A family tree. Our family tree!'

Why didn't I think to ask?

The plan had been drawn in sections over several pages in Aunty Edie's tidy, sloping handwriting, and Rebecca couldn't immediately find the name.

'I shan't be doing any more with it now,' Aunty Edie was saying. 'You keep it, dear. Now, what can I tell you about the family?'

Rebecca forced herself to close the exercise book and hold it on her lap while she listened.

'Well, there was only Aunt Cicely on my mother's side,' Edie began, back in her chair and comfortably settled. 'The two boys died in infancy, you see. Terrible, but quite common then, of course. Cicely was wild, drove her parents mad. Wouldn't settle down with anyone. Travelled all over the world in her twenties, I think I told you, and that wasn't common then. But she came back with wonderful stories.'

Rebecca saw her aunt's hand move up to settle on her chest, patting the soft jersey beneath which lived the golden vine leaf.

'Any other aunts?' she prompted.

'Oh yes, lots on my father's side. He came from a very large family. Two of my uncles died in the first world war – Father was the eldest of his family, you see, so although he was – let me see – thirty-ish in 1914, his brothers were that bit younger and went straight into the trenches. Infantry, you know. Terrible. But my father was behind the lines most of the time, although I know he did see some action.'

This wasn't what Rebecca wanted to hear. 'And your grandfather, he married again, didn't he, after your grandmother died? Do you know anything about his second wife? Did you ever meet her?'

'Oh yes, we always stayed in touch. Weddings, you know. And funerals. Wonderful chance to catch up, funerals.'

'So you met their children as well,' Rebecca ploughed on, working her way slowly towards Michael. 'Do you remember any of them? Or their children?'

'No, dear. They died before I was born. In the 'flu epidemic after the first world war. Dreadful. Whole family was wiped out. Well, the children, I mean.'

'But not all of them,' Rebecca persisted. 'Surely not all of them?'

'Weren't they?' Edie looked confused for a moment and passed Rebecca a dubious glance. 'Have you been researching the family tree as well?'

Rebecca tried not to squirm. 'Well, not really. A bit. I'm sure', she carried on swiftly, 'there was a boy, wasn't there? Who survived into adulthood? Michael?'

'Michael… Oh yes, Michael. He was a bit different, that one. I remember. I met him at some family gathering, I can't remember what now. Oh yes, I do, it was Cicely's funeral. She was killed in the blitz – refused to leave London. She was working in the WVS cooking dinners for all the poor bombed-out families in the East End. Another tragic death – she should have lived to be a hundred.

'Michael was there then, home on leave from the RAF. I was

fourteen and he was twenty-nine, which is a world away of course
when you're that age – he was a grown up and I was just a school
girl, but I thought he was utterly gorgeous, a real dreamboat,
unbelievably handsome. Made us all swoon.'

Rebecca stared at the shrunken old lady sitting in the armchair
with her cup and saucer on her lap.

'Very black hair and eyes, and such long eyelashes for a man.
Perfect skin. Very slim and upright but not quite tidy, you know?
A little bit bohemian. And lovely manners – so courteous but with
just enough humour to loosen us up, if you know what I mean.'

'Yes,' Rebecca said, 'but what I wanted to know –'

'But without ever going too far. And very sensitive, you just
knew that by looking at him. At his eyes.'

'Yes, but – '

'Very intelligent, too.'

'Right.'

'Graceful hands.'

'I – '

'Very good teeth.'

Like father, like son. Rebecca pulled herself together. 'Was he
– did he – do you remember anything – '

'I've never forgotten how that flowering cherry came into
blossom just before his mother died. We went up to visit her and
pay our respects – she had been ill for a for a few weeks, cancer I
expect – and all you could see from her window was that tree with
all the blossoms. It was far too early for it to be flowering, but
there it was, and the petals drifting in when there was a breeze.
There always did seem to be a breeze when Michael was about –
just a light breeze, a gentle one, full of lovely summer scents…'

A breeze …

'He lived a charmed life, I used to think,' Rebecca's aunt
continued, her gaze on the window opposite but her mind's eye in
the past. 'Do you know he went right through the war without
ever being injured? And he was shot down more than once… And
I don't remember hearing that he ever died. I wonder if he's still
alive. He'd be in his nineties now, of course.'

That thought hadn't occurred to Rebecca.

'He married an American girl and moved to Scotland, I

believe.'

Scotland! That thought hadn't occurred to her either!

'So take care, dear.'

Rebecca snapped to and found her aunt looking at her and the mood changed. 'I'm sorry?'

'Be careful. With what you're doing. Take care.'

'Yes, of course.'

Aunty Edie sighed and put down her cup. 'It's so easy to get caught up when you're young. Not that you shouldn't get caught up, of course, but it's a tricky business and things may not always be all they seem. You must keep a sharp eye out. And, here...'

Edie fumbled behind her neck and then held out the gold chain, unfastened, with the exquisite vine leaf swinging. 'You have it, Rebecca,' she said. 'You wear it now.'

Rebecca stared. 'Oh, Aunty Edie, I can't. It's beautiful. It's yours. You must keep it.'

'Yes, it is beautiful. But Cicely gave it to me, and now I'm giving it to you. Wear it, Rebecca, and be careful.'

Chapter Fourteen

'CONNOR!'

His sister's voice held the note that meant trouble.

'What?'

Shauna's head appeared around the door. 'Dad's back.'

'Shit.' Connor dropped the book, grabbed his jacket and leapt down the stairs three at a time. He was out the back door while his father was unlocking the front.

At the bottom of the yard – you couldn't call it a garden – Connor scrambled over the sagging fence and dropped into the alley behind the lots. He could do this easily even in the dark – knew exactly the place in the long grass where the old milk crate lay to give him a bunk up, knew exactly how high to swing his legs to clear the curling top of the fence. He landed neatly on the broken tarmac of the alley and ran. It was unlikely Dad would take off after him, but it had been known and Connor didn't risk it.

He did not know for sure that his father wanted him, but he usually did and it was never good. Either he had done something or he hadn't, basically it came down to that. It used to mean a smack round the head if he was lucky, a belting if he wasn't, but now that Connor was taller than his father, fighting back was a possibility. He didn't want to think about it – violence against a parent, no matter how rotten the parent – but if he got caught…

No, it won't happen. There's not much longer…

The GCSEs were all that was keeping him now, them and this business. He would sit the exams – he found he actually wanted to, as if they mattered – but that would be it. He didn't need to know the results. He had a passport – he was well used to forging his father's signature on anything official – so that Shauna believed him when he told her he was going abroad, and he had been keeping from her a portion of his wages from the burger chain for the last year, which made him feel rotten but which was essential.

If I don't get away I'll kill him.

Reaching the street, Connor slowed to a walk. His father wouldn't come after him this far – wouldn't know which way he'd gone. Now all he had to do was hang around for an hour or two until his family had all turned in. He had his key.

No book, though. He wished he'd kept hold of it when he took off.

He had no money so couldn't use a coffee shop. Not the modern sort of coffee shop, of course, like those American sit-com ones, with sofas and cushions and a coat stand in the corner – way too expensive – but there was an old café not far along. Otherwise at this time of night there were pubs – not good as he was under age – or game halls, where at least he could keep warm even if he had no cash to feed into the machines. Not that he would if he had – mug's game.

There was a bus shelter Connor had used in the past, giving the impression that he was waiting for a different bus from the one that arrived. He could last for ages that way, eventually at the head of the queue but never getting on. Now he perched on the plastic ledge and stared at the litter underfoot.

Michael. Michael Seward. And Rebecca Mulligan. 'Mulligan' didn't suit her, it sounded too heavyweight – some girl with big-framed spectacles and bad skin, or a boy, a skinhead with a tattooed scalp. 'Rebecca', though – that suited her. Not Becky, she wasn't a Becky.

And Michael. Raphael Michael Seward. Both angels' names, of course – two of the Archangels that all sources agreed on, the other two being Gabriel and Uriel.

Odd that Michael had become a humdrum, everyday name with even its pronunciation changed, in English at least, for surely it ought to be said with a short first vowel and a diphthong second – Mik-aiel. Whereas Raphael was instantly the painter of the Renaissance. Gabriel was Gabriel Oak the shepherd in 'Far From the Madding Crowd'. And nobody ever used Uriel.

He was wandering.

He had taken up with both of them – Michael by choice, Rebecca when she was foisted on him, definitely not his choice. No doubt she felt the same about him. It had been a shock for her when he walked into Michael's flat, that was for sure – he'd seen her face before she had it back under control. A shock for him, too. And now Michael – the one they'd both said yes to – was gone, at least for the time being, and he had to work with this girl, this artist, who considered him just a no-hoper from a local sink school.

Which was about right.

Connor checked his watch. Fifteen minutes since he'd bolted. Three times that to go at the very least, safer to make it longer.

Did he look like them? He had black hair, remarked upon by all and sundry, but what about the rest? What he saw when he looked in the mirror was just the face he lived in, but the other two...

Michael was confusing. From a couple of things he had said – brief references which might have gone unnoticed unless you were paying close attention – Connor had deduced that he was in his forties, but no-one would ever believe it from looking at him. Although there was something in his eyes – something not young. Something that made you want to know him, and made you hang back at the same time. Enigmatic. Wistful. When he smiled there was always some sadness about the smile.

And then Rebecca.

Connor shifted uncomfortably, getting pins and needles from perching on the hard seat.

She was amazing. He had never seen a girl as beautiful as that in real life. She was like a movie actress, or a model from a glossy magazine, airbrushed to perfection, so confident she didn't need to try. Connor was sure that she wore no make up, not even eye make up which practically all girls wore. And her hair, cropped short like that – all it did was show off the bone structure of her face and her long neck and her perfect, delicate ears.

Of course she thought he was a worm. Worse than that – a worm she had to pick up and carry about with her.

Except that she hadn't, of course.

He had almost burned with resentment when she pushed off to Oxford like that to stay with her old school pal. As if he was just the workforce, the sniffer dog, the instrument that told her where to go before she waltzed off and got all the glory. Well, not next time. Next time he was going along whether she liked it or not, even if he had to sleep rough.

Watch out, Rebecca, this worm's going to turn!

THE grouse were about and the taxi had to crawl up the hill in a series of stops and starts to give the birds a chance to run out from under its wheels. And run straight back again. The original bird-brains. One, sitting dumpy and dark on the fence, watched the car approach and then flopped onto the loose shingle directly in front.

The driver braked and another bird escaped whole, ready for sacrifice on the Glorious Twelfth.

The driver hissed. Michael said, 'I know. Don't worry, it's actually quite rare for any to get squashed. And no-one'll blame you if they do.'

'Stupid little blighters, aren't they.'

'They are. You're from down south?'

'That's right, Hounslow. Came up here five years ago to get away from the crowd. The wife wanted a quieter life. Well, we both did. Cleaner air, you know?'

'Yes, I know. My parents the same. Longer ago, though. And do you like it?'

'Oh yes,' the driver said emphatically. 'Wouldn't go back now. Wouldn't know how to cope with the numbers. You get used to the space, don't you?' He braked again, jerkily, and the grouse waddled and flapped away into the grass. 'Could do without the wildlife, of course... Kilts and all that!' he added, inviting his passenger to laugh.

Michael smiled.

'Your mum and dad up here, then?' the driver asked, nodding his head towards the hill in front of them. The drive wound to and fro to cope with the steep incline and they couldn't yet see the top.

'That's right. They don't own the land, though, just the barn.'

His mother had been the driving force. She had never settled in town, missing the wide skies and plains of Iowa, and Scotland had seemed the nearest landscape that would do. The heather-clad mountains and long lakes were not remotely like the American mid-west, but they were relatively unpopulated and enjoyed proper weather – blue skies in summer and snow in winter. Rose was instantly happy – it had been like flicking a switch, Michael remembered. And with Rose's happiness came his father's.

Michael might have settled in Scotland too – there was a thriving craft culture in the Highlands and probably enough tourist trade to keep him in business. But he had wanted access to the exhibitions and shows in the south, and needed the secondary sources he used for inspiration – the recurring designs of other cultures, the ancient symbols of the elements that could be found in the great London collections. And he had wanted – felt necessary – to be close to the Victoria and Albert Museum with its secret code.

It had seemed impossible that he would ever solve it. And yet now they were on the way.

'This it?'

Michael snapped to and saw the roof of the barn rising above the ground ahead. 'Yes, that's it. You can turn down here.'

Outside the barn Michael paid the driver and hauled his rucksack out of the boot. 'Thanks.'

And there was his father, opening the door and welcoming him into the kitchen.

Chapter Fifteen

IT can't be as easy as this. It shouldn't be as easy as this. Why is it as easy as this?

Rebecca was on the train for the second time, heading back to Paddington with her bag on her lap. The strap was looped round one wrist, but even so from time to time she moved her hands to feel the nylon against her skin, hugging it to her. So precious. Unbelievable.

Having run out of time the first weekend, she had returned to Steph's to try to find the candle. After a day of chapel-creeping, during which they tramped from college to college, crossing quads large and small, with and without trees or fountains or sundials, peering round oak doors during choir practices and organ recitals and cool, remote silences, they had finally identified the chapel Rebecca needed as that of St Mary's College from a combination of the stained glass windows and decorated organ pipes.

So it was indeed Oxford again. Well, there was a certain logic to that. There were few universities in England in the mid-nineteenth century and most of them very young by comparison with Oxford and Cambridge. It seemed quite plausible that the kind of people who had formed Michael's Mundus Caecus would have been Oxford graduates, and the college buildings would have provided obvious security and continuity. After all, they had already stood for four or five hundred years and were hardly likely to be redeveloped in the foreseeable future; they would not be sold into private hands, or sacked, or appropriated for some other use. The items were not intended to be lost, just securely stored.

Even so … imagine that key hanging there for one and a half centuries. Hadn't any porter ever wondered what it was? And this candle, now wrapped in a scarf and zipped securely inside her bag – how could it have lain in its paper at the back of the vestry cupboard for so long, tucked behind the hymnals and orders of service? Didn't anyone ever clean? It was difficult not to believe that some kind of force was at work here, quietly blinding everyone to the presence of these things, maintaining a sort of cloak of invisibility around them until the day she, Rebecca Mulligan, should open a door, reach in her hand, and lift them.

'Lift' as in 'pick up', of course, not as in 'steal'. It couldn't really be classed as stealing if nobody knew of its existence. And anyway, if this story were true then the objects had been tucked away specifically in order to be found and used in the future. It wasn't theft if the original owner intended you to have it.

Rebecca shifted, moving the bag on her lap. She was absolutely not a thief and she had nothing to worry about.

Except the next five items, one of which they didn't even know.

Seven objects, Michael had said. Magic number seven – seven swans in Hans Christian Andersen; seven brides for seven brothers in the musical; seventh son of a seventh son. Seven objects necessary to understand what had to be done to access and fix the leaky door, and Michael knew six of them: a candle, a key, a clock, a telescope, a book, and some thread.

The problem was that he did not know the seventh item, and there didn't seem to be any way to find it out. All they could do was hope that something would link to something else and reveal it in some way, and in the meantime bring together the other six.

Four now. Rebecca was going to have to start a file, a treasure chest to store them in. She couldn't put this candle in her biscuit jar, much less a clock and a telescope.

I wonder if those will be in Oxford too. Good thing they didn't all live in Edinburgh.

Back home, she unwrapped the candle and ran her finger over the hard wax. There was a thin metal band about an inch below the wick which resisted when she picked at it. On looking closely she was inclined to believe it wasn't a band around the candle at all, but a disc, a wafer of metal running through the centre of the column. Could you make a candle that way? Rebecca imagined dipping the wick repeatedly into molten wax. Provided the metal disc was fastened securely to the wick so that it didn't slide down – above a knot, for example – then it ought to stay in place while the candle formed about it. But why would you do such a thing?

Presumably to tell someone something. If the disc was supposed to be secret the candle maker would have continued dipping past the edge of the metal, so that the candle continued to grow fat around it and cover it from view. This maker had taken care to cease dipping at the moment that the edge of the disk was reached, so that the sliver of metal was visible.

So what might it tell?

No good, don't even think about it. Only Michael can set light to this wick.

That Michael was the boss was unarguable, and Rebecca felt no inclination to cross him. She couldn't quite say why – he had never been anything but friendly and courteous in her presence, but there was something... what? Not dangerous, more – masked. He has a hidden agenda, Rebecca thought; something in mind that he hasn't told me – us – I'm sure of it. But what?

She needed a home for the candle. If she were to follow the line taken by the Victorians, she would keep it in a candlestick on the mantelpiece, but she didn't feel quite up to that. After rewrapping it and putting it for the time being in her underwear drawer – surely no burglar would take an old candle even if they did break in? – Rebecca rang Michael's number, but was diverted to voice mail.

'It's Rebecca. I've got the candle. It was really easy – feels like it ought to have been harder. Anyway, we'll go for the other things tomorrow.'

'So.'

'What does that mean? 'So'?'

Connor shrugged without meeting her eyes. 'So.'

Rebecca stared at him. His hair was very long, far longer than was fashionable for teenage boys, thick and straight but with what hair stylists call movement. Very attractive, actually. She supposed that when she had allowed her own hair to grow it had probably been like that. Ironic that she kept hers cropped short and both these men wore theirs long.

Men? Wrong – one man, one boy.

There had been a bad atmosphere from the start. Connor

arrived at the museum almost half an hour later than they had agreed so that Rebecca had to kick her heels in the entrance hall. She had rung him, of course (thank heavens Michael had sorted him out with a phone), but he had given no excuse, and when he arrived had barely glanced at her before climbing the stairs, leaving her to follow.

Which she had. What else could she do? But it was extremely aggravating to have him responding to her in mono-syllables when she expected an explanation, an apology for having made her wait.

'What kept you?' she asked eventually. She spoke to his back because he was ahead of her and she couldn't get round in front without actually running, which obviously was out of the question.

'Nothing. Stuff. They have books in here.'

And Rebecca had to trot to keep up with him as he strode through the Ironwork Gallery, past the keys and the candlesticks, to the British Galleries.

It wasn't easy, this part of the job. Apart from the candlestick, which Michael had known about, all the pointer objects were unidentified. Connor had to tour the museum very slowly, tentacles out, straining to pick up an aura from almost any kind of exhibit.

The key had not been difficult, because all the keys in the museum were displayed in two cases next to each other. The clock was proving to be a nightmare because the few they found were distributed throughout the museum – a glass one in the glass gallery, a silver one in the silver hall – and they had agreed to postpone it for the time being and concentrate on the book.

Books also were not straightforward. There were masses in the art library, but after two hours in there alone, while Rebecca was in Oxford, Connor had drawn a blank and was disinclined to try there again. Besides, those books were in use, being handled and read, and he didn't believe the pointer book would have been subjected to that.

In the British Galleries, however, there was a nineteenth century bookcase filled with leather-bound books safely locked away behind glass, probably never touched from one decade to the next unless the galleries were reorganised, and then no doubt handled with great care. Surely that was the place to hide a one-off.

He explained this – briefly – to Rebecca, and she agreed. She was anyway obliged to go wherever he chose to lead because when all was said and done he, Connor, was the sniffer dog and she merely the recorder. So they wound their way through the period interiors of the British Galleries to stand in front of the bookcase, and Connor took up his stance, gazing blankly downwards, focusing his eyes on nothing in particular so that he could channel his receptivity into this sixth sense he was using.

Rebecca watched him lift his head a little as if he had caught something beyond her hearing, and positioned her pencil ready to transcribe what he said. But after a few moments he broke away, pushed past her, and said, 'Okay.'

'Okay what?' Rebecca, fuming, jammed her pencil through the spiral binding of her notebook and followed him. 'Didn't you get anything?'

'Yep.'

'Well what?'

'I want a coffee.'

Maddeningly he made his way still ahead of her – always damn well ahead of her – to the café, managing by some fancy footwork to weave through a school party and get far enough in front to have paid for his cup of coffee before she had got to the till. She then had to look around before spotting him, already at a table, and was close to erupting point when she finally caught him up.

'Alright, what's this all about?'

Connor shrugged.

Rebecca sat down. She said coldly, 'You obviously got something back there so why didn't you speak? How am I supposed to write notes if you don't tell me what to write?'

'If I tell you where the book is you'll push off and get it on your own. So I'm not telling you.'

Rebecca stared. After a moment she said, 'Is that it? You wanted to come to Oxford?'

Connor shrugged again, something he excelled at. 'I could

have come to Oxford.'

'No, Connor, you couldn't.' Rebecca spoke flatly, as if to a kid, because frankly he was behaving like one. 'I sleep on the floor in my friend's room. Even that isn't actually allowed. There certainly isn't room for two. What would you do? Stay in a hotel?'

That was cruel.

He stonewalled her, stubbornly silent.

Rebecca glared. 'Well, what?'

'I'd have found somewhere. We're supposed to be doing this together. And if you don't want to work together, well, maybe I don't want to work together either. So.'

'What does that mean? 'So'?'

'So.'

She couldn't browbeat him. Irritatingly, he refused to defer to her greater age, experience and wisdom. A week ago she'd have added 'intelligence' to that list, but honesty compelled her to drop that one.

There was no denying he was intelligent – intelligent to a precocious degree, so that Rebecca had fallen into the habit of holding her tongue until he had pronounced on anything even vaguely literary. For a kid at a sink school he seemed to have read acres of print, and to have remembered most of it too, a talent Rebecca lacked and for which she had great respect. He ought to be aiming for a place to study at Oxford instead of just visiting it for a stolen weekend, but higher education didn't seem to feature on his agenda.

She had considered asking him why, probing a bit into his background, but felt warned off by the invisible fence around him, eight foot high with barbed wire on top and a notice saying Guard-dogs – Beware!

Although Michael seemed to have found a way under or over or through.

Rebecca sipped her coffee thoughtfully. *I shouldn't have said that about the hotel.*

After a while she said, 'Okay, I won't go without you next time, although there might not be a next time in Oxford anyway. But if there is, you can come too.'

And that had better be magnanimous enough for you because it's all you're getting.

Connor took a drink, too. 'Okay.'

Hallelujah. Rebecca recognised her relief and decided to ignore it. 'So are you going to tell me what you saw?'

To her stark amazement, Connor gave her a small, sideways smile, and the clouds parted and the sunlight came through. She realised she had never seen him smile before.

'I can't. I can't remember. I see it, but I can't hold it. I'll have to go back and do it again.'

'So you do need me to transcribe?'

'Oh yeah.'

Chapter Sixteen

THIS time Rebecca was permitted to write. But what she wrote didn't make sense.

'Are you sure about this?' she asked, scanning her notes. 'It's a bit contradictory. Wooden shelves and metal racks. Upstairs, underground. Computer terminals – what did the Victorians know about computer terminals? Have you any idea what this is all about?'

'Wait a minute.'

Rebecca waited. It occurred to her that obedience was becoming habitual, and she wasn't sure she liked it. Connor covered his face for a moment, then dropped his hands and said, 'Okay, I'll tell you what this is. They hid the book in the British Library.'

'The British Library?'

'Of course. Why not? The largest collection of books in the country, with the best cataloguing system. Foolproof.'

'But?' Rebecca said, sensing the caveat.

'But the British Library moved, didn't it?'

'Did it?'

Connor pulled a face. 'Yes. In the nineteen nineties. These Victorians hid the book in the British Museum Library, which later formed part of the collection of the British Library. The whole lot's at St Pancras now. But I was getting flashes of the old round reading room at the BM as well. That's amazing!' He paused as it struck him. 'The information I was getting just now, it's been – well, up-dated. As if it was live. How could that be?'

Rebecca shrugged. 'How can any of this be? It's all unbelievable, when you get down to it. Magic.' She glanced back at her notes. 'So this book is in the British Library at St Pancras. Do you know it, then?'

'I've been,' said Connor, 'yes.' It was another free place to go to be quiet and write or just think.

'And you can just walk in?'

'To the building, yes. They have an exhibition hall and a café.

You can't get access to the stacks.'

'The stacks?'

'The books. The documents. They call them stacks.' How could she have got to – whatever age she was – without knowing these things? 'And it isn't a book anyway. It's a document. A manuscript. A single page job.'

'So how do we get it?'

Connor said, 'I don't think we need to.'

THE library was quiet during school hours. The red-haired librarian was on duty at the check-in desk, and it occurred to Rebecca that most of the staff would recognise her as one of the regulars. She had always been alone before, though.

She'd better not think he's my boyfriend.

She strode ahead, projecting detachment, and slipped into the chair at the first free monitor.

Connor lurked at her shoulder, watching the screen as Rebecca logged on. She searched for the British Library and, clicking swiftly through the options, found her way to Manuscript Services and, hoorah, the link to How To Order Reproductions.

'Right. What's it called?'

'It's a letter. It's addressed to Walter Spencer and signed by William Dwyer. Dated 1852, of course.'

The letter was there in the catalogue, with all details correct and a British Library reference code: their manuscript, the manuscript prepared by Mundus Caecus and buried for them to dig up. Rebecca grinned as she typed the reference into the on-line form. 'I can't believe it.'

'Yeah.'

Rebecca paid with her debit card, disconnected and swung round in the swivel chair. 'A wonderful thing, the internet.'

Tactless again.

'Look,' she said. 'I'm sorry about Oxford.'

'YOU know that I won't leave your mother now.'

Michael and his parents were sitting in the evening sunshine that lay now at one end of the house, where the land fell steeply to the tops of trees. A short sloping lawn gave way to pasture where small, red Highland cattle wandered.

Above was only sky. It was why they had come here, twenty years ago, to take a converted barn with downstairs-upstairs arrangements which allowed them a monarch's view from the living room. The sky might not have been able to match that over Iowa, but it was generous enough and Rose was happy.

She sat with the men but took no part in their conversation, and Michael knew his father spoke as if she didn't hear.

He glanced across to where she sat, humming quietly and looking outwards, as lost to them in her dementia as if she had been physically absent. She sort of knew who he was, Michael thought, or at least knew his name; whether she matched him with her son was anybody's guess. The pain came not from the implied rejection, but from his loss of all she had been. His mother was gone, leaving this shell.

'You don't need to,' he said.

'And these children are really going to help?'

Michael thought of Rebecca's haughty confidence, of Connor's contained aggression. 'They'll help. I'll manage.'

'I'm sorry I can't do more.'

But the time for his father to get involved had passed. Michael had known that he was alone in this. He was accustomed to being alone, so it didn't much signify.

His father was ninety-six years old, born twelve years into the twentieth century, two years before the outbreak of the first world war. The span of his lifetime seemed immense. A child in the Roaring Twenties; a young man during the Great Depression of the Thirties; an airman in the Battle of Britain, shot down three times and with eye-popping stories to tell; already in his fifties when he watched the eruption of pop music and mini-skirts, and in his seventies by the time most households had a computer and video cassette recorder.

Now he was four years short of his centenary, yet probably nobody in the town below would have put him at much over seventy – a fit and youthful seventy at that.

Michael considered his father's face, longer and sharper than his own but strongly similar. Same dark eyes, for a start, and the same black hair, although with silver finally appearing in it. His skin was toned, though crows' feet spread out from his eyes, and he was fit enough to climb the drive on foot if he chose. Michael couldn't remember him ever being ill.

How much difference would the thinning of the blood make? What would he, Michael, look like at ninety?

Pointless to speculate, as it always had been. You can't know until you get there.

Michael said, 'I guess you haven't remembered the missing piece?'

His father shook his head. 'Can't get anywhere with it. There was something odd about it, that's all I can recall. Something different from all the others, but I don't know what. Believe me, Michael, I've been trying. Nothing.'

If he didn't remember, what were they going to do? Seven objects were needed to locate the breach, and if they could only manage six, what then?

Don't think about it. There will be a way. Only a few weeks ago it had all been impossible, and then not just one but two mixed-race descendents had arrived from nowhere to kick-start what had seemed a hopeless project, bringing with them possibilities undreamed of.

Except that he had dreamed them, had dreamed them all his life.

No. The seventh would be found.

There was a butterfly visiting the planted tubs. Michael watched the delicate wings beat.

He said, 'Have you noticed anything up here?'

'Not specifically. I get feelings sometimes, premonitions. Sometimes it seems to me that there are too many coincidences. Like the village shop taking in extra copies of Scientific American the day I want to buy one. Like your mother choosing to send pink roses to Milly for her birthday and the roses I thought were white coming into bud pink.'

'Nice coincidences.'

'Nice, but strange. I wonder, that's all. Just wonder.'

The sun was moving round and the shadow of the house

creeping towards them. Michael senior looped all three mugs onto the fingers of one hand and offered his other arm to his wife, younger than him by fifteen years but so much older.

Michael junior moved their chairs back against the wall under the eaves. He had come to Scotland for a number of reasons, not least to see if by prompting he might succeed in unlocking his father's memory of the missing item. Apparently not.

Also, of course, to entice that meddlesome estate agent away from London, which had certainly worked – he had telephoned the hotel in Aberfeldy claiming to wish to check his reservation and giving Geoffrey Foster's name, and the hotel had innocently and obligingly confirmed that he was booked to arrive that evening.

And there was the other reason, which he did not choose to mention, although he suspected – just at times, at odd moments, intercepting a pensive look or a half-begun, quickly-stifled comment – that his father had guessed.

IF only she had found this place before he died.

Celia felt the familiar signs and made herself breathe slowly. She spread her fingers, watching them on her lap for signs of trembling.

This is no good. He's gone. Just wait for someone to arrive.

'... a shock, as we'd lost contact with that branch of the family back in the seventies, really. I feel guilty, to tell the truth, but there – the money's ours and I admit it will be very welcome.'

Would the woman never shut up?

'Have you ever had a legacy, Celia?'

Celia closed her hands tightly. 'Never.'

Only Robert's, which Olwen wouldn't have recognised as a legacy at all but which had always felt like one to Celia, despite thirty years of marriage. She had taken him for his money and his lifestyle and had inherited it when he died – early, happily.

This is my legacy. This should be my legacy. He gave us nothing while he lived; this should be mine now.

A visitor smiled in passing and Celia forced herself to reciprocate. Stewarding was at least a way of keeping close to the

house… His house…
   My house.

Chapter Seventeen

THE Rannoch Hotel sat square half way along the high street – grey stone with a lot of dark wood, red carpets and sporting prints. Par for the course, pretty much.

'Good evening. Can I help you, sir?'

And Scottish accents.

The estate agent smiled and reached for his wallet. 'You should have a reservation for me. Geoffrey Foster.'

Within ten minutes he was installed in a corner of the bar with a gin and tonic and a newspaper, and a view through the half-glazed door to the lobby. It was pleasant to relax after the long drive and play with the future's potential.

Geoffrey Foster leaned back comfortably to think.

James Josiah – and God bless him, he couldn't have understood much – had written that it all hinged upon light. They had all believed that light from this other world, state of being, whatever you wanted to call it, had been leaking into this world and causing mischief. They believed it was less as though light were creeping through a crack than that light beams from both worlds were colliding and becoming confused. Mingling, as James Josiah put it.

So let's think about that for a moment.

Light was just light to the Victorians – an amorphous wave. It was only in the early twentieth century that Einstein identified individual particles of light. Now, suppose light particles from one world met light particles from another – suppose they interfered with each other in some way. Instead of carrying on their original trajectory they would be diverted, heading off in a completely different direction. Into another dimension, even. For that to happen, the separate light beams would need to come at each other along different paths – at right-angles, for example. Where they crossed, most of the photons would continue on their original course, but those that came close enough might influence each other.

But – and here came the crunch – this kind of influence would only become a problem if the photons were already linked, or entangled, at a quantum level. How could that be? Could they become entangled simply by meeting? Or were the two dimensions already entangled, in which case any connecting doorway or portal could hold the solution to one of the highest potential money-spinners in theoretical physics.

So what was old James talking about here? What apparatus had they concocted to make everything secure again? Angled mirrors, he said, positioned to deflect the beams. Mirrors, plural, which made sense because that would permit the light to revert to its original path once the danger zone was crossed.

He doodled idly on a corner of the newspaper, sketching a series of ninety-degree bends down, along, and up again, like a hard-cornered letter U. Light being bent around space. Is that what they had done?

Separating the light beams this way would mean there could be no interaction at all. Did that mean neither world could influence the other?

And then, what about this other business? Foster smiled as he recalled his ancestor's written confession: '*I suppose I should not include this, we did agree, after all, but who would read my journal?*' After which he had proceeded to document, in considerable detail, the plan to find secure resting places for the seven clues that would tell their descendants where to find the door to the other world. It was over-elaborate in Foster's opinion – very Rider Haggard – but perhaps they had all been carried away by the adventure that had come upon them – which in fairness was exceptional, if you believed it at all.

He still wasn't sure that he did, but the possibilities, if it proved true, were too tempting to ignore.

Unfortunately James Josiah's diary left a great deal unexplained. Despite the group's agreement he had written about his hiding the clock in Oxford, and Foster suspected he would have been equally ready to reveal the locations of the other six items. But he didn't know them. In true cloak-and-dagger style, each member had assumed responsibility for one item and had dealt with it confidentially. Nobody appeared to have considered the possibility of their descendants either dying out or simply disbelieving their fantastic story.

Yet Seward had kept to the faith.

James Josiah's incautious disclosures had not been restricted to the key. Foster had been delighted to read that he suspected the woman among them to have been up to no good with the immigrant, the traveller who was guiding them. Victorian hanky-panky with an alien life-form! And now a man walking about in the twenty-first century who was the same age as Geoffrey yet looked young enough to be his son...

Foster smiled.

'I THOUGHT you said you know this place.'

'I do. Shut up. Let me think a minute.' Rebecca's turn to put her hands over her face. *Think, think. Where else is there?*

The problem was that the Victoria and Albert was a maze, a labyrinth. There was always another corner, a staircase, an archway into another gallery. It just went on and on.

Never brilliant with spatial awareness – even the expression made her stomach sink – Rebecca couldn't carry the layout in her head, and the maps the museum handed out were less than helpful, with colour codes and numbers in boxes instead of names. Rebecca was accustomed to wandering until she saw something she liked enough to stop and draw: recipe for happiness. Now she was being asked to know her way around and it was proving a trial.

Where could the instruments be?

Not musical instruments but mathematical instruments, optical instruments, that was what they needed to find and Rebecca couldn't recall ever having come across them. Yet clocks and compasses and orreries had been highly decorated in the past, so where were they?

It didn't help to have Connor standing there, breathing.

She took her hands down and marched off, leaving the boy to follow, which was a change at least. Rebecca made her way to the end of the gallery where she hoped to see a steward. Sure enough, parked on a chair at the entrance was a man in a dark suit and a museum tie.

Rebecca said, 'Excuse me.'

'Yes, miss?' The steward uncrossed his arms and sat forward hoping no doubt for some nice juicy question.

'Can you tell me where to find the scientific instruments?'

'Scientific...?'

'Clocks, telescopes, that kind of thing?'

'Ah, yes.' The steward gained confidence. 'We don't have any of those here, madam. They were all moved.'

'Moved?' Connor repeated.

'Aye, that's right. Sometime before nineteen twenty-eight.' He pronounced the date with great satisfaction. Almost as if he's going to add, And I Remember It Well, Rebecca thought sourly.

'Where to? Where did they go?'

'Next door,' the steward said. 'The Science Museum. They got all that kind of thing. Started moving them across the road at the beginning of the century.'

The Science Museum! How obvious. She hadn't been going potty, the V and A didn't have such a gallery. Self-respect restored, Rebecca headed downstairs, Connor alongside. 'Should have guessed,' he said.

'Well, yes, I suppose. Anyway, we've got it now.'

With one difficulty.

Connor was frowning. 'There's going to be an awful lot of possibles there, though. A lot of candidates for the job.'

And there it is.

In the V and A there might have been a gallery of instruments including telescopes and clocks – a single case of one, maybe three or four cases of the other. But in the Science Museum there were going to be dozens of cases, hundreds of exhibits, surely? It was going to take hours for Connor to trawl for the message he had to seek out, the silent, invisible aura that announced to him the presence of a pointer to part of the key. It could take all day. It could take all *week*.

But in the event the Science Museum proved difficult for the opposite reason.

As they entered the museum the level of noise was ferocious, the primary colours and in-your-face signage jangling to the sensibilities.

A tape strung between posts forced entering queues to snake back and forth, as if in a theme park, never necessary at the Victoria and Albert. Once through and onto the floor of the museum itself, the target demographic appeared to be aged approximately ten. The place resembled the Lego aisle in a toy superstore.

Ugh.

They found the clocks quickly, in a gallery above the open floor where clocks and watches in cases displayed their exquisite brass movements and filigree hands. There were grandfather clocks and carriage clocks and alarm clocks, and rows of watches with their faces removed to reveal their mechanisms. And not one of them was the pointer.

'Are you sure?' Rebecca couldn't quite help asking.

'Of course I'm sure. There's nothing.'

'It isn't because the noise is...'

'No.'

Right.

They stood in the midst of the timepieces, Rebecca unsure what to do, Connor apparently lost in thought. She dared a sidelong glance. He was frowning into the middle distance.

After a moment or two, she said tentatively, 'So...'

Connor shook himself. 'I'll find the telescope.' He looked at her. 'You can stay here if you like. I'll come for you when I've got it.'

Whether he was fed up with her or simply being generous Rebecca didn't care to wonder. She swiftly accepted the offer, and settled herself to draw the delicate instruments beneath the glass.

After half an hour she was interested to observe that no vines had tried to infiltrate her pencil, and the sketches, though not her best, were certainly far better than they had been of late.

Why? Because Michael is absent? Because it was only temporary anyway, and I was panicking needlessly? Or because I've committed to this, I'm on track and doing what they – it – he – wants me to do?

Perversely, she drew a pretty little ivy strand climbing over the cogs and looping round the wheels. She made the leaf variegated, and then perused it thoughtfully. It seemed to look straight back at her with disarming innocence, like a pansy. Very disarming flowers, pansies. Innocuous. Mild.

Now I really am going bonkers.

She closed the book. A coffee would have been nice. Alternately she could have faced finding Connor and finding out how the search was going, but that was not a good idea as the arrangement was that he would return here to find her when he was ready. He was oddly reluctant to use the mobile phone and kept it turned off most of the time, which Rebecca found incomprehensible.

A peculiar boy, and that was putting it mildly. She suspected dark and unpleasant things in his life, but wasn't prepared to find out exactly what they were. Although fond of imagining her home was less than perfect – her mother deceased, her natural father unknown, an awkward and interfering stepfather – she knew very well that she had never been ill-treated or neglected the way Connor very likely was. It made her uncomfortable, and she generally chose not to dwell on things that made her uncomfortable.

It was four forty-five when Connor finally came back and broke the news.

'AND where on earth is Blythe House?'

'Don't worry. It isn't the north pole. Ten minutes' walk from either West Ken or Barons Court.'

He seemed unfazed. Rebecca forced herself to cool down. 'And we can go there now?'

'No.'

'No?' Rebecca grabbed Connor's wrist in order to halt him. 'Why? Isn't it open to the public?'

Connor stopped and faced her. 'Yes, it's open to the public, but only by appointment. You can't just wander in off the street. It's their storage facility. You apply to see specific items and they get them out for you.'

Storage facility. She had been right – the Science Museum was a theme park. With acres of floor space devoted to hands-on play areas, reconstructed ship's radio rooms and moon landings, mere historic objects had been sidelined into a warehouse out in the sticks which you had to apply in writing to see.

Although perhaps Barons Court wasn't quite in the sticks. But it was a further delay, and very frustrating.

'And the clock we want, and the telescope, they are definitely there?'

Connor looked at her coolly. 'How could I possibly know?'

Chapter Eighteen

THAT Michael Seward was not staying in the Rannoch Hotel Foster knew for certain by now. The reception staff had been a little too worldly after all to reveal the names of the other guests, but after dinner the first night, breakfast, lunch, and dinner the second night, and an inordinate amount of time loafing in the lounge spying on the lobby, Geoffrey had to concede that his quarry had some other place to bed down.

The telephone directory revealed no Sewards in the district, or at least none that were not ex-directory. Geoffrey visited the town post office and newsagent, bakery, butcher and two greengrocers, all of whom refused to be drawn on the identity of their customers. He then tried the dentist, asking to fix an appointment and claiming the practice to have been recommended by friends named Seward, but to no avail. He had even considered the same ploy at the doctor's clinic but was forced to take a reality check; there was no way a doctor's receptionist would release information to him.

So no local leads at all. But since he was here, and there was always the remote chance of running into his quarry in the street, he took himself out into the town and walked.

The weather was perfect and the air, cliché or not, was sweeter in Scotland than in London. Remember this, Foster thought, and when you're a multi-millionaire you could do worse than have a place up here as a retreat.

Walking lifted his spirits and increased his optimism; notions which had been remote began to seem, if not probable, at least distinctly possible.

If an alternate world truly existed and was indeed interacting with this one, then it raised all manner of intriguing questions regarding quantum entanglement and Heisenberg's Uncertainty Principle.

It seemed that light particles – photons – were causing the rift, and if any sub-atomic particles could become entangled, why not photons? He had always read widely and was reasonably abreast with current thought. There was no doubt that the man who found his way to understanding and harnessing quantum entanglement, thus removing the fundamental obstacle to quantum computer technology, would effectively rule the world in financial terms.

Computers which did not have to operate sequentially... The prospect had not so far moved beyond the confines of research institutes, but it was captivating. Imagine – every code broken in an instant, toppling the financial operation of the globe, not to mention national security, defence systems, the internet ...

Life as we know it ...

We'll have to carry gold in our pockets.

And all to be replaced by – what? Something new, something other, something way, way better. Something controlled by himself.

HERE we go again, Rebecca thought, as they waited to be admitted. It was becoming tedious. Nevertheless she had her fingers crossed inside her pocket. The blanks they had drawn at the Victoria and Albert and then at the Science Museum had knocked dents in her confidence, and suddenly it was as easy to imagine failing to find the pointers here as succeeding.

The electric gates opened and they stepped into the yard. Blythe House had formerly been the headquarters of the Post Office National Savings Bank, and retained its impressive security. Rebecca and Connor signed for visitors' passes before the curator appeared and led them through the corridors. She seemed a little miffed.

'You can have until ten thirty,' she told them, without looking round. 'I'm afraid there is a school party booked.'

Rebecca was amazed that they were there at all. Connor had telephoned and it had apparently not been easy.

'They normally require a minimum of two weeks' notice,' he told Rebecca.

'So how did you...'

'I begged.'

Rebecca suspected begging would not be her strong point.

The room they were taken looked industrial – wood floor,

brick walls and huge steel racks containing the vast collection of objects that the museum proper had no space to display. There were no windows and the air was chill.

'Telescopes,' the curator said. 'And the clocks are at the far end. I'll take you when you're ready.' She hitched herself onto a stool at one side of the racks and watched them.

It was disconcerting. For a start it meant that Rebecca felt she had to give the impression that she was as interested in the telescopes as Connor, instead of merely waiting to take dictation. She gazed at the rows of brass and wood cylinders, wondering whether one of them was theirs, hoping fervently that one would be.

'Here.' Connor spoke quietly. He parked himself, waited while she took out the notebook and gave him the nod, and then lowered his eyes, stretched out his psychic tentacles and reached with his mind towards what the telescope on the shelf had to impart.

Rebecca scribbled. Then she whispered, 'This is ridiculous. We will never get away with this, we'll be locked up.' She put away her pencil. 'Let's get the clock quick and get out of here.' Louder, she said in the direction of the curator, 'That is very interesting. Very helpful. Thank you very much. Could we see the clocks now?'

But yet again there was no clock.

For twenty minutes Connor trawled the racks while the grumpy curator fidgeted and Rebecca's anxiety rose, and finally he shrugged and said, 'No good. It isn't here.'

'What do you mean? Where is it then?'

'You tell me.'

For a moment Rebecca stared at him in dismay. Then she pulled herself together and marched past him to the curator. 'Thank you so much. And thank you for accommodating us at such short notice.'

The curator slid off her stool and Rebecca skipped up alongside her as they retraced their steps to the lobby. She almost had to run just to keep up.

'I suppose there aren't any more clocks – or timepieces of any kind – anywhere else here?'

'No, no, we catalogue everything together.'

'And there's no other storage facility for the Science –'

'No, no, just us. Please sign out.' The curator held out her hand for the passes.

They were practically ejected into the street.

'Lovely lady,' Rebecca said. 'Now what do we do?'

'LOST.'

'Lost? How can you know that? You can't possibly know that!' Rebecca realised she sounded accusatory and tried to bring her voice down a notch. 'Seriously, how can you be sure?'

Connor, on his mobile phone somewhere, said, 'I'm not making it up. I asked.'

'But –'

'I went back to the V and A. I asked how the scientific exhibits were moved to the Science Museum, and he went off and got a book, a history of the museums, and it turns out they were moving things across for decades. It's not impossible that one packing case might have got mislaid in transit. Probably pinched. And our clock must have been in it.'

Rebecca considered. She supposed it was possible – incredibly bad luck, but possible. She said, 'You really think –'

'It must be. It must have been. Otherwise why can't I find it?'

After a moment Rebecca said tentatively, 'I suppose it wouldn't do any good to go back–'

'No.' Connor said. 'There was nothing. No hope.'

No hope.

'Either we'll find a way to manage without the clock,' Connor said, 'or we've had it.'

WHEREVER Michael was, they had rubbish mobile reception. Rebecca sighed, and began to key in a text message to reach him when and if he picked up a signal.

Telescope in museum in Oxford. Clock probably lost before 1928. What now?

Chapter Nineteen

IT had been raining more or less continuously for two days, but the rain in the highlands was quite different from London rain. It was soft, more a mist, really, and didn't seem to matter.

Milly had come up from the village and was sitting with Rose. Michael and Michael, son and father, put on rain jackets and walked down the hill, scattering grouse before them. The moisture they breathed was sweet, like grass or pine needles or apples, and bathed their faces.

This must be how toads feel after a dry spell.

They walked side by side, looking ahead. The older man swung a walking stick, but didn't lean on it. At the corner, where the drive began its zigzag down the side of the hill, he rapped the stick on the tarmac. 'Do you know what needs to be done?

'Not yet.'

He looked at his son, staring ahead. 'I presume the book will tell you?'

'I guess.'

They walked on .

'And you understand what might happen?'

Michael glanced at his father and read the concern in his eyes. Concern for whom, though, or what? Mankind? His son and heir? Himself and his wife?

'Not really. Do you?'

'No. But I suppose we'll find out soon enough if it fails. Or perhaps not.'

Perhaps not. Michael asked, 'What do you think? Guess, I mean? How much of a risk is there?'

'Of them finding a way through in Alaska before you can shut it down here? I don't know. I'd have thought it would hit the news if they discovered anything significant. Or do you mean risk if the door breaks down?' His father shook his head. 'If there were a mutual interdependency of some sort, it might not be so bad. Perhaps our elected leaders will rise to the challenge. Who can say?'

His father gazed ahead, and Michael had the impression he was seeing much farther than the edge of the forest at the next bend.

'I remember the Cuban crisis, how scared we were. I woke every day wondering whether we'd be alive that night, or wake up again the next morning. The Cold War was no joke. And then what did they have in store for us? Meteorites! Well, that would be quick enough if one hit, but we'd know about it a few days in advance, watch it coming, smell our doom. Danger is always on hand. Keep it in perspective. This is just one more threat to add to the list.'

Yes, keep it in perspective, Michael thought, but it didn't make it any easier. Perhaps fighting in a war had given his father that ability to step back, detach himself, see the longer view; or perhaps it could be put down to fifty years of marriage with the woman he loved.

Lucky man. Yet they had met when his father was scarcely younger than he was now himself, so perhaps...

But he had made his decision months ago. When they got back home, and his father was putting away the odds and ends they'd bought, he went to the bedroom he had been using and packed. The message from Rebecca had come through in the village, where there was at least partial mobile coverage, and he had replied briefly and booked his flight.

Rose came to the door to see him off, although it was plain she didn't understand where he was going or for how long. She felt frail and insubstantial in his embrace. His father ... he thought his father might have guessed, but when the taxi pulled up in front of the house, all he said was, 'Try not to worry'.

REBECCA was not happy. For a start, Connor arrived at Paddington only three minutes before the train was due to leave, and Rebecca had to wait for him on the platform, while everyone else swarmed past and boarded the train. She hated cutting things fine.

As a consequence the best places had already been taken and they ended up facing each other on aisle seats, Rebecca next to a woman in her thirties who had looked okay at first glance – not fat, not dirty, not chewing anything – but whom she quickly found to smell strongly of garlic.

She had grabbed the seat quick, forcing Connor to sit next to the large shabby bloke spilling over his seat and eating something synthetic-looking out of its plastic wrapping – Rebecca's idea of a passenger from hell. But two stops later the fat guy had got off, so that Connor had the luxury of an empty seat next to him and Rebecca still had garlic.

Truly not fair. She tried to stare out of the window, but at this angle the buildings flashed by too fast and threatened to make her sick, and she had never been able to read or draw while travelling.

She gazed blankly down the aisle. No way was she going to make small talk with Connor, who thankfully gave little indication of wanting to chat with her either.

Which wasn't flattering.

What were they doing together? How on earth had this all come about? Her exhibition at the Impact Gallery looming up, her bank balance shrinking, and what was she doing? Waltzing off to Oxford for the third time with a schedule of petty larceny.

I hope it's petty. I'm calling it petty. What was the correct term for theft from a public institution of learning? Fraud? Vandalism? Treason?

What if I don't actually do it, Connor does? What do you get for aiding and abetting? Perhaps it wouldn't come to that because it would prove impossible even to try to remove the thing.

They had Steph to thank yet again for finding it. However would they have managed without her local knowledge? When Rebecca had described the display cabinets, the staircase and the grandfather clocks Connor had seen, Steph had immediately suggested the Oxford Museum of the History of Science.

The name sounded forbidding.

Without having been there, Rebecca nevertheless had a strong notion of what they would be facing. How could they deal with alarmed cases and patrolling stewards? This wasn't some cosy university college, with undergrads strolling about and an old guy with a dog. It wasn't like lifting something from a room full of elastic bands and teabags.

This was going into the public store house of objects worth collectively thousands and thousands of pounds, and even more in terms of irreplaceable historical evidence. This was Mission Impossible, and the closer the train came to Oxford the more Rebecca felt inclined to decline the assignment and walk away.

'It'll be okay.'

Rebecca jumped. 'What?'

'Don't worry. It'll work out okay.'

Rebecca frowned. *Since when have my thoughts been apparent from my face? Nip that one in the bud!*

'Of course,' she said airily, and turned to look out of the window whether it made her sick or not.

He's a school kid. Why can't he behave like a school kid?

But school kid or not, his presence was a relief to her when they reached the museum and she did not have to mount the steps alone. They did not pause to look at it from the street because Rebecca had to stick to her maxim of tackling the unpleasant by going at it without pausing. Hesitate and you have to get going again, and that invites the possibility of your not being able to. Nope, start walking at the station and don't stop, that was the only way. Besides, it had started to rain.

So they crossed the road, crossed the pavement and climbed the steps to the door. There Connor's arm came past on her near side and pushed the door open ahead of her. Annoyingly, he seemed to have picked up good manners from somewhere.

The Museum of the History of Science was not exactly as Rebecca had anticipated. In fact it wasn't remotely like she had anticipated.

There was no wide, light hall, no uniformed stewards, no school parties; only a room barely the size of a classroom, old varnished display cases, and an attendant behind a desk who smiled at them and returned to her book. It was dead quiet and rather sleepy, with just one other visitor – a woman in a long skirt at the farther end. A fly was buzzing fitfully at a window.

Entry was free, although donations were invited. Rebecca knew that if they managed against all odds to get the telescope she would want to gallop out of there like a Grand National winner.

They dawdled round the room, acting like genuine visitors.

Despite her anxiety, Rebecca found her attention waylaid.

This wasn't at all like the Science Museum in Kensington. The cases held historical scientific instruments of all sorts, many of which she couldn't identify. They were mostly very old, made from wood or brass and extravagantly decorated, and the instruments were jumbled up, different kinds together in the same case, instead of being categorised and themed. Some of the identification cards were handwritten, and those that weren't had been typed on a manual typewriter.

'Spectroscope,' she read, and then became aware that Connor was looming at her side. He was frowning. 'What?'

Connor said softly, 'Are you sure about this?'

'You're the one who saw where to go.'

'No.' He made a small movement which managed to combine a shrug with a nod towards the attendant. 'Don't you think we should ask?'

'*Ask!*'

'Isn't this like stealing?'

Rebecca raised her eyebrows. 'Oh sure. 'Excuse me but we've come for the antique telescope, the one with the fairy iron in it'.' It was difficult to inject sarcasm into a whisper. 'Come on.'

She brushed past him and climbed the steps out of the room, floorboards creaking, into a much smaller room to one side, about the size of Aunty Edie's back parlour. There was a stone fireplace on one wall, and a wrought iron spiral staircase. Next to the staircase were two grandfather clocks, silent and still, waiting.

Not behind glass. Not even behind a scarlet cord, although there was a cord looped across the staircase, so presumably nobody would be coming down it into their midst.

She glanced over her shoulder. Although the door to the room was open, the angle made it impossible to see more than a foot or so of the stairwell beyond, and nothing at all of the entrance room or the desk. To all intents and purposes they were invisible, and they were completely alone – no stewards, no visitors.

Trusting.

On the other hand, all the small stuff here was inside locked cabinets, and who would try to run off with a grandfather clock over his shoulder? But of course they didn't want the grandfather clock. They just wanted what was inside.

Rebecca rummaged for and found her notebook. She flipped through the pages. 'Dark brown,' she read. 'Roman numerals.' Both clocks qualified. 'Brass hands.' Damn – how could they work out which one was theirs?

'How –'

She tailed off. Connor had knelt in front of one of the clocks and now, gently, he slid his fingernails into the crack of the door and prised. After a moment of resistance, the door complied, easing open without much more than a whisper of a creak. Rebecca watched motionless as Connor reached inside and brought out a slim bundle of cloth.

Old cloth. Pale green brocade, tied about with a plaited cord. He began to work at the knot.

'Come on!' Rebecca hissed, 'Look later!'

Connor persisted. 'Need to make sure,' he mouthed. Rebecca watched him part the knot and open the brocade, revealing the slim brass cylinder, barely twenty centimetres long, that was the telescope. Then he passed it to her, closed the grandfather clock and stood up.

Rebecca took the bundle, feeling the cool weight of the instrument inside, and placed it securely in the bottom of her bag, dropped the notebook on top and zipped the bag closed. Adrenalin was coursing through her system, making her heart thump. How could he be so calm? The by-product of years of shoplifting, probably.

Feeling like a drug smuggler approaching customs, Rebecca followed the juvenile delinquent through the entrance room and past the desk. Smiling brightly, she dropped two pound coins through the slot in the donations box and skipped down the steps.

The rain had stopped and the wet pavement shone. The Broad in Oxford on a Tuesday in early July was suddenly the most delightful place to be.

Rebecca took a deep, delicious breath. 'Let's have lunch!'

Chapter Twenty

52 King's Road
London

12th of June 1852

Dear Walter,
    Thank you for your letter. It was kind of you to remind me
everything must be allowed to have more than one purpose
in life. It is so easy to forget at times. And it was good to receive
news of your return from Scotland, and that you are in London,
staying at the Lion's Gate Hotel, because we wish to invite one
or two close friends beside our immediate family to celebrate with
us our forthcoming Silver Wedding Anniversary. I am having
Mary's favourite gem-stone set in a ring by Wilson's, and
do not doubt it will turn out very well. Do try to come,
Walter, as it is only right that our oldest friend should be with
us. I hope I have not left it too late to invite you, but life has
been rather an uphill struggle since Mary's illness, although
she is on the road to recovery now. The party will be on the
24th. There is a fine inn in the village, but I regret that we
shall have no room left to offer you since all of the
children will be staying over with us. The King's Head stands at the
crossroads besides the bridge on the north edge of the village. If
you are able to stay for two nights then it would be most congenial
to walk with you the three miles to Penny Hill, a landmark which on
a clear day offers views right across the county. We could eat at
the Bull in Dene and after return along a path that approaches
our house along the elm avenue, which is very fine. In any
case I look forward to your confirmation that we may expect to
welcome you to our house in the very near future.
                        Yours truly,
                        William

William. Walter. Mary and her favourite gem stone.

Rebecca threw down her pencil, scraped back her chair and stomped into the kitchen to put the kettle on.

The British Library facsimile of the manuscript they needed had arrived in the post and it dumbfounded her. It really was a letter, for heaven's sake! Having expected the letter format to be a disguise for a series of instructions (Put the clock on the sideboard, light the candle, use the key to unlock the cupboard) she had been presented instead with some long-dead bloke's plans for a thrilling weekend with a chum. *'It would be most congenial'*... *'We could take luncheon'*... What had this to do with Michael's other world? Where was the magic? Surely it must be in code?

So she had spent the evening trying out code-breaking techniques in vain. She had tried extracting the first word of each line. Then the last. Then she tried the second word, the third, the penultimate word, and each time was left with nonsense.

Next, she had tried linking together every other word, every third word, every fourth, fifth, sixth. Nope. What about backwards, from the end of the letter up? No, not that either. First word of the first line, second of the second, third of the third? Rien. Nichts. Zilch.

It was hopeless. Rebecca abandoned the problem and made a cup of coffee. All this brain work required biscuits as well. She was on her third when a stroke of brilliance struck her and she froze.

Suppose the whole thing was one giant metaphor? Suppose nothing was to be taken at face value? Suppose 'return from Scotland' really meant – um – okay, meant 'Go south'? She dusted the crumbs from her hands and seized the photocopied letter.

'Staying in London' could mean, perhaps, 'It all takes place in a city'. 'Lion's Gate Hotel' ... actual lions? Or was it metaphorical – just 'danger'? Like putting one's head into the lion's mouth? A Silver Wedding Anniversary must mean twenty-five – twenty-five years, or twenty-five hours, or twenty-five people, perhaps? Anyway, twenty-five somethings. Gem-stone... But it didn't say what kind of gem-stone. She knew stones, like many things, had symbolic associations – diamond for longevity, ruby for fire – but without being told which gem-stone this Mary favoured how could any information be inferred from that?

And who were the Wilsons?

Good grief.

Well, words were not her forte, of that she was well aware.

She was a right-brain person, intuitive, artistic and non-analytical. Whether this ridiculous sheet of paper bore a message concealed in numbers and patterns or in metaphor, it needed a left-brain person to read it – a scientist, or a wordsmith.

Connor.

Damn.

Rebecca dropped onto her bed and sat cross-legged, her elbows on her knees and her chin on her fists.

Connor wrote. He wrote close and tight, squeezing as many words to a line as he could in that spiral bound notebook he took everywhere. She thought – guessing, but pretty confidently – that he wrote poetry. She also guessed he'd die rather than admit it, but she had never felt the urge to open him up so had never been tempted to goad him about it. But poetry requires a very careful choice of words, and frequently involves metaphor and subtle references and connections. Would a poet have a better chance at unravelling the message this letter held? Better than an artist? She should let him have a go.

Blast and damn. She didn't want to. It was enough of a pain to have to accept him being in charge at the V and A, the last thing she wanted was to hand over this fun part to him as well.

Every children's mystery story worth its name included a code to be cracked, and the hero inevitably had a brainwave in the middle of the night and leapt up with a torch to read off the vital clue. And not just children's books, either. Who doesn't thrill to the call of a coded message? – Indiana Jones reading the disc at the top of the staff; Daniel Jackson deciphering the stargate; Alice holding the poem up to the mirror, and Bilbo Baggins interpreting the knocking of the thrush. Riddles in the dark. Crossword puzzles and anagrams.

I want to do it!

She'd never been any good at crosswords though.

I can do anagrams.

Rebecca visualised the letter in her head, its ragged edges and stained paper reproduced in the facsimile. Could the whole thing be an anagram? No, because an anagram that big isn't an anagram, it's a code.

What, then?

Rebecca saw the answer clear as writing on a blackboard:

A s k C o n n o r.

Well, there was no great rush, they had three other objects to get hold of and an enormous problem with two of them. The thread Connor would deal with – hoped to deal with – tomorrow. But the clock had vanished without trace and they had no notion of how to find the hiding place of its partner.

And nobody even knew what the seventh item was.

MICHAEL started working on the problem on the flight. He did not doubt that Foster would soon be on his heels, but he needed to see the others face to face; it was not something he could handle remotely. He couldn't go himself without raising suspicion, but if he stayed behind, stuck in his studio, surely Connor and Rebecca would be undiscovered?

His father's warning had been a blow he could have done without. 'You know that your grandfather always suspected there was another line, that Emily wasn't the only woman to have given him a child?'

No, Dad, I didn't know that. So now there's the possibility of another descendent, unconnected to Mundus Caecus, about whom we know nothing. There wasn't even a name, just a shadowy notion of another mixed-blood line capable of throwing up an individual in whom the genes remained strong.

Too much to worry about, this has to go on hold. First we must get the clock.

It would cost a bit, but if they were frugal, were in and out quickly, it wouldn't break the bank. And what alternative was there?

In London he checked prices and emailed Rebecca. 'Don't worry about the clock, there is a way. I need to see you both. Don't ring. Meet me at the V and A Wednesday 10.30 am. Small Sculpture Gallery, carved ivory. Michael.'

REBECCA arrived first. She had aimed for ten, wanting the half hour of solitude before facing Michael. There were things she had to sort out in her head, and the cool, quiet space of the museum seemed more conducive to thought than her cluttered flat. Now she walked along the Small Sculpture Gallery, between the cabinets with their terracotta busts, alabaster horses and religious icons, to the far end and the case of carved ivory.

She sat on the bench and gazed at the Celtic box with its vine roundels that she had been trying to sketch over two months ago, when the drawing had taken charge and rampaged over her book.

It had been the day she first met Michael, and had thought him worth looking at twice. Had put him in his mid-twenties.

Ha!

Why was she here really? How much had it to do with this parallel world business, which even now she could not altogether believe, and how much because her work had become stuck – the artist's equivalent of Writer's Block? Or rather, Writer's One-Track-Mind, because the problem had not been an inability to draw, just the inability to draw what she wanted.

And how much of it was because of Michael?

Forget it, she told herself, he's forty-four. *Forty-four.* He could be your father, if he'd begun early enough. And he probably had. Boys walking around looking like that, like he must have looked at eighteen or nineteen, would not be short of opportunities. He gave the impression of being quiet and quiet-living now, but what did she really know? Had he left a trail of broken-hearted women? He didn't have a partner, Rebecca was certain of that. There was a distance about him always – a kind of No-Man's Land that was not to be crossed, and if she was aware of it then perhaps other women were, too.

And not just distance. He seemed trustworthy, felt trustworthy, and yet she was sure he was holding something back. Sometimes he seemed almost to check himself, as if taking time to consider his words before he spoke them, screening them for content.

What content, and why?

How sensible was she in trusting him at all? How sensible was Connor?

And that was another thing. How old was Connor? Sixteen? He looked older, and he certainly talked older when he talked at all, but it had been GCSEs he'd been dodging around recently, not A-levels, although he seemed to spend most of his time bunking off.

Did his people know? She hung back from using the word 'family', because whatever relations he had and wherever it was he lived – slept and got his meals – they didn't seem to conform to her own ideas of 'family' and 'home'.

Intuition is one of those qualities everybody likes to believe they possess, like a sense of humour and the ability to untangle string. In truth Rebecca had a sneaking suspicion that she was not the most intuitive of people, and was even prepared to accept that sometimes others – Steph, for example – might be better at judging people than herself.

But even to Rebecca it was plain that Connor came from a bad background. It was one of the things about him that made her so uncomfortable, but you couldn't raise the matter – Connor kept up his own No-Man's Land that was every bit as forbidding as Michael's. Was it something in their genes?

In which case, do I have it too?

Brought up short by the notion, Rebecca considered.

Surely not. She had friends – well, Steph – and she had had boyfriends. Well, two or three. At least, she had been out with boys once or twice, although nothing you could call a relationship had ever developed.

They had all seemed a touch nervous of her.

Am I scary?

Rebecca tightened her lips. *I don't want a relationship with anyone who's scared of me anyway. Forget it.*

Back to Connor. What she really wanted was for someone in authority to come along and take over, sort things out, give him a bed-sit somewhere and some clothes that didn't look as though they'd been scrounged from a skip.

That was one thing. The other was even harder, and not what Rebecca wanted to think about, but it came cantering into her brain anyway.

What had Michael looked like aged nineteen? Not a million miles from what Connor looked like now, probably. But if he was sixteen then he was three years younger than she was, and at nineteen that's a gulf. He could also be sullen, suspicious and not invariably clean, although in fairness that was quite possibly the clothes rather than the body inside.

What she was thinking was simply unthinkable and she must stop thinking it right away.

Even if he wasn't scared of her.

Rebecca glared at the ivory casket. *I'm nearly twenty. I'm intelligent. I'm talented. I'm driven. I'm responsible and I'm not frightened of either of them, and I'm here because I choose to be, and that's that.*

And there isn't a clock and there isn't going to be one, so that's that as well.

Footsteps were coming from the farther end. Rebecca turned and saw the two men, the two boys, the man and the boy walking towards her, side by side, matching step. Both of them wore their black, springing hair hooked behind their ears and both wore jeans, Michael in the denim shirt he had been wearing the first time she saw him (*must be his Carved Ivory shirt*) and Connor in a grey T-shirt with a wavy, worn-and-washed-too-many-times hem. They didn't look identical but they could easily have been brothers.

Connor seemed optimistic (*must be the Michael Effect*). Michael himself also looked fairly ebullient, or at least not crushed by the mighty blow of knowing the clock had been lost.

Why?

They sat one on either side of her – her own fault for sitting in the middle of the bench, and now she had to keep turning her head to keep track of them both.

'Rebecca,' Michael said, smiling, 'Can you fly to New York tomorrow?'

Chapter Twenty-One

'Is it Oxford again?'

'Er, no, New York.'

Aunty Edie lifted her hands in delight. 'New York! How wonderful! Aren't you lucky!'

No questions, though; not, Why on earth?, or Can you afford it?

Rebecca could afford it because Michael was paying; at least, he was buying their tickets and would reimburse them for their accommodation, which would have to be as low budget as he could find.

But still... New York! Icon of icons in this age of film and television, even if you didn't have a television and couldn't afford the cinema. Rebecca could not help the grin on her face as she ran upstairs.

With one day to get ready, she lingered at the public library after checking email. There would be two long flights and although she invariably had a book on the go, she happened to be quarter of the way through a (very good actually) period novel which had an unfortunately camp cover, and she had no intention of sitting on a plane with that open on her lap while Connor worked his way through Proust or Joyce or someone equally intimidating. Or poetry, which would be even worse.

So she roamed the fiction shelves searching for a good read which was also respectable, and in the end checked out an Anthony Trollope (reliably engrossing despite being Victorian – which come to think of it was very appropriate) and a mystery that had been shortlisted for a major literary prize. She would, of course, have her smallest sketchbook as well, and with all of that she ought to be able to keep conversation to a minimum.

She picked up a couple of travel guides too, a slim one to take with her and a fat one to bulk out her knowledge before they left.

'You must look after each other,' Michael had told her. 'I need you to do that.'

'Sure,' Rebecca had answered breezily.

It was that obvious, was it? Well, she would keep an eye on Connor, who most likely had never seen the inside of an airport before, and do her best to see that he stayed out of trouble.

'And keep wearing the necklace,' Michael added.

'Pardon?'

Michael nodded. 'Family heirloom, is it? Good. Keep it on.'

So she would.

Amazingly, Connor possessed a passport. 'Ypres,' he explained shortly, 'the Menin Gate. School trip.'

That didn't quite explain it. Rebecca, too, had done the obligatory history visit to Belgium and recalled that most pupils were put on a group passport arranged by the school, but she wasn't interested enough to pursue the matter. Connor had a passport and it was valid, that was all that mattered. There was nothing to stop them flying. Michael had managed to find them a couple of places in a small hostel down-town (*'down-town'!*) and gave Rebecca the address and booking confirmation along with their medical insurance details and an earful of instructions, which basically boiled down to Find The Clock.

Because there was still a chance. The Victorians – their Victorians – had not been quite so confident after all. It seemed one of them had suffered a devastating fire at his country home a few years after the gap had been closed and had become alive to the danger of relying totally on the set of pointers in the V and A. Unlikely, yes, but it wasn't impossible that the museum might also be consumed by fire, and to leave all their eggs in one basket was irresponsible.

This was one of the things Rebecca had guessed Michael knew but had been keeping back. With the help of the original traveller, a duplicate set of pointers had been prepared and taken across the Atlantic to New England, where the New Yorkers were delighted to welcome a respected academic prepared to found a museum of the arts and sciences, and who had even brought with him the start of a collection.

Rebecca had started to laugh at this point. 'You're *not!* You really are *not* telling us these people didn't only start the V and A, but started the New York Metropolitan Museum of Art as well? You can't be serious!'

But he could. All seven items in the V and A were duplicated in the Met, and thank providence for it.

'And what if it's hidden in, I don't know, Colorado or something?'

'It won't be. There isn't a duplicate component, only a duplicate pointer. The clock Connor's going to find at the Met will show you where to go in Britain to find its partner. You just have to go to New York to get the message.'

Another trip to Oxford, then, no doubt, Rebecca thought. But first the U S of A!

THE night before they were to fly, Rebecca read over the letter from William Dwyer again. What must she do to unlock its secret? She had not yet admitted to Michael that she had it. It had arrived in the post sooner than expected anyway, and Rebecca desperately wanted to be able to produce the manuscript together with a transcript of its message; but she was flagging.

William's signature, with its spiky capital letter and finishing flourish, lay before her on the desk.

Why did you write this? she thought. What do you have to tell me? How do I get in?

She would give herself until they came back from New York. If she hadn't solved the puzzle by then, she would show the manuscript to Michael.

NEW York was going to be sweltering, Michael had told them, but public buildings generally had air conditioning set so cool they'd need sweaters. And it might rain, and if it did the rain would be torrential.

The American-ness of America struck Rebecca as they passed through Immigration. The officials manning the stations looked like ordinary people but when their's spoke, his deep, rich, New York voice was thrilling to hear.

They emerged from the airport into the early evening, which was dark and hot and instantly alien. Hot and dark and only seven-thirty – weird!

They had agreed to take a taxi to the hostel as they were tired from the flight; in the morning they could suss out public transport. Rebecca sat in the back of the yellow cab – another icon – and watched through the window as they dropped down into the tunnel that linked Long Island and the airport with Manhattan.

And then, the magic moment: the road tipped up, the cab emerged from the tunnel, and suddenly they were in New York for real. Rebecca twisted to peer out of the window, because now it was essential to look out and up. Skyscrapers on either side rose like the sides of a canyon, and as far as she could see the road was laser-straight with traffic lights slung from gantries across the intersections.

She grinned – it was impossible not to when finding oneself in the middle of what looked, really and truly, like a movie set. *The* movie set.

Turning to see out of the other side of the cab, Rebecca found Connor also rubber-necking, and for a moment they exchanged a look of gleeful excitement, like kids arriving at Alton Towers. Rebecca tugged the corners of her mouth sharply downwards in a joke grimace, and Connor bit his lip and lifted his eyebrows in return.

The cab pulled away from the red light and turned so that they were going south on a fresh road as straight as the first. The famous New York grid pattern. It was astonishing how far it seemed to stretch ahead.

And then they were pulling up and Rebecca paid the fare while Connor lifted their rucksacks out. They stood together on the pavement – no, sidewalk – and breathed in the warm, exhaust-laden air. Traffic sounds floated, with the intermittent beat of car horns, exactly as they sounded in the movies.

They mounted the steps to the front door.

Chapter Twenty-Two

STEPPING out into the street, feeling the sharp change between indoors – cool – and outdoors – hot – was what told you that you had left England, Rebecca thought. It was still only eight fifteen, the sidewalks full of people on their way to work, with the sky and the light and the freshness flaunting the start of the day, and yet already it was hot enough for a strappy tee-shirt and sandals.

They had come out early, having for her part been awake since a little after three in the morning, which her body clock insisted was really eight a.m. It had been frustrating, because their dormitory room was full, and there was no way she could start moving around or switch on a light while everyone else – with the probable exception of Connor, of course – was still asleep. She had had to stay in bed, counting the hours until it was reasonable to slip out to the bathroom and get dressed.

At six she tiptoed out with her rucksack. It was a relief to put the bathroom light on and be active. She showered and dressed in a fresh tee-shirt and shorts, brushed her teeth, raked her fingers through her short hair a few times to ruffle it up and get it drying, and went downstairs to the kitchen.

Connor joined her ten minutes later.

The hostel Michael had found for them was pretty much like a youth hostel in Britain: communal rooms with bunk beds and a kitchen where guests could make their own breakfast from cereal, fruit and bread. The bread was sourdough, hard and full of holes, but the oranges were exactly as oranges should be.

They spoke quietly in case their voices travelled through the ceiling. Obviously the first job was to visit the Met, locate the clock, and take down whatever it had to impart. But the rest of the day was theirs to play with. Half a day to do New York... What was essential?

'Empire State Building?'

'Statue of Liberty?'

'The Guggenheim?'

'The What?'

Rebecca tossed Connor her guide book. She made herself a cup of tea using teabags from a jar labelled 'English Breakfast' while Connor flipped the pages. 'Want one?'

'What?'

Rebecca pinged the jar with the spoon.

'Oh. Yeah. Please. Thanks.'

'I think,' Rebecca said, bringing the mugs to the table, 'we need to consider the geography. We won't be able to do the north end and the south end – we'd waste too much time travelling. We need to think of what's within reasonable distance.'

Connor was frowning at the map. 'I thought New York was all 'Fifth and Forty-Third' – you know, all numbers. What's with these names?'

He was looking at the toe end of Manhattan, where there was no discernable grid and the streets made the sort of mess you get used to in England. 'Yeah,' Rebecca said. 'We ought to go down there if we can. The original bit. We have to if we want to see the Statue of Liberty, anyway.'

'You choose,' Connor said, closing the guide book and taking his tea.

So Rebecca chose, feeling a little guilty but mostly relieved.

The Guggenheim Museum of Art was only a few minutes' walk north of the Met, so she felt she could reasonably include that. Then they'd hop on the underground and go right down to the southern tip and do whatever they could of the famous sights down there, including the Statue of Liberty, before time ran out.

They would need to get the tube – subway, rather – to the Met to begin with, because it was about three miles and it would be a shame to waste an hour just walking.

The subway was strange to someone brought up with the London Underground – only one short flight of steps from the platforms back up to the street, where the trains were clearly audible beneath their feet. The noise in the station was aggressive and the heat intense, but at least the trains were air-conditioned and getting down to them and up away later was very quick.

And the entrance to the Met was lovely: giant columns and vast stone steps – gosh, what you could do when there was the space to do it in. About the only street in London Rebecca could think of wide enough for this was Whitehall.

Inside they put on the sweaters Michael had advised them to take, picked up a floor plan, and began to hunt for clocks...

THE Victoria and Albert began to take on the aspect of a cottage. *How could I have ever got lost there? What kind of country bumpkin am I?*

The Met was enormous, palatial. It was also in some way fresher and cleaner-seeming than the Kensington museums – cool and echoing and dust-free, the colours pale and remote.

I'd like to spend a week here. A month.

It was well signed and the map was easy to read. They headed for European Sculpture and Decorative Arts and found it where it was supposed to be, without any surprising corners or stairs, and there Rebecca supported her sketchbook along her left arm and drew details from eighteenth-century porcelain while Connor roved the cases.

It took him half an hour to find the clock they wanted – a 1720 wall clock, oak with walnut veneer, which according to the label had been donated to the collection in 1870 by Henry Cuthbert Bullinger.

Rebecca swapped sketchbook for notepad and Connor glanced along the gallery in both directions. Nobody near. There was a steward at the farthest end, behind one of the freestanding cases.

It didn't take long. But Rebecca said dubiously, 'A pelican?'

'A golden one.'

Rebecca pulled a face, then tucked her notepad back in her bag. 'Okay – play-time!'

THEY spent another hour in the museum, touring the galleries quite swiftly just to get the feel, and then sat on a low wall surrounding an entire reconstructed Egyptian tomb and debated what to see next.

Connor consented to the Guggenheim, and to riding downtown to see the oldest part of the city afterwards. Rebecca found she felt awkward about dragging him around another art gallery, and settled for a swift walk down the astonishing spiral that formed the main building before riding the subway (she was getting the hang of this now) to the southern end, where they wandered around the crooked, cobbled streets. Strange streets, some of them – one seemed to have shops selling only chess sets, and another mostly smoking paraphernalia.

It was very hot and Rebecca wished she had a hat. Was it worth buying one now, with only a few more hours to go? She had remembered to bring sun-block, and offered some to Connor, who looked wary but deigned to smear a little along his arms.

They bought sandwiches and ate them under a tree in a square of grass.

'I think we should ride the Staten Island Ferry,' Connor said offering a suggestion for the first time. A welcome change; it's hard spending much time in company with no conversation.

Rebecca therefore agreed. The guide book had listed the trip as one of the Musts, and it was free – a short ride across the water right past the Statue of Liberty to Staten Island (whatever that was) and back again, offering the single most iconic view of Manhattan: the giant skyscrapers outlined against the sky.

There turned out to be nothing much for tourists on Staten Island, and like a number of passengers they simply disembarked, crossed the terminus and waited to get back on board for the return trip. Bonkers, but fun.

'You realise we're daft?'

'Of course. So what?'

After the sea breeze on the ferry the city felt even hotter. Small wonder the rich leave the island and retreat to their country mansions for July and August, Rebecca thought. Wasn't there a film, an old film about some poor businessman left in the summer city while his wife and children evacuated? The one with Marilyn Monroe's white dress being blown about above the ventilation grill in the pavement? That would have been before air conditioning, of course.

Thank heavens for air conditioning.

They hopped into public buildings from time to time to cool down, working their way gradually north, and eventually realised they were hungry enough for supper.

Chapter Twenty-Three

AT least restaurant and take-away prices were relatively low. 'Here?'

They ordered pasta. Rebecca fanned herself with the menu. Not all places turned the temperature down as much as she'd have liked. It went with the money, no doubt – high prices and wealthy customers equalled expenditure on cooling the air. Cheap prices, poor customers, who wants to pay?

She was beginning to feel sleepy. She'd had only a few hours' sleep last night and a long day on foot. She yawned.

Connor said, 'Me too.'

Rebecca looked at him in surprise. Had he really, actually instigated a conversation for the second time? True, he appeared to be responding to her yawn, but a yawn wasn't really speech, was it? 'I could go to sleep right now,' she said.

Connor nodded, his eyes roving the restaurant. Rebecca considered him. He didn't say much, but it hadn't been as bad as she had feared, dragging him around all day. She hadn't even remembered to worry that they might be taken for a couple.

One thought led to another. She said, 'I hope they don't think we're anti-social, the others at the hostel. I hope they don't think we're weird to have breakfast so early and push off.'

Hostels were traditionally sociable, chatty places, she understood, where travellers were expected to swap stories and pool information. She and Connor had hit the sack long before anyone else and were likely to do so again tonight.

Oh well.

'They're just people,' Connor said, which was less than crystal clear. What did he mean? Just people, so it doesn't matter what they think? Just people, so we can ignore them?

'Don't worry about it.'

So now he thinks he needs to reassure me?

What kind of background does he come from? What goes on when he's not here?

Too difficult to think about. They ate and paid, and went to the subway. Six forty-five – after the commuter rush hour; fifteen minutes before midnight at home. The soles of Rebecca's feet ached in her sandals and she had worked up a blister on one heel. She felt sweaty and unpleasant, and urgently wanted a shower.

Please don't let anyone else be using it when I get in, please let it be free for me. I'm sure Connor won't mind waiting.

She decided to walk towards the end of the platform where the front carriages would be, to save time at the other end. So noisy in these stations, where several lines ran side by side with open platforms between, and oh so hot.

Despite having bought two bottles of water during the day, Rebecca suspected she had become dehydrated in the heat. She felt the beginning of a headache, and blinked, screwing up her eyes for a moment. Oh thank goodness, the train.

As the doors opened she was vaguely aware of Connor's voice behind her, and she waved. 'Come on, this is ours.'

'*No!* Rebecca!'

What was he on about? Of course it was their train. Rebecca boarded and sat down. Connor jumped on just before the doors closed, having had to run.

Oops, nearly lost him there.

Connor dropped into the seat opposite her, stretching his long legs across the centre aisle so that she had to move her own back. He looked sullen and unfriendly, staring at the floor.

What have I done now?

Well, if he wanted to be sulky, let him. The train moved off, and Rebecca leaned back. The carriage was virtually empty and blissfully cool. 'What a pity we don't have air conditioning on the London Underground,' she said, thinking aloud.

'Too old. Too much bother.'

Well, yes. Rebecca opened her eyes again and looked idly around the carriage. Connor was sitting forward now, still staring at the floor, his hands dangling between his knees. There were only two other passengers yet there was quite a strong smell of booze, she slowly realised, and now that she came to look at them, they might have been supporting actors in an American crime movie.

They didn't look exactly – respectable. Or safe. Not the sort of person one might turn to for help, should one need it.

And now the nearer of them, the taller one, said to her, 'You got something for me, missy?'

'Something for you?' she repeated, because years of good manners had brainwashed all the commonsense out of her, and she saw Connor shift.

His companion, shorter but stocky, got up and swung between the posts to loom over her. He stank of alcohol and unwashed skin. 'Yeah. What you got in that nice bag, uh?'

If she stood up now she would touch him. How could she get away? All the slick little tips she'd heard for self-defence seemed unlikely to the point of impossibility. How could she really jab him in the eyes? Tug down on his earlobe? Knee him in the groin? The man was twice her weight and had probably been fighting since the school playground. Rebecca had never hit anyone in earnest in her life; she simply couldn't do it.

For a moment she stared up at him – at both of them – and then the man dropped his hand and started to worm it under the flap of her bag, and Connor stood up and slipped between them.

It was a horribly tiny gap – six inches? – but he managed it, sliding his lean body over the top of Rebecca, separating her and her bag from the two men, knocking the groping hand away. Rebecca squeezed out from behind and shot over to the door, her pulse galloping, and watched in amazement as the sixteen-year-old school kid fronted up to two New York low-lifes tanked up on who knew what drugs and booze.

Where was the next station? *When* was the next station?

'Hey, look at this! *You* got anything for us then?' The tall one shoved at Connor's chest, and Rebecca squeaked, but rather neatly he ducked sideways and kept his balance while the thug rocked.

Oh please, Rebecca thought, *where is the station?*

There was a growl and one of the men drew back an arm, and Rebecca watched horrified as Connor suddenly dropped his shoulder, twisted and drove himself sideways into the man, like someone breaking down a door in a movie. Rebecca suspected trying that in real life would leave the door still locked and you with a broken shoulder, but against a person it seemed pretty effective. The man swayed, off-balance and clutching at his partner, and both men lurched as the train began to decelerate. Connor backed towards her, poised on the balls of his feet, his arms readied.

'Get out when it stops.'

Did he think she was mad?

The train slowed, and neither of the men showed signs of following. Too many witnesses now. The doors opened and Rebecca practically fell out onto the platform, Connor spinning and jumping after her.

Chapter Twenty-Four

'THAT was *stupid! Really stupid!*'

Rebecca, still shivering, flinched. 'What do you mean? What was stupid?'

'Taking that empty carriage! Almost empty. Didn't you *look?* Weren't you paying any attention at all?' Connor was nearly shouting, his eyes hard and his colour high. He was not able to keep quite still, shifting from one leg to the other, taking two strides and coming back again. He had shoved his hands into his pockets, and Rebecca, her own hands shaking, thought she knew why.

'I didn't notice... I didn't think...'

'Too bloody right!'

Rebecca was contrite. It was true, she had even read the advice in the guide book – the subway is safe but don't enter an empty car or one with only one passenger. No doubt two together counted the same.

She had forgotten, left her guard down, her brain on hold, whatever. She didn't have any excuse – especially as she now realised, with a sinking feeling, that that no doubt was what Connor had been trying to shout to her. And what had she done? Ignored him, got on board and brought them both into trouble.

It could have been worse, of course. They might have pulled out knives, or guns even, she supposed, although guns seemed altogether far too melodramatic. Still, this was New York. Suppose when Connor confronted them they had threatened him with a weapon? Rebecca rather thought he would have stayed between them and herself even then. After all, just the two big guys were scary enough.

They had scared her.

They had scared Connor too. That was why he was so angry and why he couldn't keep still.

Somewhere inside her, Rebecca became aware of a peculiar, curling, twisting sensation that was not entirely unknown to her.

Doubt. She didn't get it often, but it always signified an

imminent change of opinion. It was time for a reappraisal.

The next train was still several minutes off, according to the display. Rebecca retreated to a bench and sat down. She watched Connor stand where she'd left him, slowly cooling down – his temper, that was; the station was dreadfully hot and he must be sweating just as she was.

It had needed courage to take on the two thugs, outnumbered and unarmed as he was. She hadn't even asked for help, too confused and idiotic, yet he had stepped in and provided an escape route for her.

He didn't seem quite the school kid any more. He certainly didn't seem a burden.

She stood up again and went across.

'I'm sorry.'

Connor stared at the ground, non-committal.

Rebecca said, 'I didn't think. I forgot about taking care. Sorry.'

They were both subdued now, the after-effect of adrenalin, and rode the train in silence, sitting in a well-populated carriage.

The sun had gone down by the time they emerged into the street. They walked side by side to the hostel and somehow, Connor was always on the kerb side – as he had been all day, Rebecca now realised.

The bathroom was free and Rebecca nodded in its direction. 'Do you -?'

'In a minute. You go first.'

Well, she wanted to shower desperately, so she collected her towel and shampoo and went. But whereas yesterday she had assumed Connor was just a teenage boy unconcerned about personal hygiene, now it seemed likely that he was simply putting his own wellbeing second to hers.

Again.

REBECCA emerged from the bathroom pink and glowing, with her weird spiky hair standing up and her towel wrapped round under her arms and tucked in, like a sort of fleecy sarong. Her shoulders were bony and bore signs of a white strap mark. She threw him a slight smile as he slipped off his bunk and grabbed his stuff.

All the time under the water, his eyes shut against the stream, he saw her in his head, drying off and pulling her tee-shirt on. He adjusted the shower to run almost cold, and presented his face to the spray, letting it run over his eyelids and throat and shoulders.

She has no idea. No bloody idea at all.

Rebecca Mulligan. Rebecca *Maud* Mulligan – he had looked over her shoulder at Immigration and read her middle name. It was odd, and she probably loathed it, but he found it strangely attractive.

It was Alternative. It suited her.

When he had spent so long in there she absolutely must have had time to finish whatever she had to do, he turned off the flow of water and towelled roughly dry before getting into the tee-shirt and boxers he slept in and taking his bundle of clothes back to the dormitory.

She was in bed, sitting up with a book open on her lap while she ran her fingers through her hair, over and over, removing moisture and opening it up to dry.

Neat trick. Maybe he should get his cut that short.

Connor attacked his hair with the damp towel and climbed into his bunk.

'They'll think we're useless,' she said, 'the other guests. Going to bed so early again.'

She was bridge-building.

He said, 'Give Brits a bad name,' and saw the relief in her eyes.

Well.

She closed her book, keeping her finger in the place. 'What do you want to do tomorrow?'

Their flight left at five p.m. Even allowing plenty of time for the taxi ride to the airport, they still had all the morning to fill. He noticed that she had left the question completely open this time – not 'I thought we might blah-blah-blah-, what do you think?' Definitely bridge-building.

Connor said, 'I'd like to see the New York Public Library', and watched her register surprise and then swiftly smother it.

She made him feel old.

ONCE again they had finished breakfast before any of the other guests emerged, and had paid and gone out into the city, this time lugging their full rucksacks with them.

There would be no chance to take another shower before the flight, and they agreed to take it easy. The library – apparently famous – had a cool, marble interior where it was easy to spend a couple of hours, and was almost next door to the hostel. After that they took another short walk to Grand Central Station – which even Rebecca had heard of – where they bought lunch and rode the subway – carefully choosing populated carriages this time – to Central Park to sit in the shade.

They were now sweltering, but they lay on the grass for an hour to recharge before taking the taxi to the airport.

On the plane, Rebecca reclined her seat as far as it would go – not enough, of course, never enough – and wriggled herself into a reasonably comfortable position.

I don't want to think about it. I don't want to think about anything for the moment. I'll think about it another time.

But just before she fell asleep, Rebecca did think about one thing: the manuscript still in her flat. She decided what she would do about it.

Connor angled himself in his seat so that he faced the aisle. Shortly they would be in England again, and normal life would resume. There would be questions and opinions and incessant noise, and no doubt Rebecca would be back to her usual haughty self. Eight hours left.

Eight hours, and how many more days?

Chapter Twenty-Five

BY the time she arrived home Rebecca had recovered from her scare, but in one respect at least her change of heart – well, opinion anyway – had a lasting effect.

It was true she would still love to produce the manuscript and its message in one flourish, but if it wasn't going to happen it wasn't going to happen, and it really wasn't going to happen.

She stopped off at the library to make two more copies en route to meeting Michael and Connor, so that they could all work on it.

If either of them gets it straight off I'll cut my throat.

No I won't, I'll beat them up and then cut my throat.

'Beating up' reminded her. She swiftly changed the subject in her head.

Today they were going after the thread. Michael was sure it was decorative thread, rather than a strand from a rug for example, so Rebecca had suggested the Textile Study Rooms where hundreds of textiles from all over the world resided in glazed panels shelved vertically, like books: threads galore.

She hoped Connor would be able to detect the aura through the racks without having to pull each one out to be scrutinised, or they'd be there for a week.

She also hoped Connor hadn't ratted to Michael about the subway. 'Look after each other,' Michael had told her. It was unsettling that most of the looking after had been done by Connor.

She thought she could trust him not to tell.

She was the last to arrive and found the two men (*'men', now? Oh, whatever*) on a bench in the Ironwork Gallery. She sat down on the nearest end – Michael's end – and handed them each a photocopy and Michael the original facsimile too. 'It's come,' she said, omitting that it had arrived the previous week. 'I can't make anything of it. Any ideas?'

She waited while they read the letter through for all the world as if the information could be presented plainly and yet somehow have eluded her.

Michael said, 'William Dwyer was one of the original Victorians, I'm pretty sure.'

'I guessed that much.'

Connor asked, 'Why is the left hand margin so ragged?'

'I noticed that too. No idea. I've tried extracting words and letters and going upwards and backwards and inside out. Nothing.'

'What about Lewis Carroll's code?'

She looked past Michael at Connor. 'Lewis Carroll? Alice?'

'Yeah.'

'He had a code?'

'Made one up, yes. It relies on a key word or phrase – I think it can be a phrase. Provided both parties have the word it's straightforward to transcribe. If you don't then you're back to pure cryptography – counting the percentage of letters, looking at punctuation, that kind of thing.' Connor glanced back at the paper in his hand. 'I didn't think you could come up with proper, sensible script, though.'

Michael shook his head slowly. 'I agree. I don't think this is Lewis Carroll.'

So I'm the only one who doesn't know about this, Rebecca thought, exasperated. So he didn't just write peculiar books that aren't funny.

'Well, I've tried, now it's your turn,' she said.

'Later,' Michael said, folding the facsimile and sliding it into his pocket. 'Let's go.'

Rebecca knew the textile rooms well from having spent many hours drawing the decorative satin stitch and gold-thread work. It was a silent, secret oasis in the museum, where very few casual visitors came. Pop your head round the door and you were faced with racks of anonymous wooden spines, the glories inside hidden from view, and empty tables along the wall where mounts could be propped up for study.

Actually very few serious visitors came here either, or at least very few at any one time. Usually she had been alone in the room, and curators rarely strolled through. You'd have to smash glass deliberately to do any damage in here, and there was no obvious treasure on display, nothing that would make you a mint on the black market.

And while on the subject of the criminal underworld – 'Did you see any more of that estate agent?' Rebecca asked Michael, while Connor began slowly trawling the room.

'Uh-uh. I rang the hotel in Aberfeldy and he was there, but he didn't find me.'

'I thought hotels weren't allowed to give that sort of information out.'

Michael's mouth twitched. 'Well… I scammed them.'

A new facet of Michael to mull over.

Rebecca said, 'So the heat's off?'

'Hardly. The door's breaking down, Rebecca. If we don't seal it up –'

He broke off as Connor called from the middle of the room where he stood holding one of the glazed mounts. Rebecca took a look. 'Samplers', she pronounced. 'Eighteenth century. Very domestic.'

Behind the glass was a portrait-oriented sampler – taller than it was wide – of dingy, discoloured linen worked with tiny cross stitches. At the top of the sampler was the alphabet in capital letters and in lower case, followed by the numerals nought to nine. Then there was a short verse – 'Gay dainty flowers go sweetly to decay' – very cheering – and beneath that was stitched a square house with a central door and chimney and four windows. And beneath that were an array of randomly chosen objects embroidered to show off their maker's skill with a needle – a six-petalled daisy, a dog with little wonky legs, a clock with miniature hands and so on. At the foot was stitched the maker's name and the date it was completed – Elizabeth Bolton, November 16th 1852.

The truly scary fact was that small children made these things, Rebecca knew, sewing diligently away at an age when modern kids wouldn't be trusted even to thread a needle.

Connor tapped the centre of the glass. 'It's this one,' he said, 'I think.'

'Okay.' Rebecca went into her routine, flipping the notebook to a fresh page and holding her pencil poised above the paper. 'Shoot.'

And Connor went into his. Out of the corner of her eye Rebecca was aware of Michael watching, and thought, He hasn't seen this yet – or at least, not since we've been doing it properly. We're on a production line, and for Michael it's still a party trick.

She began to scribble, and as she scribbled, realised that something was wrong.

'Connor?'

The words had petered out. The boy was leaning against the rack, his hands spread apart and his head bowed, and when Rebecca moved a step to one side she could see his face was tight and pale.

'Are you alright?' Michael had moved in and put his hand on Connor's shoulder, and at that Rebecca made the connection.

'Oh no! Michael, it's you!'

'Me?'

Rebecca shoved her notepad in her bag and took hold of the boy's elbow. 'You're the amplifier! You're the one that makes him faint!'

'*Amplifier?*'

'Yes, yes!'

Between them they walked Connor to the nearest desk and sat him in the chair, where he leaned forward and propped his head on his hands, his elbows on his knees.

'We worked it out ages ago,' Rebecca explained. 'We think you intensify the experience. Dead weird. When you were with me, right at the beginning, I managed to pick up something about that candle, but I got nothing at all without you. And Connor's fine by himself – brilliant, actually – but when you're around it's too much.' She said, 'I'm afraid you're going to have to push off.'

His face was a study, as puzzlement was followed by enlightenment and then wonder. And lastly acceptance.

'Okay. Yes. Right. Good.'

After five minutes Connor's faintness had passed and he was back to normal operating strength. There was quite a lot to scribble down, and at the end she said, 'A lion and a unicorn?'

First pelicans and now these. Had they started to hide the things at London Zoo? Not that they had many unicorns there, of course.

'I'm just describing what I see,' Connor said, and Rebecca thought he sounded tired. She hastily stripped the scepticism from her voice.

'Fine. Unicorn it is, then.' She read back the rest. 'So we're looking for a small green door in a high brick wall, and acres of gold thread on velvet. And the biggest gates in the world, by the sound of it. Where on earth...?'

It was going to be fun searching for this.

They found Michael roaming the staircase outside and broke the news.

'Ring any bells?'

'I'll think about it.' Michael said. 'When are you picking up the clock?'

Picking up... that's how easy everything had become. 'I can go tomorrow,' Rebecca offered. The sooner all this was done the sooner she could get back to real life.

Michael looked at Connor, who nodded. 'Yep.' He slid the glass mount back into place in the rack. The mount bore a small brass label on the spine – H56. Rebecca watched it slip from view, and then shook herself mentally. One more step taken.

But towards what?

'WHEN are you picking up the clock?' Michael had asked, and it had seemed like that. After all, Rebecca had picked up the candle and the key easily enough, and between them they had picked up the telescope. Getting hold of the manuscript, or at least a copy of it, had been simple, and the directions for the clock – although admittedly they'd had to cross the Atlantic Ocean to get them – had been specific. Not too many golden pelicans sitting on fancy sundials!

So Rebecca and Connor returned to Oxford and stood on the pavement outside the open gate of Corpus Christi to gaze in at the bizarre gold-painted statue and its ornate pillar with no fewer than five independent sundials.

It was extremely close to the gate, and to the lodge.

Instinctively Rebecca was certain that to say what she was thinking – How on earth are we going to get it? – would be defeatist. Instead, knowing it to be useless, she asked, 'Any ideas?'

Connor said slowly, 'Perhaps we have to ask.'

Rebecca looked at him.

Connor stared across the street. 'The sundial's always been there. I mean it hasn't been moved. Whoever chose this as a hiding place for the clock knew it would be impossible to get at without anyone seeing. So, perhaps we're supposed to ask.'

He had suggested that last time, at the Museum of the History of Science. Rebecca turned the idea over in her mind. It was hard to see how they could get at the sundial secretly and Connor's theory held a kind of logic, but she quailed at the prospect of marching up to the college porter and asking whether a hundred-and-fifty-year-old clock was concealed in the college's famous sundial. He'd think they were nutters.

Right, do it then.

Rebecca strode across the lane and through the gate. She didn't even glance at the sundial but instead knocked on the lodge door. The porter looked up from his desk.

'Hi,' she said sweetly when the door opened. 'I wonder if you can help me. I believe there is a clock inside your sundial –'

'No, no. No clock there now.'

' – because we …'

Rebecca trailed off as she took in the porter's reply: no clock there *now*.

'He came for it last week.'

'Who came for it?' Connor was at her side.

'Mr Foster.'

Rebecca watched the porter sweep his gaze over Connor, down and up again. 'Mr Seward, is it? He said you might be calling. Left something for you. Hold on.' The porter rummaged. 'Here we are. Hope it's what you're expecting.'

Hardly.

Back in the lane Rebecca stood in a state of shock while Connor opened the envelope. It was addressed to 'Michael Seward'.

'Why did he assume I was Michael?'

Rebecca had an opinion. What might Foster have told the

porter? *'He has long black hair and looks very young.'* But she said only, 'What does it say?'

Connor read aloud. 'Perhaps you'd like to discuss this? Look forward to hearing from you, followed by a mobile telephone number and an email address.'

Rebecca's heart sank. Michael's trip to Scotland had been in vain, then, because somehow, goodness knew how, the estate agent had found his way to the quarry ahead of them. 'He's got the clock,' she said, needlessly. 'What on earth are we going to do now?'

Chapter Twenty-Six

'DON'T worry about him. I'll deal with it. Just get the thread for me.'

Not 'pick it up', Rebecca noticed. 'You know where it is?' she asked.

'I'm pretty sure.'

Michael had been searching. In the end it was his own memory that provided the vital link. The main gates of Hampton Court Palace were topped by heraldic statues, balancing on their hind legs and bearing armorial shields. Searching afresh for both the palace and the word 'embroidery' had thrown up the Royal School of Needlework, founded in – of course – the eighteen fifties and originally housed – guess where – in Kensington. It seemed a reasonable bet.

'Is it open to the public?' Rebecca asked.

'I don't know. Can you deal with it?'

He rubbed his face with his hands.

Something happened in Scotland, Rebecca thought, the smile's gone. Do I have the nerve to ask?

'How were your parents?' she inquired, deviously.

Michael looked surprised. 'They're fine. How did you know?'

'You mentioned them,' Rebecca lied.

Michael's face registered a sort of 'Oh yes' look, and Rebecca thought, Crumbs, he thinks he did. He's losing it. That's scary.

It was, too, because Michael was at the heart of everything they were trying to do. *Was* the heart, in fact. Without him she and Connor would never have become involved. Without him they would have remained ignorant of this mysterious confusion of the two worlds, wouldn't have known about any other world at all. And without him they certainly had no notion what to do about it.

Even with all the key components, even if they discovered the shadowy seventh, they still had no idea how to use them. How can you save the world with a key, a candle, a clock, a telescope and a spool of thread? What on earth could the missing item be that it would make sense of everything? What message was hidden in that damned letter that would tell them about it?

Her brain was aching. Was this how Flash Gordon felt when trying to save the planet? Probably not. Oh to be a comic book hero!

And now, just as she had accepted that she was going to have to worry about Connor, it seemed like she would have to worry about Michael as well. It wasn't fair.

Perhaps that's where James Bond scores, she thought; he just has to worry about things, not people.

Rebecca telephoned the Royal School of Needlework. They opened regularly for public tours of the workrooms. Fantastic!

By 'regularly' the receptionist did mean 'regularly' – at regular intervals. She did not use the word in the way it has come to be used, sloppily, to imply 'often'. The public tours ran on four days each year. Hell.

The four days were in April, June, August and October. August – this month – fantastic!

…and were fully booked up for the whole of this year and most of next. Hell.

Rebecca finished the call and stared at her phone. She pictured Hampton Court Palace, which she had never visited in person but had seen in photographs. It was reputedly a homely palace, whatever that meant, but it was definitely not a cottage and would have all the defences you'd expect of a glorious public monument – massive walls, giant gates, and no doubt round-the-clock guards. Not a good candidate for breaking and entering.

But the thread is inside, and Michael needs it, and I have to get it.

How?

Ask, Connor had said. It had been a bit shocking to realise that Connor's instinct was to be open and above-board while her own default setting was mistrust and deviousness. And she had once suspected him of shoplifting.

Rebecca redialled. This time she said, baldly, 'Hallo, I wonder if you can help me? I believe you have something that belongs to a friend of mine, and he has asked me to get it for him as he's a bit tied up at the moment. It's a spool of thread and it's labelled eighteen fifty-two.'

She waited. After a pause the receptionist said, 'I beg your pardon, could you repeat that? A spool of thread?'

'Certainly,' Rebecca said. 'A spool of thread labelled eighteen fifty-two – probably – but at any rate dating from then – '

She paused, hearing the receptionist on the other end of the line muttering 'Eighteen fifty-two' to herself as if she were writing, then continued, ' – and it might be in your lost property box, but –' (this was crazy but she was thinking on her feet here) '– it's probably in the place you keep all the old things nobody wants any more but you can't quite throw away.'

Murder.

The receptionist murmured, 'Old things,' and then said, 'Please hold the line one moment,' and left Rebecca listening to Greensleeves.

Rebecca gazed out of the window at Aunty Edie's garden. It had been a damp and disappointing summer so far but the garden was loving it. The chap who came to mow the patch of grass was up to twice a week now.

What was the weather like in the other world? What climate made vines thrive? Fairy tales, or at any rate children's versions of them, generally seemed to be set in an idyllic version of England as it no doubt never was, with lush green hills and comfortable, unrutted roads between plump hedgerows full of flowers; deciduous forests of oak and chestnut with soft floors of golden leaves; snow as white as – snow – which never turned to slush.

Not much rain.

'Hallo?'

Rebecca snapped to. 'Yes?'

'Is it Jap?'

'I beg your pardon?'

'Jap? Is it Jap you're expecting?'

Rebecca tried to martial her whirling thoughts. 'I'm not sure,' she said, carefully, 'I'm not very knowledgeable about this. My friend didn't tell me exactly what it is.'

'Jap gold.' The receptionist didn't sound thrown at all. 'That's what we call it nowadays. Gold wire wrapped round a silk core. Yes, it's here. Are you going to collect it in person or would you like me to post it to you?'

*   *   *

'I'VE got the thread!'

Rebecca, on the train, tried to call Michael first, but her call was diverted to voice mail and leaving a message didn't do justice to her elation.

So she tried Connor, whose phone, courtesy of Michael, was switched off. He really didn't get it. She forwarded a text message to him anyway in case he turned it on at some point – pigs might fly – and then in desperation rang Steph.

It wasn't an unqualified success. Steph was outside the enterprise and behind the current situation, but Rebecca felt that if she couldn't crow to somebody she would explode.

'What thread?' Steph asked.

'*The* thread! The thread from eighteen fifty-two! The thread that was hidden at the Royal School of Needlework!'

'Is there a Royal School of Needlework?' Steph asked.

'Yes, yes! They teach people to embroider royal regalia and stuff. They're at Hampton Court Palace, in one of the Grace and Favour apartments. But I've *got* it!'

'Oh. Well, good.'

'I just *rang* them! Just rang them and said it was there somewhere and could I have it please, and they *gave* it to me! Just *gave* it to me! Just like that!'

'Well… good.'

It wasn't working. Rebecca slipped her free hand into her bag and closed it round the hard lump that was the wooden spool in its tissue paper. 'Yes. Well. Anyway, how are you?'

She spent the next ten minutes trying to imagine life back in Suffolk while Steph chatted about her vacation job in the leisure centre in Ipswich, and a concert at the Maltings Arts Centre, and all the reading she had to do before October, but none of it seemed very real compared with the cool spaces of the Victoria and Albert Museum, and the golden vine leaf she was wearing round her neck, and the urgency of cracking the manuscript.

'Steph, how are you at code breaking?'

'Code breaking?' Steph stopped short. 'It depends. What sort of code?'

Rebecca pictured the manuscript, burned into her memory. 'No idea. It's a letter'

'How many letters?'

'No, a letter. You know, 'Dear William – Yours truly'. A letter.'

'Oh. Right. And it makes sense?'

'Yes, perfect sense.'

'Have you tried extracting words or letters from it?'

'Yep. Nothing.'

'Then it probably needs a physical key.'

Rebecca pulled her attention back from the speeding landscape beyond the train window and said, 'Physical key? What do you mean?'

'Well, some physical thing that you have to do to read the meaning. Treat the piece of paper – it is on a piece of paper? – like part of the code.'

Rebecca concentrated furiously. 'I still don't get –'

'Look,' Steph explained patiently, 'if it was a straightforward case of switching letters for other letters you'd never end up with a coherent bit of text both ends. Oh, alright, perhaps not never – monkeys typing Shakespeare and all that – but it would be extremely unlikely. Fiendishly difficult. You wouldn't bother. You'd just translate your message, whatever it was, into a jumble of nonsense.'

'But I don't think they wanted it to look like a code waiting to be broken,' Rebecca argued, 'in case someone got hold of it and tried to break it. If a letter – just some random letter – fell into the wrong hands it wouldn't raise suspicion, would it?'

'Exactly. So this person used a physical key. All you have to do is find out what the key was.'

Rebecca tried not to sound petulant. 'But what do you mean, a physical key? What are you talking about?'

Steph said, 'Like the thing the Ancient Greeks used. A strip of hide wrapped round a stick.'

'Wrapped round a stick?'

'Yes.' Steph sounded maddeningly as though this were common knowledge but it was new to Rebecca. 'They had a long, narrow strip of hide, or parchment or whatever, and they wrapped it in a spiral round a stick and then wrote along one side. When it was unwrapped it read as complete gobbledegook – no pattern, no transposition, nothing to crack in fact. Then they sent that off to whoever – the general on the other side of the valley, say – in perfect safety because even if the poor old messenger got captured by the enemy they wouldn't be able to do anything with the strip because they didn't have the right stick.

'Then,' Steph continued, although by now Rebecca had caught on, 'the general on the other side had a stick of the same diameter, so all he had to do was wrap the hide round *his* stick and read off the message. Neat, eh?'

Rebecca was thinking hard. 'But this letter isn't a strip.'

'No. Well. But I wouldn't mind betting it's some kind of physical key that you need.'

A physical key. Treat the piece of paper as part of the problem. It at least gave her a new avenue to explore.

Before she finished the call, Rebecca asked, 'How do you know all this?'

'Oh, one of the clarinets in orchestra knows someone doing Middle Eastern studies, and he went to this ancient history lecture because it overlapped with one of his topics, and the lecturer was plugging a speaker who was going to be at the Union talking about cryptography and warfare. So some of us thought we'd go along too,' Steph said. 'It was really interesting.'

Chapter Twenty-Seven

IT was as well that Rebecca had spoken to Steph, quite apart from the information she had picked up about code-cracking, because by the next day all her lovely euphoria had trickled away.

Michael called in the morning, using the land line from his studio.

'Is this safe?' Rebecca had asked.

Michael sounded flat. 'Yes, it's safe. He isn't the CIA, just an estate agent.'

Put like that it sounded funny, but it wasn't, really. Estate agent or not, Foster had possession of the clock and he wasn't going to trade, or at least not for anything reasonable.

'He's a maniac,' Michael said. 'He thinks he can make a fortune – I mean a real fortune, think Microsoft – by drawing power through the link. He's fixated.'

'Power?' Rebecca queried, thinking of emperors and dictators.

'Quantum Entanglement. A way to increase the speed and capacity of computers beyond our ability to imagine.' Michael sounded as though he were quoting. 'He spent an hour explaining it to me.'

'Is it feasible?'

'I have no idea. I didn't understand a word.'

A thought struck Rebecca and she found she had spoken before thinking. 'Would Connor?'

What? Understand quantum physics? Is it likely?'

'I don't know. I suppose not. But he's...'

What was he? Not easy to define, that was all Rebecca felt she knew these days.

Michael didn't wait for her to work it out. 'I can't get hold of him anyway. His phone's switched off and I haven't heard from him. I wish I had his address.'

Connor had steadfastly refused to give out any information about where he lived apart from The Angel being his nearest station. Rebecca would have put serious money on his home not being in the posh bit around Islington. It was annoying, but there wasn't anything either of them could do about it.

'What's going to happen then?' Rebecca asked. 'How can we manage without the clock?'

'We won't have to.' Michael's voice sounded heavy. 'We'll have the clock.'

'But you said –'

'We just have to take Geoffrey Foster as well.'

CONNOR stayed in the museum until he was thrown out with the last visitors at quarter to six. As he crossed the floor to the revolving doors the steward manning them joked, 'You living here, son?'

'Pardon?'

'You were here yesterday, weren't you? I remember you. And last week.'

Connor grunted something non-committal and made his escape. One of the problems of a limited wardrobe. He didn't kid himself the guy had remembered his face, it would be the combination of black hair, faded jeans and old tee-shirt that stayed in his memory. The person inside was anonymous.

When the weather was as warm as this the absence of roof and walls was not a problem; the problem was keeping washed.

On the Cromwell Road the evening rush hour was in full swing. Connor turned up Exhibition Road and made for the park gates, leaving the traffic behind.

And the noise. It was the noise that was getting to him, and paradoxically the museum wasn't helping. Surrounding himself with quiet, burying himself in the mild, distant echoes of the museum for hours at a stretch just made home worse.

It was becoming a physical thing, a physiological reaction to the incessant racket in the house – Shauna's sewing machine, and the television turned up so that she could hear it over the electric motor, and the twins shrieking at each other the length of the stairs, and Mick running the cement mixer in his yard next door, and always, always the sub-audible throb of Aoife's bloody hi-fi. It churned his stomach so that he couldn't eat, made him tremble sometimes so that he had to fight not to run away down the road.

It was the reason he kept the phone switched off, even though he felt guilty. He couldn't bear the thought that it might ring.

The exams had been finished a month back, so why was he still here?

He sat on the grass under one of the chestnut trees and took the photocopy out of his back pocket.

From first impressions he was inclined to disbelieve the notion that a complete coded message was involved here. The difficulty of ending up with a piece of text that read correctly was just too great. He thought instead that the words, either in their sentences or perhaps chopped up into phrases or clauses, held some secondary meaning, something that would be missed by anyone not specifically looking for it.

He read the letter again, slowly, and looking very specifically indeed. Obviously the address needed to be checked, but Connor thought it unlikely that it would turn out to be the address of the gap. For one thing it was a street name that existed all over the place in London, and for another it was simply too obvious. Most likely it was William Dwyer's genuine address.

Similarly the date did not seem likely to be significant. He supposed it was faintly possible that the numerals might represent, for example, a map's grid reference. If you omitted the word – June – you were left with the day and the year: 12 1852 – six digits that could be split into two groups of three: 121 852. But then what? Ordnance Survey? You'd need to know which sheet to be looking on, and without that information the grid reference was worthless.

That left the body of the letter. Connor read it through yet again. It seemed stilted, but perhaps that was normal for mid-nineteenth century correspondence. It certainly assumed some knowledge on behalf of the recipient – references to Mary's illness without stating what form it had taken, and the children without mentioning how many or how old – and yet William clearly didn't know the area geographically. The second part of the letter read almost like a travelogue.

Then there was that odd little line at the beginning about having more than one purpose. Just general encouragement from one old friend to another? It was strange that he had put 'everything' instead of 'everyone' – 'Everything must be allowed to have more than one purpose in life'.

Event, perhaps? Difficulty? It knocks you down but you rise up stronger, that kind of thing?

Connor traced the wavering margin on the right of the text with his finger, but could make nothing of that either. Still, it was unusual to see such large spaces, where surely another word could have been fitted in. And the left margin was none too steady either. On an impulse, he pulled out his notebook and pencil and started counting the words in each line, jotting down the figures, but the sequence of numbers held no significance he recognised.

Oh sod it, it was hopeless. And he didn't believe that was the way William Dwyer had chosen to communicate with his descendants anyway, chopping everything up into numbers and juggling with them. No, there was something in the words, something in the sentences that was waiting for them to find it. Waiting...

BY eleven the sun had been down long enough for the air to be quite chill. By one or two in the morning it would be cold, but if he sneaked a blanket out of the house he'd be stuck looking after it all day. Having forced himself to return home in order to shower, Connor had bolted back out and laid claim to one of the benches surrounding the swings in the park the other side of the railway line. He had a torch to read by until he became too sleepy, when he would curl up on the slats.

His hands would get cold, but he would tuck them between his thighs.

Chapter Twenty-Eight

GOLD wire coiled around a core of silk; actual, real gold, which would never tarnish. People had worn clothes stitched with this. How fine must that wire be? How amazing that they had the technology to make this so long ago.

Rebecca held the spool in her hand and marvelled at it. She would have liked to snip a piece off, uncoil the gold and see just how fine it really was, but of course she didn't. There was very little of it and who knew what it would be used for? Suppose her having snipped off a finger's width prevented it from performing its function? Didn't bear thinking about.

She rewrapped the spool and tucked it away in her drawer, but it lingered in her mind. Was it the gold that nagged her or was it the wooden spool, so old fashioned in its shape, so unlike cotton reels in a modern haberdashery? Or was it the sampler in the museum, with its cross-stitched alphabet and little house?

Forget it, she told herself; it's done the job, I've got the thread, the pointer doesn't matter any more.

So why can't I stop thinking about it?

She even dreamed about it, its stained linen ground forming a ghostly grid on the inside of her eyelids like a pattern you might be left with after looking too long at a bright light. It was as bad as the vines had been, or nearly.

Why?

Rebecca pulled out her sketchbook and turned to the page where the manic vines poured out from the carvings on the ivory casket. It seemed so long ago now, but it was less than three months. Strange. She looked at the drawing which had become a symbol of entrapment to her.

It was actually very good. Surreal, but interesting. If I were turning the pages of a book, she told herself, and came upon this, I'd stop to look more closely. Especially here, where the weird stuff starts.

She looked now, each little image familiar: the bird's nest, and the shells, and the mouse's skull. And then the really strange stuff, candles and whatnot.

Candles. A candle with the flame blown sideways, as if by an invisible breeze.

Rebecca stopped breathing. A light pencil mark crossed the column of the candle just below the burning wick, like a band around the wax…or a disc set into it.

'But I drew this.'

And I drew it long before I saw the real thing.

Fingers walked up her spine. Rebecca tore her gaze from the pencil candle and ran it over the drawn tendrils of vine, spreading across the paper. Clock hands, but no clock face. A locket on a chain – or was it a vine leaf? And there was the spool, the old-fashioned kind, and the tail of thread floating free.

Rebecca swallowed. *Breathe deep, steady now. What else is there? What else did I draw?*

The key, that was there, although the shape of the handle was different. The wards looked broadly similar. (*That's good, be analytical.*) A scroll of paper – the manuscript, obviously. A pencil, sharpened in flat scoops by a knife. A compass.

That was it. No telescope, not even an anonymous cylinder which might have been a telescope.

So it isn't really a catalogue of what we need.

Except that I was interrupted. I didn't finish the drawing because the closing bell interrupted me. What if I had been about to draw a telescope?

Rebecca looked at the right-hand corner at the foot of the double page spread, where the spiralling stems had petered out. The last thing she had drawn, the very last pencil stroke she had made that day, was a single dead straight line…

BY morning the connection was clunking her across the head.

The sampler, the alphabet sampler also had seemingly irrelevant objects included in the picture. What were they? There had been a dog, Rebecca remembered that, and a flower…

She tried to picture it before her, staring at the blank wall across her room.

A key. There had been a key. And a clock, the hours marked

in tiny roman numerals stitched with a fine thread. What else?

She reached the Textile Study Rooms before eleven.

Mount H56.

Rebecca drew the frame out from the rack and carried it to the nearest desk. Then she opened her sketchbook to the crucial page and compared.

Okay...Ignore the pram, and the dog with its peculiar, geometric legs. There was the clock, and the key, and there was a candle in a candlestick. Rebecca's heart thumped. Beneath the house was stitched an odd little shape like a dumbbell, which could be a spool of thread. There was a cylinder, which could have been a rolling pin but could also be a telescope. There was nothing that looked like a letter. On the other hand, the entire sampler was not unlike a letter, with text and a date and a signed name.

And in the bottom left corner, just inside the stylised vine leaf border, was a stitched circle with four letters around its rim – N, E, S and W.

A compass.

Rebecca checked her sketchbook, fighting the urge to cross her fingers for luck. Of all the objects she had drawn and Elizabeth Bolton had stitched, the only duplicates were the candle, the key, the clock, the telescope, the spool of thread, the letter – allowing for the sampler to fulfil this role – and the compass.

'MICHAEL, I've worked out the seventh item! I know what it is!'

She had had to leave the museum to make the call, partly because she didn't want to be overheard and partly because she wasn't at all confident of her ability to keep her voice down. Elation filled her. The seventh item! The lost link! The missing piece of the jigsaw, without which none of it would work!

Rebecca wanted to leap the wall and throw her arms around someone. Instead she walked up and down the pavement outside the museum.

'A compass,' she said. 'It's a compass.'

'How do you know?'

Rebecca perched on the edge of the wall. 'It was in my drawing. The first one I did, the one you made turn into vines. Well, not you exactly, but you know what I mean.'

She sprang up again. 'There were a load of peculiar things in the drawing, I found them when I looked at it that night. I'd forgotten about them. I never guessed they were relevant. Manic stuff, I thought. But, you won't believe it – they were the key objects! All of them – the clock, the candle, everything! And a compass!'

'I don't remember seeing them.'

'Well they were quite small and tangled up. You only held the book for a moment. And listen, there's more. I kept thinking about that sampler. I haven't been able to get it out of my head, it's been driving me nuts. So I went back today, just now, and guess what? They're in there as well! All the same things – candle, telescope and so on. And a compass. It has to be a compass, Michael, it's got to be!'

'Okay. Listen, have you spoken to Connor?'

'No. Why?'

'He hasn't been in touch. The phone's always switched off. I wonder … Rebecca, you're at the museum now?'

'Yes.'

'Can you ask them if he's been in? Find out whether anyone's seen him?'

Rebecca pictured the hundreds of visitors pouring through the revolving doors each day. 'Well, I could, but surely they wouldn't remember?'

'Probably not. Just try.'

Just try. Well, she had just tried at the Royal School of Needlework and her success had been startling.

Definitely something magical happening. The fourth steward she approached said at once, 'Oh, the quiet lad? Long black hair? Your brother, is he?'

'*Brother?* No, no!' Rebecca was startled, not having foreseen that one. 'A friend.'

'Well, you look just like him. Yes, he's been here a lot recently. Came in soon after we opened this morning.'

'He's here now?'

'Unless he left by one of the other doors. Do you want us to put out a call?'

Rebecca recoiled from the idea, certain that Connor would hate it. 'No,' she said, 'thank you. It isn't urgent. I'll see if I can find him myself.'

Some chance though, she thought, as she headed up the stairs. *In this labyrinth? The only way I'll find him is if he's planted himself.*

She began searching, walking briskly, looking every way, trying to see round corners and through doorways and past cabinets. She cleared the British Galleries, walked through the Sculpture Court and made a quick circuit of the costumes and musical instruments. Then she climbed back to the first floor, checked out Glass and Architectural Drawings, and was wondering whether to call Michael again when she turned into the Small Sculpture Gallery. And there at the end, coming towards her, was Connor.

Just as she waved it occurred to Rebecca that he might not want to be found. After all, he had been deliberately staying of contact.

But instead of turning and beating a retreat, Connor acknowledged her with a lift of his head, and quickened his stride to reach her. They met in the middle of the gallery.

'I've got it!' Rebecca spoke as soon as she was close enough. 'I worked it out!'

Connor's face registered surprise. 'So have I. Well, I think so. What made you realise?'

Rebecca tried not to frown. 'You have too? How?'

'It was the second line. It just didn't fit with the rest somehow. It kept nagging me.'

Rebecca gave up the fight. 'Second line of what? What are you on about?'

Now Connor looked puzzled. 'The letter. What do you think?'
'The *letter?*'

There had been nothing about a compass in the letter.

Connor was saying, 'How did you get it?'

'I'd already drawn it. Weeks ago, when I first met Michael. Well, technically before I met him. And it was in the sampler as well!'

'You *drew* it?'

For a long, strange moment the two of them looked at each other. Then Rebecca said slowly, 'Oh – you mean the *code!* You've cracked the code! In the letter!'

'Of course. What are you talking about?'

'The seventh object!' Rebecca grinned, confusion dispelled. 'I've discovered the missing item! It's a compass!' Then she asked, 'So what does the letter say?'

Connor shook his head. 'I don't know, at least not for sure. I could guess. But I know how to find out.'

Chapter Twenty-Nine

'COFFEE,' Rebecca said. 'I'm buying.'

On their way to the café they passed the carved ivory, and Rebecca said, 'This is where it all started, for me anyway. I was sitting here, and Michael was drawing from the case in the middle, there.'

She gazed through the glass at the eleventh century casket with its carved roundels and leaves. So innocent. But look at all this trouble you've caused me, she told it, although not seriously. At the moment she was walking on air. So what if the code had eluded her? The code wouldn't have helped anyway if she hadn't guessed about the compass.

Now all they needed to do was locate one in the museum for Connor to go to work on, like the good sniffer hound he was. A good sniffer hound in need of a change.

'You look like you slept in those clothes,' she said as they descended the stairs, and then she paused and looked back the way they had come.

Had something moved? The gallery was empty, but her attention had been caught for a moment, as if by some glimmer in her peripheral vision, or a reflection…

Or not. Whatever.

She turned back. There were grass seeds clinging to the back of Connor's tee-shirt. Surely he hadn't been to the park this morning? Or…

Oh hell.

Rebecca bought the coffees, and also carrot cake. She didn't want it herself but had the feeling Connor would wolf his down, and if she made a show of playing around with hers for a bit he could finish that too.

They seated themselves at the end of the corridor. The café was quiet and the nearby tables empty.

'Okay,' Rebecca said. 'Tell me about the code.'

Connor drew his copy out of his pocket. 'It's the second line. It doesn't relate to anything else in the letter.' He read aloud, quietly: 'It says, '*everything must be allowed to have more than one purpose*'. That's the line, not the sentence. If you read the whole sentence it still sounds odd, irrelevant, but not enough to make you stop. But the second line on its own, that sounds like a message, don't you think?'

Rebecca turned the photocopied sheet to face her and read it over. She sort of agreed. 'You say the full sentence wouldn't make anyone stop over it, but it made you stop.'

'Well. I was looking for something.'

Rebecca said, 'So, what else? What about the rest of the message?'

Connor said, 'I think there are two messages in here. Think about it. What are the things we need to know?'

'Where the gap is, and what to do with the stuff.'

'Right. So this line tells us – well, hints at – what to do with the key items. Use everything twice. Or rather, more than once, so I suppose that means at least twice, maybe more.' Connor took his last mouthful of cake, chewed and swallowed. 'And in fact the letter itself, the manuscript, follows that rule. It has more than one purpose. It has the purpose of telling us that everything has more than one purpose, and it has the purpose of telling us where to go.'

'How?' Rebecca asked. 'Where? And do you want to finish my cake? I don't really fancy it now.'

She avoided his eyes, afraid her ruse sounded thin.

'Are you sure?'

'Sure.'

She pushed the plate across the table and Connor started in. Between mouthfuls he said, 'This information could be left only lightly disguised because it's quite general. But directions to a location would need to be hidden more thoroughly so they couldn't be read from left to right by anyone who happened by.'

'They read backwards!' Rebecca interrupted, delighted to have guessed. Then she said, 'No they don't. I tried reading it backwards. It doesn't work.'

Connor gave her a small, twisted smile. He looked immensely pleased with himself, and it occurred to Rebecca that she had never seen him really pleased before. 'Not backwards. Not horizontally at all. Vertically.'

'Vertically!' Rebecca scanned down the words at the start of each line: Thank that in news staying or us Mary's do Walter us. 'Rubbish!'

'Where's the telescope?'

'The telescope? At home, of course.'

In the shoe box with the others. I really ought to have a better place to store this stuff.

'Let's go, then.'

REBECCA fished out the telescope still wrapped in its brocade, and passed it across. 'Don't tell me there's microscopic writing in here.'

Connor shook his head. He flipped the letter over so that it lay face down on Rebecca's desk and began to roll it round the telescope. When the whole sheet was a single tight tube, he turned it to where the edge of the paper finished, and his face fell.

'Hold on.'

He released the tube and then re-rolled it starting from the other end. Rebecca watched the spirit drain from him.

'What are you trying to do?'

'It has to be the telescope. There isn't anything else.'

'You mean, the Ancient Greeks' stick?'

She had surprised him with that. He frowned. 'The message is here in the words. You don't have to crack a code at all. It's both safer and easier than that. You just have to know the diameter of the tube. If you roll the paper round something of the right diameter, round one of the key elements, the message should appear. But it isn't working.'

Rebecca considered. It was indeed the Ancient Greeks' trick, except that the sheet of paper wasn't a strip. 'But surely the paper has to be the right size as well.'

'Well yes, of course, but it is, isn't it? This is the letter.'

'No,' Rebecca said, 'this is a photocopy of a facsimile of a letter. This is the letter photocopied twice.'

The penny dropped visibly. Rebecca tried not to smirk. Perhaps she wasn't so short of spatial awareness after all.

She lifted the curled paper and took a pair of scissors out of the pencil pot on the desk. The edges of the original manuscript, secure in the vaults of the British Library, were clearly visible as a hard shadow on the copy. Rebecca cut round them and handed the trimmed sheet back to Connor. 'Now try.'

He rolled the paper round the telescope. The cut edge now came exactly beneath the second line of text. The first message was displayed.

'Alright. Proven. And the second message?'

Connor re-rolled the paper, this time from the left-hand side. He looked at the point where the edge fell, and then held it out to Rebecca.

'Ignore the top three lines, they're part of the first message. Start at the fourth line and read the marked words.'

Rebecca looked. From the fourth line on, the edge neatly bisected a word on each line. Never a space, never the start or end of a word, always exactly in the centre. Allowing the paper to lift enough to reveal those words, Rebecca read aloud: ' 'from Gate beside Silver stone turn right left uphill to inn left over bridge two miles right after elm to house'.'

She raised her eyes. 'Connor! You're a genius!'

CELIA lifted the box down from the dresser and placed it on the table. She took off the lid and folded back the cloth.

Guns must be cared for, Robert used to say. Look after a gun and it will look after you.

The oil-cloth felt unpleasant to her fingers, but the metal beneath was smooth and clean. As she had been taught, Celia opened the revolver, spun the chamber, inspected the moving parts. Then she rewrapped it and replaced it, snug against its ammunition in the box.

Not yet. But something was nagging her, and perhaps, perhaps it would be soon.

It was good to have Robert's old gun close to hand.

Chapter Thirty

'*FROM gate beside silver stone, turn right. Left uphill to inn. Left over bridge. Two miles. Right after elm to house.*'

But no village name, and without the village the directions were useless.

Michael called his father.

'No, I'm sure he never mentioned a village. I'm afraid I can't help you there.'

So the name of the village hadn't been handed down with the list of keys, which implied that it was integral with the key components.

'Everything must be allowed to have more than one purpose'.

Then one of the components had the secondary – or even tertiary – purpose of directing them to the right village. *Think logically.*

A candle. You light it and it burns. The wax melts. The flame provides light and also heat. You see by it, and you burn something with it? Sounds a bit destructive.

A key. Obviously it unlocks something. And locks it again? Or is that part of the same single function? What else… It was made of iron, so might act as a weight or counterweight perhaps. It would sink in water. You could hit something with it, although it was too small to be effective as a hammer … No, this was rubbish, you could use anything as a hammer or a weight, there needed to be a function this key would perform that nothing else could. But what?

A clock. Tells the time, although it will need to be rewound and it sounds as though the key wasn't buried with it. A stopped clock. What about the clockwork inside? Cogs and springs and levers… Or the face, and the hands…Roman numerals one to twelve.

Okay. Come on. A telescope consists of a cylinder and a magnifying lens. Well, the cylinder is taken care of, thanks to Connor. What could be the second function of a telescope of this size? What would they need to magnify? What would they need to see?

What am I going to see?

Not now, not yet.

Thread. Gold thread on a spool. A counter-balance? A plumb-line perhaps? A pendulum? That might tie in with the clock. A pendulum could measure a very precise period of time, extremely precise in Victorian terms. If the thread was tied on to the spool, that might suggest the need to let it hang... And what else? And why gold? Because of the integral characteristics of gold – never tarnishing, never oxidising? Precious enough to pay for something? No, nothing like enough of it on a single length of thread.

And then the compass. Well, obviously it points north. Gives you a bearing. Keeps you on course, lets you find your way back...

... should you want to ...

And where exactly did the village name appear in any of this?

'I CAN'T believe this is happening,' Rebecca moaned. 'Not again. Not now.'

They had searched the V&A for anything remotely compass-like and drawn a blank. They had asked a steward and had the same reply as before – mathematical and scientific instruments went to the Science Museum in the nineteen-twenties. So they had spent a couple of hours tracking slowly through the Science Museum, queuing to reach the front of displays, over-run by school parties and families, assaulted by giant advertisements for IMAX films, and had picked up no trace of any kind of aura at all. Nothing. It simply wasn't there.

Begging at Blythe House wouldn't work twice, Rebecca thought, and they couldn't wait a fortnight.

But neither could he send them back to New York. How much money did he have?

I don't want to do it again.

Rebecca realised she was losing enthusiasm, her mind worn from the constant preoccupation, theorising, guessing. She wanted to be at home with Radio 3 playing while she sank into her work.

She wanted to return to the real world, to be occupied with something she could talk to people about.

'Do you want to tell him or shall I?'

Rebecca tried Michael's studio phone and found it engaged. Connor sloped off and Rebecca wandered, killing time before she tried again. Soon she was once more back at the beginning of her journey, dropping onto the bench opposite the carved ivory, stretching her legs in front of her.

She stared blankly at the display, at the horn with its silver trappings; at the curling head piece of the bishop's staff; at the tiny pill boxes. For some reason she found this corner of the museum very comfortable. Because of the upholstered seat, more like a couch than a public bench? Funny that Michael had been here that day as well.

What was it that had caught her attention as she left yesterday? There was nothing here that would have reflected light. Rebecca leaned forward and examined the cabinet's contents, with their old typed labels – catalogue numbers and dates of acquisition, sometimes the name of a donor.

Her eye roved over the shelves. A comb, a beaker, a little book.

A book? She stood up and stepped closer. On the top glass shelf stood a painted ivory case, hinged at the left-hand side and the size of a small pocket book. But it wasn't a book because it had no pages.

Rebecca moved to one side to peer round the corner of it, and her jaw slowly dropped.

WHY was his damn phone never switched on?

Rebecca flew along the galleries, jumping stairs, almost skidding round corners, pulling up only when she spied a steward ahead. *Curse* the architect of this appalling place – how could she hope to cover it logically?

The phone in her pocket buzzed. She stopped dead and checked the screen.

Hallelujah!

'Connor! Where are you?'

'I'm–'

'Never mind. Meet me by the ivory cabinet. Quick!'

Wherever he had been, he made it there before she did. Rebecca jogged along the gallery and drew breath. 'There. On the top shelf. Feel it?'

Rebecca watched the light dawn in Connor's face as he saw what she had seen – the circle cut out of the base beneath the lid, the finely painted radial lines, and the needle floating free.

'Try it, Connor, go on.'

Oh please let it be the one. Please let it work.

It would explain why she had felt so drawn to this display, and why Michael had been here. It would settle the question of what had been calling to her yesterday. It wanted to be found, had been waiting for them, whispering to them! She had to be right...

She watched Connor concentrate, and wondered yet again what it must feel like to him. Echoing voices reached them from the large sculpture galleries below – someone was talking about a new car...

Connor was frowning.

'What? What? Doesn't it work?'

'No, it works.'

Rebecca breathed out.

'But I can't... It's confusing. Wait a sec.' Connor took a breath and tried again. Rebecca watched, silent. After a moment or two he shook his head. 'I don't get it. It's definitely projecting the image of a compass, but no location. Just a compass. And a different compass each time. Nothing specific at all. I don't understand.'

Rebecca stared at the ivory compass in the cabinet. 'It's definitely the one?'

'Must be. It's very clear. I should have felt it before, I suppose I wasn't listening around here...'

Rebecca sat on the bench. 'Suppose... Suppose it just wants us to get *a* compass? Any compass? It doesn't have to be the Victorians' particular compass because it doesn't have to do anything – tell us anything – other than what any compass can do. Does that make sense?'

'I guess.'

'Well, then, ' Rebecca said slowly, 'a trip to the camping shop and we've got the lot. We're ready.'

MICHAEL felt desperation stalking him, and the village stayed stubbornly anonymous.

The directions gave a clue to the topography, of course – a turning left that went uphill to a bridge, where another turning left was possible, and an inn at the bridge. Bridges are marked on Ordnance Survey maps, as are inns. Gradients can be inferred from contour lines. But without a clue as to where to start looking...

And it was still thin. The bridge might have been over a river or over a railway line. It might have been a stone bridge carrying a road or a wooden footway over a ditch. And there were no distances aside from the final one, and that was useless because it relied on an elm tree which would have died thirty years ago from Dutch elm disease.

And he knew of no way that a map could tell them how to locate a silver stone beside a gate.

And what was a silver stone anyway?

Nevertheless Michael had worked his way over the Landranger maps covering Oxfordshire and its environs, using a magnifying glass and checking off grid squares in turn as he excluded them. It took forever, and he didn't even know that he was looking in the right county.

Hopeless. But the original Victorians must surely have realised that it would be hopeless and included the information in the key. But how?

Candle, clock, compass, key, manuscript, telescope and thread.

Knock out the compass, because it was non-specific.

Knock out the manuscript, because all three of them had been attempting to drag this word out of it for two days and had drawn a complete blank.

Knock out the thread, because Rebecca had unwound the thread from the spool in case anything was written on the wooden core, but it remained a perfectly normal, unadulterated nineteenth century spool.

Knock out the telescope, because Connor had dismantled it and found nothing hidden, nor engraved.

So that left the clock, which they did not have, and the candle. And the candle contained a metal disc, Rebecca said. What might be the purpose of a metal disc buried in the wax?

They would have to access it, and the only way to access it would be either to cut the candle in two at that point – ruthless and possibly ruinous – or to burn it down. Michael was in favour of burning; at least that was what people might expect one to do with a candle. If there was some secondary function the candle had to perform, then there would still be another six or seven inches remaining below the disc.

Michael arranged a meeting.

Chapter Thirty-One

REBECCA had packed her bag with care, conscious of carrying a precious burden, and wondered what would happen if she were to be mugged or run over en route to Michael's flat. What happened to personal belongings after an accident? Would she be traced to Manorfield Road or to the farm in Suffolk? If Aunty Edie got the bag, whatever would she think?

Perhaps she should have left a letter in the kitchen – not a suicide note but a fatal-accident note, giving Michael's number and asking her aunt to contact him.

Distracted, she almost didn't see the motorcycle courier as she crossed the road outside the tube station, and gave herself a fright. Self-fulfilling prophesies, she thought – on no account fulfil them!

She paid more attention crossing the next side road and made it intact to Michael's door.

Connor had already arrived, and there was a loaf and a big bowl of salad on the table and a pan of soup on the hob.

Rebecca unloaded, setting each object in a line on the coffee table in the back room. If only they had the wretched clock.

'First,' Michael said, brandishing a matchbox, 'has anybody had any brilliant ideas since this morning?'

Connor shook his head. Rebecca said, ''Fraid not.'

'Then the candle burns.'

Michael struck a match and held the flame to the candle wick. One-hundred-and-fifty-year-old cotton soaked in one-hundred-and-fifty-year-old wax resisted for a second or two, and then took hold of the flame and began to burn. The scent of sulphur drifted round the room. Michael waved the match out and took it to the kitchen sink. The candle flame wavered…

It was going to take some time. Michael set a series of alarms on his mobile to remind them to check the candle so they would not miss the moment that the disc was revealed. While they waited, they took a Landranger map each, extending the area of search outwards from Oxfordshire. Rebecca found herself with Reading and Windsor, and began, obediently and methodically, at the top left-hand corner.

At each alarm all three marked their places and raised their heads to check the candle as it burned down ever closer to the tantalising sliver of metal, less easy to see now that dribbles of melted wax were spilling over and trickling down the sides of the column. After a while Michael pared away the solidified spills with his pocketknife to clean up the sides.

And eventually the disc was close to the flame.

'I think we just watch now.'

Rebecca plonked a glass over the grid square she had been examining and swivelled round to lean forward, her elbows on her knees, and stare at the flame. After a few seconds she moved her eyes away, realising even something as low-tech and old-fashioned as a candle flame produces enough concentrated light to interfere with one's vision.

Time crawled. Rebecca shifted position and stretched her legs.

'That's it.'

Michael snuffed the candle with his thumb and forefinger and Rebecca bit her lip. The metal disc was clearly visible, flat and circular with a wick-sized hole through the centre. There was a sheen of liquid wax over it, but the engraved script could be seen quite clearly.

Not very much of it, though: a very short village name.

Michael dipped the corner of a paper towel into the wax and allowed it to soak into the paper. The disc became clearer. Rebecca craned forward.

Wick.

'Wick,' she said aloud, as if the other two couldn't read.

Good pun.

'Where's Wick?'

Michael was already at the book case, tugging out an atlas. Connor said, 'There are several, I think. It just means village or dwelling place.' He caught Rebecca's expression and became defensive. 'There's a book, a dictionary of place names, with stuff like that.'

Michael said, 'There are two reasonably close to Oxford, one in Gloucestershire, one in Berkshire. That's all. Rebecca?'

Rebecca jumped and moved the glass off her map. 'Where?

Where?'

'North-east of Newbury. To the right of the A34.'

Rebecca scanned the map. 'Got it. Gosh, it's tiny.' She marked it with her finger and started looking for a bridge. 'Yep, a bridge over a stream. Streamlet. No pub though.'

The other Wick also had a bridge at the foot of a gradient, although it looked too gentle to be described as a hill. Still, safer not to rule anything out. They would have to visit both and decide from the ground.

Rebecca left the key components with Michael. She didn't want to walk under a bus because she was worrying about street crime. It felt odd to be without them now, to have them no longer in her keeping, as if a little piece of the action had been taken from her...

She kept the key as a precautionary measure. It had been easy at the last minute to thread it onto the chain that held Aunty Edie's gold vine leaf and wear it round her neck, tucked inside her tee-shirt. She mentioned it to Michael as she was leaving, and then skipped down the stairs quick before he could protest.

She half expected him to chase after her, but he didn't. Still, she would be taking the train with Michael and fully intended to watch him all the way.

Or not.

'Why?' Rebecca demanded, trying not to sound petulant.

'Running out of time,' Michael said over the phone. 'Everything's taking too long. This makes much more sense.'

He was right, of course. Anyway, Michael couldn't actually do anything without the key that was around her neck.

Rebecca toyed with the idea that he had somehow taken an impression of it in plasticine the evening they were at his flat while ostensibly heating up soup, but rejected the notion on the grounds that he'd have had no reason to suspect that she would run off with it. He must just be playing it cool.

Or maybe he intended to keep Connor and herself in on it to the end after all. Perhaps it was going to be something that needed more than one person to carry out. Because, in all honesty, what on earth were they expected to do with some wax, a couple of lenses, a handful of cogs and springs, and a length of thread? Wallace and Grommit contraptions sprang to mind.

And why would they have to know where north was?

'WELL, it was a nice day, anyway.'

Connor grunted.

Rebecca leaned her arms on the rucksack on her lap and looked out of the window. Under the circumstances, grunting was probably the more appropriate response.

It wasn't the right Wick. But it had taken them several hours to be sure.

Wick – this Wick – was one of those villages far enough from London to be considered countryside and close enough to the motorway for determined people to commute to the city. It had, as the property brochures say, excellent connections and as a consequence had received a scattering of modern housing developments and the associated upgrading of its public amenities. Rebecca and Connor emerged from the station into a thriving village centre that had a mixture of traditional shops – a baker, a greengrocer, a hardware store – and some definite newcomers, with chic names and cool, colour-coordinated window displays.

'No bookshop,' Connor said.

They had checked their orientation against the Ordnance Survey map and headed out of the centre. Their intention was to start at the bridge and then try to work backwards, following the letter's instructions in reverse to see if they could identify a silver stone of any kind. If they were successful they would then retrace their steps to the bridge and go on from there, always aware that the crucial landmark of the elm was going to be missing.

Gauging distance by counting steps – a shaky business at the best of times – they nevertheless came upon the bridge at about the right point, and there was indeed a pub on the corner opposite – The Pig and Whistle, with a tarmac car park on one side and a beer garden on the other, where people were already enjoying lunch in the sunshine.

Taking a few swallows from their water bottles, Rebecca and Connor turned their backs on the pub. According to the instructions in the manuscript they needed to be able to turn right when they had their backs to the bridge and find themselves facing downhill. They tried it. Well, kind of, although it was a very gentle hill.

Okay, back down the road to find this silver stone.

And there they drew a blank. There was nothing that could remotely be described as a silver stone, or indeed any stone come to that. Just tarmac and pavement and front gardens, mostly belonging to mid-twentieth-century semis. Near to the village centre there was a short row of Edwardian villas, but nothing made of stone.

Rebecca said, 'Let's go over the bridge anyway. We might as well see.'

So they trailed back again, feeling hard done by when they passed the pub for the second time, and began to plod up the hill the other side of the bridge.

The letter stipulated two miles, and it was hot. The village was left behind and the road had no footpath, so they were forced to go single file, listening out for traffic. Connor went in front and Rebecca plodded along staring at his back and feeling quite sure now that they weren't going to find any kind of landmark to guide them towards the house, even if this was the correct village. She checked her watch from time to time to keep track of the distance they had come, and after an hour said, 'That has to be two miles, you know. More than two. We're not walking that slowly.'

'What's the time?'

Recently he hadn't been wearing a watch; another unasked question.

'Two thirty,' she said. 'We were at the bridge an hour ago, nearly. If it's here, we must have passed it.'

Although I personally don't think it is.

There had been no trace of anywhere that a landmark elm might have stood, and no indication of a turning. Surely the drive to a house would not have vanished in one and a half centuries unless it had been deliberately razed? Besides, the land each side of the road was pasture occupied by sheep, and a hedgerow ran between the road and the grass. Hedgerows don't spring up overnight.

And so they had walked back along the road to the bridge, and then into the village, and then to the station, where they arrived just as the London train was pulling out and had to wait an hour for the next one.

Michael had been spending the day in Gloucestershire. Rebecca wondered whether he had had better luck.

Chapter Thirty-Two

'No good,' Michael said, crushing their hopes. 'The bridge was a modern thing over one of the later railway lines – long after our guys were operating. The pub's new, too. The whole damn place is, pretty much.'

He was treating them at the restaurant he had taken Rebecca to before, the restaurant from which she had walked out.

Connor opened his mouth to speak and then paused as the waiter brought the pizzas. They waited while the plates were set down.

'Enjoy your meal.'

They murmured thanks and picked up cutlery.

Connor said, 'It was a waste of time anyway.'

'Why?' Rebecca asked, surprised.

'We've been misreading the directions. The hill has to be before the bridge, not after it.'

Rebecca saw Michael's eyes narrow. He put down his fork and reached into his back pocket to pull out another photocopy of the facsimile, with annotations in pencil. Connor reached across and took it.

'Listen: 'silver stone, blah-blah, turn right. Left *uphill* to inn, left over bridge.' The uphill bit comes before the bridge. It doesn't matter whether the hill continues after the bridge or not. The crucial point – the direction part – is that the bridge is not at the lowest point.'

'Damn.'

Rebecca watched Michael breathe out and close his eyes momentarily. This was obviously a big thing. Why was it a big thing? Surely, it was just a case of …

Oh. They had to be starting out from somewhere lower than the bridge in order to climb uphill to it. But bridges are either built across water, and water courses are at the lowest point, or over railways, which are also allowed to remain low. If they were going uphill to a bridge they would have to have started underwater or underground.

But how could that be?

'Then –' she began.

Connor cut her off. 'This isn't in the home counties. It isn't anywhere in the south.'

'Cumbria,' Michael said. 'Derbyshire. Maybe Yorkshire.'

'But –'

'The land down here is basically flat,' Connor said. 'We want somewhere that the stream, railway, whatever, runs at the bottom of a gorge. Then the bridge across it could be uphill.'

'Oh. Right. A gorge.'

More map scouring then. Not to mention horrendous train fares.

Or perhaps not.

'I'll rent a car,' Michael said.

BUT it wasn't straightforward. There were no villages named Wick up north. Michael had a copy of the dictionary of place names Connor had referred to, and it was apparently Old English – Saxon – whereas most northern place names were Old Norse. So if 'wick' was not, after all, the name of the village, what was?

'And nothing in the telescope?' Michael said. 'Nothing on the spool?'

'Nope.'

'Then it has to be the clock.'

REBECCA remembered the curly hair, too long for the business suit although not so noticeable now he was wearing casual. She had forgotten the voice, which was deep, cultured and easy on the ear, and she hadn't expected him to be such a charmer, approaching her with his hand extended and a warm smile. The hand was warm too, and the grip exactly right. He knew what he was doing, did Geoffrey Foster.

Aunty Edie would swoon on first sight.

Although... Rebecca recalled her great-aunt's dazzling description of Michael's father. *Perhaps not.*

'And Connor.' Geoffrey Foster turned his charm on the boy,

who had stood up, and Rebecca watched with interest to see how it was received. Hmm – shields are up, she thought. He'd be using a Romulan Cloaking Device if he had one.

The clock was wrapped in a square of thick velvet inside bubblewrap plastic, inside an antique tin inside a plastic storage box kept closed by spring levers at each end. Not quite the way Rebecca had been toting her bits and pieces around.

Well, clocks are more delicate.

Now Foster parted the layers to reveal a small carriage clock in a wooden case with button feet and a ring at the top for hanging it. The face was white, with roman numerals and ornamented hands. The manufacturer's name was written in small, spidery cursive just above the centre, and the hands were stationary at twenty-five past two.

'Have you altered anything?' Michael asked.

'By no means. What you see before you is what I took out of the wall.'

He had a flowery turn of phrase, Rebecca thought.

'Scout's honour.'

Ingratiating, too.

'No key with it?'

'Nothing with it.'

'How was it wrapped?'

Foster indicated the table with a graceful movement of his hand. 'There's the cloth and there's the tin. The plastic is mine.'

Nobody smiled.

He has no idea how we feel about this, Rebecca thought. He thinks it's a joke, a lark, a bit of fun.

She looked surreptitiously at the other two. Connor, she was sure, felt as she did – his face was taut as if he had swallowed a lime. Michael was intent on the clock, leaning forward. He picked it up, moved it in his hands, peering at all sides and underneath.

'Two twenty-five.'

Connor jotted a note in his pad. Michael prised off the back plate with his fingers and glanced at the inner side of the metal disc. Foster was watching closely, and Rebecca wondered whether Michael realised and would be consciously preventing his face from registering a reaction to what he might find. Was he a good poker player? Probably, she decided.

He moved the clock again, frowning slightly as he looked into the workings at different angles, searching for something – anything – hidden inside. Then he shook his head and replaced the back plate. 'I don't know. It tells us a time, sure, but I don't know what else it can be telling us.'

'And the significance of two twenty-five?' Foster asked.

Michael shrugged. 'It's a time. Happens twice every twenty-four hours. Maybe…'

'Maybe?'

'Maybe it'll become apparent nearer the time.'

Michael looked up to meet the businessman's eyes, and Rebecca thought, That's a poker face alright. But how good is his hand?

PRETTY damn good, as it turned out.

Michael saw Foster right out of the building – he was the sort of person you would not care to leave skulking in the hall. When he came back he said, 'He'll follow us, of course. I'd like to think we could lose him, but I don't think we will.'

'Follow us where, though?' Rebecca asked. She had collected the coffee mugs and left them next to the sink. Connor waited by the book case, the dictionary of place names open in his hand.

A glint had suddenly appeared in Michael's eyes, and Rebecca remembered with a little shock how he had seemed to her when she first met him. 'Ashendon Wyld.'

'What? *How?*'

She was aware of Connor already flipping to the start of the dictionary.

Michael smiled, stretching luxuriously. 'Ashendon Wyld. You'll find it's in the peak district, or maybe Yorkshire. I hope.'

'Got it. Derbyshire. Wyld with a Y.'

'I know.'

'I don't,' Rebecca said. 'How did you – '

'It was on the clock face,' Michael said. 'It looked like the manufacturer's name. But there was another manufacturer's name engraved on the back plate. Sheriton and Son. The name on the face had to be the village.'

Rebecca thought 'had to be' was pushing it, but provided there was indeed a village in the north of England with that name – and it appeared there was – she was happy.

Michael was already at the bookcase running his finger along the map spines. 'I've been walking in the peaks. Hold on. Got it.'

He spread the map on the table and referred to the atlas to locate the village.

'This shaded area is the National Park.'

Everyone leaned over the map.

'There.'

Ashendon Wyld. Pretty small place, Rebecca thought, with hardly any pink to indicate built up areas.

'Is there a bridge?'

'There are two,' Connor said, 'Both half way up the hill.'

Chapter Thirty-Three

BY the time Rebecca stepped out of the car she felt as if she had entered an Enid Blyton story, or perhaps Arthur Ransome. It had been like slipping back in time to drive up here in the hatchback Michael had rented using minor roads instead of motorways in an attempt to throw Foster off the scent.

Rebecca did not drive, having moved away from home immediately after leaving school, so Michael had to do it all and that had meant stopping twice on the way to give him a break. The weather was perfect – watercolour skies and sunshine without being too hot, and the breeze now they had arrived was balmy.

Rebecca stretched and went round to the back for her bag. There was a reasonably level area for parking to the side of the hostel, but the land around was steep and the views over the valley were ridiculously beautiful.

I need to draw, Rebecca thought. Whatever else we do I must get some time to draw.

They were not in Ashendon Wyld. The village was small and had nowhere for them to stay. Michael had located a hostel four miles south-west that had space for three, and they would drive to the village tomorrow. They had set off from London after the morning rush hour, and now it was mid-afternoon. Everyone was feeling both tired and in need of exercise after the journey.

They signed in and laid claim to their bunks. Rebecca found she was in a jumble about staying overnight in the same small hostel as the boys.

For some reason New York had not counted – the dormitory had been quite large and very full, and despite being mixed sex, it had felt more like travelling with a younger brother than a man.

This hostel segregated the sexes but it was tiny, with just the two bedrooms and only four bunks in each, which meant that between them they would account for nearly half of it. Michael represented a whole eighth. And if no other travellers showed, it would be solely theirs.

Oh well.

They stowed the box with the collection – minus the clock and minus the key – in Michael's bag. Rebecca felt the weight of the chain around her neck and wondered when Michael would ask for it.

She also wondered how much of a problem the lack of the clock would be. How many functions would it prove to have? It had provided the name of the village – vital – and had indicated a time; or was that merely chance, simply the place where the hands happened to have stopped when it ran down?

By mutual agreement they took a walk into the village below, mooching around the cottages and shops, and had supper as soon as the pub started serving so that they could turn in early. Rebecca changed in the girls' dorm and scrambled into bed. No-one else had turned up, and she lay feeling isolated, the low murmur of the men's voices just audible through the wall.

I'm the outsider here. What are they planning?
Nothing; don't be paranoid.
But the voices were still murmuring when she fell asleep.

TWO bridges and both of them uphill from the village, which was in a breathtakingly lovely spot, with water tumbling down the gorge and into a stream which ran through the settlement. There was a third bridge in what amounted to the high street.

'So we need to find the silver stone,' Michael said. 'Anybody know what stone is silver?'

He spoke rhetorically, of course. If either of them had known about stones they would have said so before now. Geological research at the library and on-line had brought forth nothing at all.

'There has to be a gate beside it,' Connor pointed out.

'True. Okay, let's find a gate.'

They walked the length of the high street, turned down a lane past an old smithy, now a shop selling barbecues, bird tables and garden plants, and left again along the third side of the triangle in front of tiny cottages, until they were back at their start point. The only gates were those belonging to the cottages.

'That way?'

They crossed the road, skirted a Celtic cross – stone, but not silver – and walked along the edge of a short but broad street in front of the church. There was a post box set into the wall around the graveyard. At the end they faced a choice – out of the village up an extremely steep road between houses, or back along a lane parallel to the high street

Where was this gate? Where was the silver stone? *What* was the silver stone?

'Ask?' suggested Rebecca, won over by this new concept.

Connor said, 'Ask what? 'Where's the gate?' They'll say, 'Gate to what?' and then where are you?'

They took the parallel lane, turned left at the end and passed a pub and a tiny haberdashery with faded knitting patterns and a dead bluebottle in the window, before meeting the high street again. No stones. No gates.

It was very warm. They strolled back to the church and sat on the low wall, drinking water from the bottles they carried with them. The breeze had died and Rebecca was ashamed to realise she was feeling drowsy even though it was ten thirty in the morning. A result of the poor sleep she had suffered the previous night, no doubt. It was quite difficult to stay focused, and really difficult to remember how important staying focused was.

She let her eyes close, enjoying the warmth on her face. Connor disappeared from her side – she heard the scrape as he left the wall and his footsteps retreating. Then Michael went too, letting himself down the other side, straight into the churchyard.

Whatever. She wriggled into a more comfortable position. It wouldn't be long before her backside complained about the stone wall, but for the moment...

'Wake up!'

She almost fell off the wall. Michael was in front of her, his voice shockingly close. 'We've got it.'

'Got what?'

'The stone. The gate. Come on!'

Michael had made the connection. Connor said, 'We should have been paying more attention. The letter didn't call it a silver stone. It called it a Silver stone.'

Rebecca wanted to smack him. 'Your point being?'

'Silver with a capital S. A name? A name on a stone?'

'A name on a stone,' Rebecca repeated.

'Stone, as in headstone?'

Rebecca looked behind her, at the church graveyard with its ranks of headstones old and new (though mostly old) and at the names carved into the granite.

Connor said, 'It's the name Silver.'

There were two gates in the wall around the church. The closest grave to one of them belonged to an Eleanor Jane Silver, 1792 to 1844.

JUST as the moment when she had closed her hand round the key from one and a half centuries ago, the sight of the name carved into the headstone acted on Rebecca as a shock, a spur, a call to arms. It told her that what she was doing was real. The warm, sunny sleepiness vanished and she felt energised and excited.

They set off, walking faster, striding out and looking ahead for the next landmark.

'From gate beside Silver stone, turn right.'

Done.

'Left uphill.'

Shortly there was a gap between two of the cottages on the left of the road and a signed footpath led quite steeply upwards. The houses just managed a level footing, but their back gardens sloped sharply and some had been terraced. They started to climb, and the paving slabs gave way to loose shingle and then to turf as they arrived at a stile. On the other side the path followed the boundary between pasture and woodland.

'Can this be right?' Rebecca asked. 'Should we have left the road behind?'

Michael shrugged. 'I don't see why not.' He looked again at the directions. 'Left uphill to inn. Then left over bridge.'

Within ten minutes the footpath had curved to the right and dropped into a narrow tarmac road with stone walls on either side. Twenty metres ahead of them on the upward slope was a pub. The Wild.

The wild what? Clientele? Stag nights? Fancy dress parties?

Rebecca saw Michael and Connor exchange looks. 'What?' she said. 'What don't I know?' Then hurriedly, before that unfortunate question could begin to be answered, 'What does 'wild' mean here?'

Connor said, 'According to the dictionary of place names it comes from the Old Norse word "wil", meaning engine or contrivance. A windmill, for example.'

A windmill.

'Or?' Rebecca said. 'What else could it mean?'

Michael said, 'A contrivance. Or a trap.'

They had passed the pub and there was no left turn or bridge to be seen, but there was another fingerpost pointing to the left and a gap in the stone wall. In single file they followed the sign and immediately came upon a ditch running parallel to the road and a mossy wooden beam about the width of two railway sleepers laid across it, embedded in the bank either side.

Some bridge

'... over bridge. Two miles. Right after elm to house.'

Two miles. Michael paused and reset the pedometer on his belt. 'This won't be dead accurate,' he said. 'If the terrain is tricky it'll throw out the stride length. But it should be close.'

THE elm – or rather the absence of elm – was not a problem. Before the two miles were up, Rebecca had seen the chimneys above the trees and knew the others had too. As the footpath wound on, sometimes steep, sometimes level, occasionally – quirkily – dipping for a few strides, it became ever more clear that the house beyond the trees was going to stay on their right and was the only building for some distance.

When a second footpath branched away across the well-tended orchard on their right they did not need the ivy-covered stump that remained on the corner, nor the weathered fingerpost pointing to Ashendon House. It had become obvious to them all that the quarry was in view.

Chapter Thirty-Four

THE house was a grey stone rectangle with wings that extended back on either side of a courtyard. The roof had a low pitch and symmetrically placed chimneys, and there were five shallow steps to the front door, with clipped box trees in containers on either side.

The view from the footpath, running towards the house at an oblique angle with an orchard on one side and falling pasture on the other, had been mainly of the side of one wing and the high wall that continued beyond it, enclosing the courtyard. To their right and to one side of the house, screened by a high holly hedge, was a single-storey cottage in a picture-book cottage-garden, complete with lupins and hollyhocks.

The footpath ended at the boundary of the orchard. They passed through a kissing gate onto the gravel of the main drive, where a green-painted fingerpost pointed in various directions with destinations written in white: House; Tea Room; Car Park; Lavatory.

Ashendon House was open to the public.

Although not at the moment. The doors at the top of the steps were closed and when they walked towards the car park they found it empty. There was a large noticeboard at the entrance:

EASTER TO END OF SEPTEMBER
THURSDAY TO SUNDAY AND BANK HOLIDAYS
2.00PM – 5.30PM
NO DOGS IN THE HOUSE EXCEPT GUIDE DOGS
DOGS IN THE GROUNDS MUST BE KEPT ON A LEAD
PICNICKERS WELCOME – PLEASE TAKE YOUR RUBBISH HOME

'Anybody expecting this?' Rebecca asked.

Everyone had gone very quiet. She stole a glance at Michael, who looked preoccupied.

Nothing new there, then.

'Well, at least we'll be able to get in,' she said, aware she was stating the obvious. What was happening to her these days?

Where had that renowned acerbic wit shuffled off to?

'True.' Michael sounded as if he had come to, given himself a good shake and started off afresh. 'And today is Thursday, lucky us.'

Also true. But they were almost three hours too early.

It seemed the footpath ran through the grounds and then followed the line of the drive, presumably meeting the road further on. Not unheard of, but unusual in such a remote place as this.

Rebecca was hazy on the nitty-gritty of statutory rights of way, but was pretty sure that if a path had been proved to have been in general public use for long enough it became enshrined in the maps and could not be closed off by the landowner. It was a romantic, egalitarian aspect of England that she approved of, but appreciated that it must be very annoying for a landowner to have strangers tramping around the place at any time of the day or night.

With hours to kill, they strolled around the outside of the house and its associated buildings, getting a feel of the place. It was large enough to qualify as a stately home and a fair-sized platoon of servants would have been needed to run it.

The wings proved to have been stables and carriage houses on one side of the courtyard and 'household offices', as they are called, on the other – a laundry, a dairy, a room for hanging meat. Standing on tiptoe to peer through one of the high windows, Rebecca saw domestic paraphernalia displayed in the laundry as if in a museum. The stables had been converted into a tearoom.

The grounds were steep and mostly wooded, but there was a cleared area about the size of a playing field where forest gave way to grass with shrubs and benches, and there were the orchard and walled gardens which would once have supplied the occupants with fruit and vegetables.

The cottage seemed not to be open to the public. Perhaps somebody lives there still, Rebecca thought – a caretaker or estate manager. The curtains were drawn, and it was very – really, extremely – quiet.

The boys had separated off, Connor no doubt scribbling, Michael... Michael what? Brooding. Plotting.

Well, he couldn't do anything yet. Rebecca found a pleasant corner out of the sun and made herself comfortable on a bench facing across the courtyard. She took out her sketchbook and began to draw.

'EXCUSE me, miss?'

The voice drifted into her head from beyond, reaching her from out of the singing summer heat. Slowly, reluctantly, Rebecca opened her eyes and blinked.

'Miss?'

An elderly man stood in front of her, dressed rather formally for a sunny afternoon in a tweed jacket and a dark tie. Rebecca peered up at him, finding her way slowly back to the present. 'Mmm?'

'Are you waiting to see the house? We opened ten minutes ago. Do you want to come inside?'

Ten minutes ago. Good grief, she must have fallen asleep *again!* Last night was really taking its toll. Embarrassed, Rebecca straightened herself up. 'Yes,' she began to say, but then had to stop and clear her throat. 'Yes,' she said again – much better this time. 'Thank you. Er – right, thank you. I'll be there in a moment.'

He smiled and walked away. Rebecca became aware of the sketchbook open on her lap and looked down.

'Oh no.'

It was the ivory casket all over again – the ivory casket with knobs on. Vines poured across the double page spread, flowing like lava from a volcano, buds and flowers opening and spreading and multiplying. And it wasn't only that page. Flipping back through the book Rebecca was stunned to find this was the third spread she had filled.

With shaky hands she closed the book and stowed it in her rucksack. Then she took a long drink from her water bottle – she was already feeling a touch headachy and they had to walk back later – and got up to search for the others.

She found Connor first. He was standing propped against the rail fence where the drive opened out in front of the house, staring at his notebook. He looked as dazed as Rebecca felt. As she approached he raised his head, and she saw the startled expression in his eyes.

'What?'

'I...' He paused. Rebecca saw him conduct some sort of inner struggle with himself, and then he said, 'I've written a whole load of stuff I – well, stuff I didn't know I was writing.'

He thinks I don't know about the poetry, she thought. That must have cost him something, then.

She said, 'Let me guess. Vines? Ivy? That sort of thing?'

Connor nodded, as if amazed by her perception. Rebecca took out her sketchbook and drily flipped the pages for him. 'Welcome to the club!'

They found Michael outside the cottage. He wasn't exactly trying to peer through the curtains, but he wasn't exactly not, either. He seemed to have ground to a standstill, staring into the stone wall four foot in front of him. He looked, to tell the truth, somewhat batty.

Rebecca said, 'Michael?' and put her hand on his arm. It was the first time she had ever dared touch him. She expected him to jump, but instead he looked at her slowly and consideringly, and then equally slowly swept his eyes around, taking in the garden and the edge of the car park, the cars beginning to arrive now, and the side of the house, and the orchard behind. Then he nodded slightly.

Rebecca said, 'They're open. We can go in.'

THE house was extraordinary, not at all like any stately home Rebecca had visited before. It was impossible to see how anyone could have lived in it.

It was a museum. A museum of the most anarchic, jumbled, crazy kind imaginable.

Every room, including the kitchen and the bedrooms, was stuffed – absolutely stuffed – with, well, stuff. Nothing was labelled, very little was ordered, everything was piled in together. The only way you could describe it, Rebecca decided, was to list.

There were masks from every continent. There were weapons:

spears, shields, bows, pistols and hunting knives in tooled leather
sheaths. There were musical instruments, including ancient,
decorated woodwind and an amazing, curling monster Michael
said was a serpent. There were dolls' houses with dolls, and bald
teddy bears, and a beautiful wooden horse on old-fashioned
rockers and two more, less beautiful, on wheels. There was an
open paint box with dried up squares of pigment, and a
blackboard with chalks, and an easel. In one glass case there were
several items of costume, including an elaborate and surely
uncomfortable dress for a child, and satin slippers, and pockets –
the independent sort that women once tied around their waists like
panniers – and bonnets decorated with folded straw, and fans.

There was a small room taken over by Japanese armour and
Samurai costume, and another with dozens of clocks, including
one with an astonishing wooden mechanism. Orreries and
astrolabes and sextants and – yes – telescopes. Horse harness with
brasses to ward off the Evil Eye. A set of blacksmith's tools, a
mangle, an early treadle sewing machine, some kind of bobbin
winder (probably) and three looms. Glassware, including a goblet
with a fish curling round the stem, and porcelain, and a china dog
bowl. Board games, cards and dominoes. A wall full of mirrors,
the silvering patchy and dark, and another covered with framed
maps, and over the stairwell the architect's drawings for the house
– this house – and a cross-section of a modern warship.

It was intriguing and irritating and brilliant and bonkers. Who
on earth had collected all this, and why?

Michael had bought the guide book. They clumped together in
a corner of one room, between an eighteenth century baby-walker
and a rack of woodworking tools.

Michael skim-read, speaking aloud the salient points.

'Uriel Passenger built the house and lived here until he died.
Never married. He bought all this stuff from visitors, it seems – he
never travelled, never left Britain. Just collected, obsessively.'

'Uriel Passenger!' Connor repeated, eyebrows almost in his
hair line. '*Uriel!*'

'The locals must have loved him,' Rebecca put in. 'Imagine –
any old thing you want to throw out, just bring it up the hill to –
what was it? Uriel? – and he'll give you money for it! Great asset

to the neighbourhood.'

'When the house got too full he moved into the cottage – ah!'

'But he's not still alive?' Connor asked.

'No, no. He built the place.'

'Then who owns it now?'

'Er...Left a trust fund to run it. Some complicated settlement drawn up by solicitors, no doubt. It doesn't say.' Michael flipped ahead. 'The rest describes the collection. Well, gives an idea of it. It would take a bigger book than this to list everything.'

They stared around the displays.

Rebecca said, 'I've been drawing vines again. Or rather the vines were drawing themselves. Through me. Worse than before, by miles.'

Connor cleared his throat.

Michael dropped his eyes to the floor.

After a moment, Rebecca said, 'What do you –'

'Let's look at the rest.'

Michael moved off and they followed.

More stuff. Model trains and needlepoint cushions and a very early typewriter with round keys. A hammock.

Bizarre.

Eventually they spilled out of the back door into the courtyard, where a party of visitors was emerging from the tea room. Rebecca felt a sudden yearning for a cup of tea and a scone, but felt reluctant to suggest it. The prices would be outrageous, no doubt.

Then she realised she was alone because the others had not spilled out with her. She retraced her steps to the last room of the tour, where Michael was talking to the steward. Rebecca recognised him as the one who had woken her earlier. She hoped she hadn't been sleeping with her mouth open.

He nodded and smiled to her as she joined them, which probably meant she had.

'... so there is a search being conducted now, but I don't know whether they'll find him. Or her.'

'A search for what?' Rebecca asked.

'The heir,' Michael said briefly.

'Oh.'

Imagine being called out of the blue and told you had a huge house in Derbyshire filled to the eaves with junk.

'And there is the password, of course,' the steward added, with a well-practised twinkle.

Rebecca said obligingly, 'A password?'

Michael and Connor seemed unsociably subdued, she thought.

'Yes indeed. The Trustees have a copy of a document that must be matched. When somebody can tell them the information that matches what is in the document, we'll have the heir. Like a glass slipper, don't you see.'

It seemed a haphazard way to deal with your property. And Cinderella was a poor analogy.

Michael said, 'Whom does one speak to about the password?'

'In the first instance, to the manager on duty. After that, if you had the bare bones straight, so to speak, you'd be referred on. No-one ever has, of course.'

'No,' Michael agreed politely.

Then he said, 'Where do I find the manager on duty?

Chapter Thirty-Five

IMPOSSIBLE to get her head around it. And he seemed so calm!

They walked down the hill in single file, Michael in front, for all the world as if nothing had happened, and Connor at the rear, silent and closed up. Rebecca, between them, felt ready to explode.

'What made you think of it?' she had demanded, when they first emerged from the manager's office – the smallest room imaginable on the second floor of the house, presumably the only bit of space they had been able to reclaim. But Michael had just shrugged as if there were no question to answer.

It had taken a moment for Rebecca to understand even after he asked to see the manager. More detail on the story? The background on the house and its contents, and its eccentric, now-deceased owner with the far-out name?

They had been conducted upstairs to the office, where the steward had left them with a middle-aged woman wearing a crisp white shirt and dark green skirt, who immediately struck Rebecca as headmistress material. She was certainly of the same breed as her own headmistress had been – an archetype really, efficient and precise, willing to listen but managing to imply that her time was not unlimited.

They had entered like a trio of action heroes, in a spear head with Michael at centre front and Connor and herself in the flanks. Michael had crossed the two strides to the desk and offered his hand at the same time as Mrs Kerrigan was standing and doing the same. 'Michael Seward,' Michael had said, 'and Rebecca and Connor.'

'Denise Kerrigan. What can I do for you?'

As there was only the one visitor's chair and Michael was too polite to sit while others stood, everyone had to stay on their feet. Michael rested his fingertips lightly on the edge of the desk. 'You hold some information I understand that would legitimise an applicant as the heir to Mr Passenger.'

Rebecca remembered thinking, What is the point of this?

'Yes indeed. Such an intriguing story, isn't it?'

And that isn't genuine, Rebecca had thought. She's wondering why we're wasting her time.

'Yes, it is,' Michael said, and then, 'I believe I have that information and am that heir. Can you tell me how we proceed to verify this?'

Rebecca suddenly found that she wanted the chair, but Michael was in the way.

Denise Kerrigan glanced around for her own chair. 'You have...' She sat down. 'Excuse me. You believe yourself to be Uriel Passenger's descendent?'

'Yes.'

Her eyes flicked over Rebecca and Connor. 'And your sister and brother.'

'Oh, no,' Rebecca answered swiftly, 'He's not my brother.'

'Cousins,' Michael said, stretching the point a little.

'I see. Well, initially you might tell me broadly what the subject of the information is. I know that much. Then I can arrange for you to meet Mr Passenger's solicitor to take it further.'

If necessary, is what she didn't say. Rebecca felt stifled, and then realised she was holding her breath and forced her lungs to work.

Michael said, 'Arrangements for a friend to come to a wedding anniversary celebration,' and Rebecca opened her mouth and shut it again.

The letter. He thought the letter held the password to – to all of this, this enormous house and everything in it, and the land around it, the estate. Everything.

She reached past Michael and pulled the single chair towards her and sat down. Her heart was racing, her brain teeming.

He had been intending this all along. The whole thing, the whole exercise, had been to get his hands on this fortune. She and Connor had been dupes, kids taken in by his superior age and experience and intellect. He had used them from the start, sending them here, there and everywhere on madcap errands, chasing wild geese, risking all kinds of embarrassment, not to mention theft on at least two occasions, and all for this – to pass himself off as the heir to some poor old bloke who had filled his house with so much flotsam he had had to live in the next door cottage.

She thought she felt sick. She certainly felt faint. There seemed to be no air in the room at all, and despite the heat her skin felt cold.

Mrs Kerrigan said, 'Are you alright? You look pale.'

Both Michael and Connor looked at her now as well. She felt foolish and uncomfortable. 'Yes. No. I felt a bit odd for a moment, but I'm fine now.' She stood up to prove it, and found her head clearing but her legs like string. 'But I think I'll get some fresh air.'

Michael's eyes caught Connor's, and the next moment the boy was following her down the stairs and through the house into the courtyard.

Rebecca sat on the bench she had used earlier. Presumably no vines would attack her if she didn't have a pencil in her hand. 'It's okay, I'm fine. But what the hell is going on?'

'What do you mean?'

'That!' Rebecca snapped, and realised she had raised her voice. She lowered it. 'That. The password and everything. What does Michael think he's doing?'

Connor frowned. 'What is he doing? He's getting on with the job. What's the problem?'

Rebecca was squinting. 'Sit down for heaven's sake, I can't look at you up there.' Connor obediently sat next to her, leaning forward with his elbows on his knees. Great, thought Rebecca, now I can only see your back.

'The password,' she said, more quietly now, forcing herself to be calm. 'The manuscript. The letter. Michael is trying to lay claim to this. All this.' She waved her arm, meaning to indicate the courtyard and the buildings and the orchard and car park and gardens.

'Yes.'

Rebecca stared at the back of Connor's head. You're the bright one, she thought. The boy genius. Wake up and look!

'He's been using us. He told us all that guff about a – a parallel world – so that he could inherit this place. It's worth a packet. Millions.'

Connor sat back and turned towards her. His face didn't

display any of the dawning knowledge Rebecca expected to see, just puzzlement and faint concern. 'What are you talking about?'

Rebecca, exasperated, opened her mouth to speak but was cut off before she had begun.

'Where does the candle fit in? Who has said you need the password *and* a candle?'

Rebecca narrowed her eyes. 'I –'

'Why did you see a vision of a candle buried in an Oxford college chapel when you were standing next to a candlestick in the Victoria and Albert Museum?'

Why did I? Rebecca tried to think, but Connor was still going.

'And the key? And the telescope? Okay, so you didn't see those, only I did. But how would I have known there'd be a key labelled 1852 in the porter's lodge at Cardinal's College? How did I know about the telescope in that clock? And the manuscript itself, how did I discover that?' He paused. 'Come on, how?'

Rebecca said, 'I don't know. But –'

'And anyway, have you ever heard of anyone leaving their estate to somebody completely unknown on the strength of a password? I mean outside of Enid Blyton, of course – I concede that the Secret Seven might have run up against something like this.'

Now he was being sarcastic. But Rebecca was thinking. It was true she couldn't see where the key and the thread and all the other stuff fitted in. 'Then why did this Passenger guy do it?'

'Because he left no descendents and he knew somebody some time would have to deal with the gap. It's here, Rebecca, the gap's here. How do you suggest Michael gets at it if he can only come as one of the paying public?'

'Well...'

Then Connor said, 'Look in your sketchbook.'

'Pardon?'

Connor nodded towards her rucksack. 'Look in your sketchbook. Look at what you drew.'

'I don't need to, I remember very well thank you.' It was hard not to shudder.

Connor nodded. 'Right. Where does that fit in with a simple case of intent to commit fraud?'

Well, it didn't. Nothing accounted for the rampaging vines either today or three months ago, nor the coincidence of Michael's tattoo and Aunty Edie's gold charm.

Oh shit. I've made an ass of myself.

'It's just...' She paused, staring across the courtyard, searching for words. 'It's just that he was so – single-minded. Deadly, almost. He hasn't laughed for weeks,' she added.

'He is single-minded, he has to be. It's serious. That's why he isn't laughing.'

'Oh Lord,' Rebecca had sighed, and at that moment Michael appeared, his expression considerably lighter than earlier, as if to defy them.

'Tomorrow,' he told them. 'The solicitor's coming tomorrow. We're into the final straight.'

THEY spoke little as they walked, single file not being conducive to conversation. Rebecca was still running it through her mind, restless and probably over-excited like a child on Christmas Eve. What was Santa going to bring tomorrow? What indeed!

Connor, as usual, seemed turned in on himself, and Michael was enigmatic. She had to acknowledge that from the outset she had never had much of a handle on him. She hadn't even been able to guess his age or nationality.

But she had guessed something, and she intended to keep a very close eye on that.

It was late afternoon by the time they reached the village. Rebecca was looking forward to shedding her rucksack and letting the air get to her back. And a drink of something other than water – orange juice with lots of ice would be nice, or a Coke. They swung round the corner of the churchyard and a voice said, 'Ah, just the people I want! How are you?'

And Geoffrey Foster walked to meet them, hand as ever extended.

Chapter Thirty-Six

HOW? How on earth had he tracked them here? It wasn't possible.

And it was true, it wasn't possible and Foster hadn't tracked them at all. He had taken his own path and arrived independently.

They went for a coffee; at least, the others had coffee but Rebecca succumbed to a cream tea – well, it had been two miles up that hill. 'My treat,' Geoffrey Foster said smoothly, but there was no chance of that – all three of them, Rebecca was convinced, would sooner have eaten their paper napkins than accepted his paying the bill.

They took a table in the garden, where striped parasols offered shade, and placed their order. Connor had ginger cake with his, so she wasn't the only greedy pig.

It was the clock, of course. 'The information had to be sufficiently apparent for you to have found it while you were looking,' Foster explained. 'Clearly it didn't require the clock to be taken apart or weighed, for example.'

Rebecca could not refrain from asking, 'How did you know for sure that Michael had found the information?'

The estate agent turned his easy, infuriating smile on her. 'He gave it back to me. Therefore he must have been finished with it.'

Oh.

Foster leaned back in the café chair, making it creak. 'Obviously the name was the first thing to consider. And here we are.'

Here they were indeed.

'I take it you've found the place we're looking for?'

We're looking for – the nerve! Sourly, Rebecca spread jam on her scone. This was definitely an occasion to leave the talking to Michael.

Michael himself seemed commendably composed. 'Yes.'

'Care to share the secret?' Foster's eyebrow quirked up, an amused smile lurking in the shadows. He was behaving like an actor in a nineteen-sixties caper movie – Cary Grant in 'Charade', only without the charm. 'I'll be able to tail you quite easily now, you know.'

Michael said, 'No need. It's Ashendon House. It's signposted and open to the public. You'll have no problem finding it.'

'And yet the public haven't fallen through the back of a wardrobe?'

How strange, Rebecca thought, that he knows that; that once upon a time he was a little boy who read stories. It didn't fit with the impression he gave now, the man of the world, all business projections and spreadsheets.

'I haven't yet located the gap,' Michael said, calmly.

'I see.'

They drank their coffee or tea. Anyone watching would have assumed them to be a group of friends enjoying the summer afternoon.

'So what do you propose?'

'I propose,' Michael said, 'to meet with a solicitor tomorrow, after which I will know whether or not I own Ashendon House. If I do, it shouldn't be too difficult to find the exact location of the gap. If I don't, I'll have to think of an alternate course of action.'

To Rebecca's delight, Foster swallowed the wrong way and put his cup down, coughing. Michael remained impassive, without a flicker of reaction, simply waiting for the coughing to subside before carrying on.

'There seems little point in keeping it from you since the story is published in the guide book. The owner left a trust to continue running the property after his death, but with a proviso that if at any time someone should present himself or herself as a possible heir, and be able to provide specific coded information to back up the claim, then the estate would pass legally to that person.' He said steadily, 'I believe I have that information.'

As do we too, Rebecca thought. And then she checked and thought again, in words that she heard in her head: We – Connor and I – we do too. We all know that letter off by heart. Michael put two and two together, guessed it was the password they were waiting for, but we all know it. And we're all descended from the same stock.

So surely the estate is no more Michael's than mine or

Connor's?

Images flew unbeckoned into her head: owning a pile like Ashendon House. Of course, it would cost a fortune and a half to maintain, she wasn't quite so unworldly as not to know that. It was the reason so many properties were donated to the National Trust. Land duties, inheritance tax, the never-ending cycle of building maintenance and the high cost of labour all made owning and living in such a house prohibitively expensive.

But you could sell it. There were millionaires who would take it on – footballers and film stars and software giants. Or a hotel chain – it was in a fantastic spot for tourism. What would it fetch on the open market?

Geoffrey Foster would know, or at least could make a shrewd guess. Of course it was impossible to ask him. But still...

What would a share of money like that do for her at this point in her life? Independence. A flat of her own instead of two rooms in a house belonging to a batty great-aunt. Freedom, temporarily at least, from the continuous grinding worry about money.

And what about Connor? She still knew nothing about his background, despite days spent in his company. She had found in New York that you could have quite a decent conversation with Connor about what was around you, or even about the abstract, so long as you never touched on the personal. One step in that direction and the conversation was over, finished, the door slammed shut. For sure, a large injection of cash would turn his wretched life around.

'I have that information,' Michael had said. No mention of anyone else. She looked across the table at him, and saw the flat expression and heard the flat voice. But were his eyes cool or cold? Was his voice steady or dead?

All her doubts, so soundly squashed by Connor, came flooding back.

*   *   *

So it was to be now. Late August early in the twenty-first century. Ten days before her birthday, which she would, as always, lie about – not through any inane coquettishness but because nobody would believe the truth and it would ignite curiosity. She had lived her life avoiding the idle – and on occasions not so idle – inquisitiveness of others, and had learned the most effective strategies.

The password fulfilled at last. Despite her lifelong control she had been unable, in the event, to prevent herself from asking.

'I don't know,' Olwen had said, still excited. 'I don't suppose they'll say, do you? Certainly not before it's all been verified and made legal and so on. But who would have thought?'

Who indeed.

What does he look like? she had wanted to ask. Dark, presumably. Handsome, undoubtedly. And fooling everyone as to his age, which would be what? Was he as old as herself? Or had the enigma dragged its weary way to another generation?

Well. Tomorrow she would find she had an empty day and would drop in for a few extra hours.

Chapter Thirty-Seven

BRUSHING her teeth, Rebecca suddenly found herself remembering her favourite children's fiction from ten years back. Before some momentous occasion – the first day of the holidays, the school sports day, a gymkhana – the reader was always told how the heroine had slept. 'Ginny lay awake in her bed for hours before finally falling asleep as dawn began to break;' or 'Alison thought she would stay awake all night, but despite her excitement she was asleep as soon as her head touched the pillow'. Which am I? Rebecca wondered wryly, nervy and highly-strung or phlegmatic and dull? Neither was particularly flattering.

If I ever write a book I shall simply say that my heroine slept, and let them guess.

Nevertheless it was difficult at breakfast not to sneak glances sidelong at her companions and wonder how they had fared. Michael was being so consistently, unceasingly composed she was becoming quite unsettled.

He cooked eggs for them all – they had discovered that he seemed able to fry eggs forever without breaking one – speaking when he had to with perfect good grace yet all the while managing somehow to discourage questions. Connor was taciturn, saying next to nothing and never meeting anyone's eyes.

Am I the only normal person here?

Michael's appointment with the solicitor for the Ashendon House Trust was at eleven-thirty. Once again they had more than two hours to fill.

Well, there was one distinct advantage in being an artist. Rebecca took her sketchbook down the lane to where a heartrendingly beautiful stone bridge rose over the archetypical babbling brook, and drew. No vines appeared, and she filled several pages with long views, middle-distance compositions, and close studies of the texture of stone and the vein structure of leaves and the movement of water, and for a blissful while the simple process of engaging her right brain and observing drove all thought from her head.

She had no idea how the others spent the morning, and was disinclined to ask. Since the revelation in Mrs Kerrigan's office she had felt detached in some way she didn't understand, and uncomfortable in company. For the moment she was better by herself.

They met in the kitchen at eleven, and then they were driving to Ashendon House, and her poor mind was teeming once more.

REBECCA had wondered what she would do while Michael was closeted with the solicitor. If I sit down and start drawing now those bloody vines are going to get me again, she thought.

But Michael said, 'My cousins need to be present as well'.

Startled, Rebecca tried to pretend she wasn't, and tried also to look like a cousin. All cousins together. But of course.

The meeting had to take place in the manager's office because no other room was available. Three extra chairs had been scrounged from somewhere and shoe-horned into the room, so that Denise Kerrigan and the solicitor, who looked encouragingly young and undusty, sat cosily on one side of the desk and Michael, with Rebecca and Connor on either side, sat opposite.

They had more width to spread themselves, which was good, but the desk was the heavy, old fashioned kind with a plinth of drawers at either end, so while Michael had a space for his legs, she and Connor rammed their knees against solid mahogany.

Rebecca shifted her chair to an angle and skewed herself round.

But in the end they didn't have to sit there for long. What Rebecca had expected to be long and drawn-out turned out to be over swiftly and painlessly. For some reason – too much exposure to Dickens, perhaps? – she had anticipated a fight, with Michael versus the stubborn, stalling might of the judiciary, instead of which the solicitor seemed happy to be present at the closure of an irregular and awkward arrangement.

Michael named the author and the recipient of the letter, its date, and William Dwyer's address. With this information cleared, the solicitor opened a sealed envelope in which was a copy of the letter, which he referred to while Michael pretty much quoted the text verbatim. After that, all Michael needed to do was prove his identity, for which his driving licence was considered acceptable in the short term, so that his descent from one of the seven names on the solicitor's list could be proven.

'So far as I'm aware,' the solicitor said, 'nothing links these people other than that they were chosen by Mr Passenger.'

We know, though, Rebecca thought: Mundus Caecus.

The final verification of descent would be required before ownership of the property could be legally transferred, but that could be dealt with in a matter of days. All in all everyone seemed content. And then Michael ended the interview by saying quietly, 'Please understand that this claim is being presented by myself on behalf of the three of us. We are equal heirs in this matter.'

It took a few seconds for the words to reach her brain. Her skin turned icy and her heart gave one almighty thunk. She had enough presence of mind to think, Don't go fainting again or everyone will think you're a washout, and to take a few discrete deep breaths while the solicitor queried Michael's statement and Michael clarified it ('We are all descendants of Emily Seward. If the legacy doesn't permit joint inheritance, perhaps you will draw up a separate document to provide for my sharing the property with them').

And then they were standing up and shaking hands and she was following Michael out of the house and along the path to the cottage.

The cottage? She must have missed something in the blur. Mrs Kerrigan was unlocking the door with the proficiency of someone who knows the exact angle to insert the key and the little sideways jerk needed to get it to turn. But when the door swung open, she did not go inside and instead stepped back and handed the key to Michael. Smiling, she said, 'I'll leave you to it, then. If you need anything, please ask.' And Michael stepped over the threshold.

Rebecca and Connor followed.

IT was musty, but smelled okay – dusty but not disgusting, so no dead mouse in the trap or dead bird down the chimney.

Connor drew back the curtains. The cottage had low ceilings

and very low lintels which Michael only just cleared. Connor had to duck, and Rebecca had to squash the urge to warn him at every doorway.

The walls were wood-panelled – unusual in such a small building – and the floor carpeted with a succession of overlapping rugs. Rustic but homely. Rebecca opened doors and peered into rooms – a bedroom; a kitchen with a solid fuel range cooker and an airing frame suspended from the ceiling; a bathroom with a vast claw-footed bath; what looked like a best parlour because it felt less worn and lived in than the rest of the cottage; and a couple of rooms that were basically giant cupboards.

There were pictures in frames and plates on hooks and maps and a couple of tapestries, and in the parlour one wall was almost covered with old mirrors. There were books everywhere – on shelves, in cases, stacked on tables, standing in a ragged line on the floor against the wall. Some of them looked like handwritten notebooks, and some of them, Rebecca was excited to see, looked very much like sketchbooks.

She didn't know what to say. The situation seemed wildly unreal. Connor was frowning – why frowning? – and Michael was still irritatingly impassive. What was wrong with them?

'I can't believe it,' she said, mostly for something to say, although it was also true.

Michael glanced at her, and after a beat turned one side of his mouth up in a half smile.

Rebecca's stomach lurched. He can have no idea, she thought, what he looks like when he does that. If he had any idea at all ...

She bit her lip. Then she sat down on the couch, which was surprisingly modern and squashy. The cottage was not the time capsule it had first appeared. Lots of the things in it, from furniture like the sofa to the equipment in the kitchen, were contemporary.

In fact now something jumped out at her and she leaned forward, stretching, to take the top book off the pile on the table.

'I've read this.'

It was a paperback novel she had enjoyed the previous year, which had won a literary prize. She flipped the pages. The first two-thirds of the book had been read – the spine broken, the pages opening easily; the last section was pristine.

'When did this guy die?' she asked.

'Fifteen months ago. The third of May last year.'

Michael's voice was distant. Rebecca looked sharply at him, where he stood next to one of the tables with his back to her, and then saw that Connor too was watching him with narrowed eyes. Briefly they exchanged glances. Then Rebecca, because she realised it had to be her, said, 'Are you alright, Michael?'

Michael turned round and looked at her as though he wasn't sure what she was doing there. Then he seemed to come to himself, lifting his eyebrows suddenly and saying, 'Yes. Yes, of course.' He took a breath. 'It's just… '

They waited. Michael's eyes roved the room, and then came back and settled on Connor and Rebecca.

'You don't realise who he was.' He smiled the peculiar half-smile again, and Rebecca saw something in his eyes that disturbed her. 'He was the only owner this house has had. He built it, in eighteen fifty-three. He was our mutual ancestor.'

Rebecca's thoughts caught up at last. She almost choked. 'You mean, he was the fairy!'

Michael's smile reached his eyes. 'Yes. He was.'

Chapter Thirty-Eight

IT was dusk by the time they left and there was little traffic on the road to the hostel. The lane twisted and swooped, dark beyond the headlamps.

It had been tempting to stay overnight in the cottage, but not practical. There was no running water or power, the mains supply having been disconnected, and there was nothing to eat either. They had done without lunch and it was likely, Rebecca thought, that the fluttery feeling in her stomach now was hunger as much as excitement. She decided to postpone bed long enough to make herself a fat cheese sandwich.

Also the cottage had only the one bed, and couches are not comfortable to sleep on for long. But it had been hard, nonetheless, to drag themselves away.

Rebecca had opened every window wide – voices and footsteps from the visitors to the house floated in with the fresh air and the scent of the wallflowers and stocks in the garden. They had been too engrossed to notice lunch being served in the restaurant, but late in the afternoon one of the stewards kindly brought over a tray with tea and a plate of biscuits. She gave the strong impression that she would have liked to stop and chat, refusing to hand the tray to Connor when he opened the door but instead walking straight through, barging him aside using the tray like a cow-catcher on an American locomotive.

'So this is the inside!' she had said, eyes on stalks.

Michael had put down the book he was holding and taken the tray from her. 'Yes. Thank you very much, you're very kind.'

She hadn't taken the hint. 'And you are the heirs.' She gestured gracefully, implying the cottage and its surroundings. She was a very graceful woman, Rebecca considered, very slim and upright and sleek, much more polished than you'd expect of a volunteer steward in a stately home. Very Wallis Simpson, she suddenly thought, recalling photographs of the late Duchess of Windsor, only taller and much prettier.

None of them quite knew what to do with her. It seemed ruder than any of them could manage to just turn her round and bustle her out of the door. She was off on a tour of her own now, repeating what Rebecca had done – opening doors, checking the passages, peering everywhere.

I suppose curiosity would have built up over the years, Rebecca thought – stewarding the house, never allowed to get a look inside the cottage. Knowing the old guy lived here but never seeing him. According to Mrs Kerrigan he had been a recluse for decades – one way to stop people asking awkward questions like 'How old are you?'

Eventually Michael had scooped her up as she came back into the sitting room, his hand light but irresistible on the back of her waist, guiding her to the door. 'Thank you for the tea,' he said firmly. 'We'll bring the tray back when we're finished.'

After that they had attacked the books in earnest. Not the published books, not the shelf-loads of fiction and non-fiction that the – the what? You couldn't possibly carry on calling him a fairy. The alien? The immigrant? Rebecca decided on The Traveller as being sufficiently neutral – that the traveller had collected, but the notebooks he had compiled himself.

There were dozens of them, handwritten and filed in order of date. Somewhere, Michael was sure, would be found the information they needed to deal with the gap, the instructions for using the objects they had collected – the key, the candle, the thread.

Unfortunately the traveller had remained anxious about security, and even the earliest books, which covered the eighteen-fifties, made no mention of any of the items. Perhaps he had been too worried that someone might gain access to the books to put anything down in black and white. So they took a year each and began to read, or at least to skim, trying not to become side-tracked on their search for the key.

Which was difficult. Some of his jottings were fascinating. 'Hey, listen,' Rebecca couldn't help saying. 'He was on the roadside at Queen Victoria's funeral procession! He saw it! Can you imagine!'

Shortly afterwards Connor was kick-started out of his silence by discovering that the traveller had met Isambard Kingdom

Brunel. 'Brunel! And this guy only died last year!'

Only Michael remained fully focused, never pausing, never exclaiming over what he was reading.

After an hour or so Rebecca and Connor also fell silent, saturated by the strangeness. Some time after four Rebecca took the tray back to the tea room and bought some bottles of water, and at half past five Mrs Kerrigan knocked on the door to tell them that the place was now closing for the evening. The house would be locked and the alarms switched on, but the cottage was separate and theirs to do with as they wished.

They wished to go on reading. It was becoming increasingly frustrating to have come so far and still be in the dark. Michael had explored the cottage again, staring at every wall, internal and external, sometimes laying his palm flat against the plaster or wood panelling or stone as if against the flank of a living animal, feeling for indications of – what? Its state of health? Its personality? Or trying to communicate his own intentions?

Then Connor said abruptly, 'Here! '*Remember that everything must be allowed to have more than one purpose*'. That's from the letter.'

They gathered round. The sentence appeared in its own separate paragraph disconnected from what had gone before and what came after. It was a reference, but pretty oblique. Michael flipped to the flyleaf at the front of the book – 1863.

'How sure are you that he did write the instructions down?' Rebecca had to ask. 'Perhaps we're supposed to work it out for ourselves. Otherwise why put this reminder in everything?'

Michael frowned. 'I don't know. Could be. Maybe we should start thinking about how the things might be used.'

'Starting with the key,' Connor said.

'Why the key?' Rebecca asked.

Connor shrugged. 'Seems obvious. It must unlock something we need to have unlocked.'

The sitting room was lit by the late afternoon sun, but by now rooms on the other side of the cottage were becoming quite dark and it was not sensible to begin searching afresh. Besides, as Rebecca discovered when she stood up, they had spent too much time sitting still and needed to stretch and move and turn their thoughts to something else for a spell. Or at least try.

Geoffrey Foster, for example. Where had he got to? They had found him at Ashendon House waiting for them to arrive, and had expected him to be laying siege outside afterwards to hear the result of their meeting.

But he wasn't. In the excitement of having Michael's – their – claim ratified and gaining admittance to the cottage she had forgotten to wonder why, but now it seemed very peculiar.

Where was he? And what was he up to? Something, for sure. It was simply not believable that he should have given up and cleared off, not at this stage.

'Where do you suppose Geoffrey Foster is?' she asked, as the car turned out of the drive.

But nobody had any suggestions.

SHE was a goodlooking woman even now; she must have been a cracker in her day.

Geoffrey Foster closed the car door for her and stepped back as she started the ignition. He smiled as she pulled away, and raised one hand in a salute, watching the Lotus slide neatly into a slim gap in the traffic of the high street. Bold driver. Bold all round.

Which was why it was interesting to discover she was also nervous.

They had driven to the hotel separately as she intended to return to Ashendon House afterwards, and met in the lounge as agreed. He had fetched drinks – pink gins, very nineteen-thirties – and listened with increasing interest to what she had to tell him.

For that he would give a little in exchange. Not too much, but enough to give the impression that he was playing fair. He spoke a little about quantum entanglement, giving his words the veneer of authority that experience had taught him reeled in the punters like children to chocolate. He had expected her to latch on quickly – she clearly understood money, as was evident from the car she drove and the size of the diamond on her right (not left) ring finger – and was surprised when she waved aside his proposition.

Careful not to show it though.

'You understand that it is very important to me that these people do not gain access to this? That it must be left to me – to us – to handle as we see fit?'

Confident that he could deal with the woman when the time came, Foster smiled. 'Of course.'

'Then you will have to join them tomorrow, and stay close until they've found what they're looking for. They appear to trust you, at any rate.'

Foster smiled again. 'I wouldn't call it trust exactly, but they accept me. I am an unavoidable evil.' He found it amusing.

She looked at him sharply – a lot about her was sharp, from her intellect to the heels on her shoes. 'I don't want conflict.'

'I know.' Foster raised his glass. 'To the future.'

Her lacquered fingernails were sharp, too, and her hand holding the wineglass was very slightly trembling.

Chapter Thirty-Nine

IT was well after midnight before Rebecca finally managed to sleep, having lain helplessly awake for hours trying to think how the different components could be used. There had been no blinding flashes of inspiration, but in the morning, when she awoke, she recalled the disk in the candle and the engraved word 'wick'.

So had Michael, and so had Connor.

Before breakfast they took the candle out of its wrapping and examined it afresh.

Wick.

Alright then, presume it not to have been a pun. The dark, scorched wick projected a few millimetres above the level of the wax. What, pray, could be done with that?

Draw with it? Rebecca touched it with her fingertip to see if it would behave like charcoal. It didn't. Her skin remained clean and unmarked. She pinched it. Still no mark, but the wick flopped over and tried to come with her.

'Oops.'

'Careful!'

Too late. The scorched wick separated from the candle and Rebecca's stomach did a flip as she realised she had just destroyed something vital.

Or had she? The wick didn't fall off but stayed, dangling. Michael nudged it gently and it rolled on the slope of the candle without falling.

It was attached. The wick continued into the candle, but not as a proper wick should.

With infinite care, Michael took hold of it and drew it away, and as it came a thread followed. Rebecca peered closely. In the centre of the wax column, in the hole where the wick should have been, was a bundle of fine thread, folded many times until it reached the approximate thickness of the regular wick. Michael was unfolding it, drawing it out to its full length.

'Good grief.'

Michael's hand was now a foot from the candle and the thread continued to unravel.

'How long can it be?'

Eventually he met with resistance, and the thread stopped. Winding it carefully around his fingers, Michael brought the bundle back to the candle and they inspected the hole in the wax. The thread was scarlet. At the bottom of the hole it had vacated, the remaining wick was white. Michael opened his penknife and cut off the thread. They looked at each other.

'Ingenious. What do we use it for?'

They needed to measure it. Rebecca, ingenious herself in a small way, used the length of her sketchbook, which gave its dimensions on the front cover – 305 mm. The thread was about thirty-five centimetres long.

If all the items had secondary functions this obscure they were going to have endless fun.

'HAVE you tried all the doors?'

What a moron.

Rebecca said, 'Of course we have. What else can you suggest?'

The estate agent had rejoined them, clearly determined to be part of the enterprise after all.

'Sorry I couldn't be here yesterday. Business. Rather out of the blue, actually.'

It had been disappointing to see his BMW in the car park when they pulled in, and Rebecca was disappointed again to see that he remembered to duck at the cottage door; she would have enjoyed watching him brain himself on the lintel.

Once inside he listened attentively to what Michael told him, looking at each of the objects carefully, apparently giving them his full consideration. Rebecca could almost hear the cogs turning in there, click, click, click.

He was most interested in the key.

Every internal door in the cottage had a key hole, and the key fitted every one of them. Fitted, turned, locked and unlocked. No help.

The man had an irritating ability either not to notice that she was being rude to him or not to mind it. He maintained an aggravating calm and – worse – that hint of a smile. An amused, indulgent, patronising smile. Rebecca would have liked to throw something at him.

Now he said, pleasantly, 'May I?' and put out his hand, palm upwards.

Michael looked at Rebecca. Rebecca unthreaded the chain and gave Foster the key. She was reluctant, but frankly any input at all would be welcome.

As they had done, Foster weighed it in his hand and stroked the smooth metal with his thumb. He inspected the cloverleaf design of the handle, with the thin ribbon threaded through, and the irregular series of right-angles that formed the wards. Then he said, 'Have you considered that this might represent a floor plan?'

A floor plan? All three of them perked up, Rebecca noticed, and (if they were like her) wished they hadn't; so uncool, and you could just see how it pleased Foster.

'It does look rather like the floor plan of a building, don't you think? This one, perhaps?'

And it did. There was the main room, with the kitchen at one end, and then the passageway along one side from which the smaller rooms opened. The numbers were correct, and the proportions approximately right. Damn – who but an estate agent would have thought of that?

There was a small projection, a tiny pip, on the side of one of the smaller rooms: the best parlour. But when they went to the room there was nothing to be seen there, not on the wall nor the floor nor the ceiling. The ranks of mirrors reflected their own frowning faces.

Rebecca made a conscious effort to lift her eyebrows.

'Okay, so what's next?'

The thread? They now had two threads, of course. What can you do with two lengths of thread? Rebecca, as the sole stitcher present, felt the burden of responsibility. She needed to solve this one. How?

'I'll keep working on it,' she said briskly. 'What about the telescope?'

No one could think what to do with a telescope except look through it. At what?

'The primary purpose of each of these things is the obvious purpose,' Connor said, slowly. 'The manuscript had to be read for its superficial sense to get us access here, as well as hiding the directions.'

'And the clock gives us a time as well as a name.' Michael took up the theme. 'So the candle?'

'Burns,' said Rebecca.

Why should you want to burn a candle? Well, for light, obviously. Why would you want light?

'Why do we need light?' she said aloud, standing in the sunny parlour on the east side of the cottage in the morning.

Michael said, 'Because it will be dark when we do what we have to do.'

Foster said, 'Two twenty-five in the morning, not two twenty-five in the afternoon.'

'Maybe.'

The candle, the clock, the manuscript, the key. The telescope they had used cryptically, as it were, but not yet in its straightforward way. The thread – the gold thread on its spool – and the compass had yet to be used at all.

Perhaps, Rebecca thought, the compass would have only the one function after all – it was any old compass, nothing special or individual. But what could be done with thread?

Or with gold?

'What is special about gold?' she asked.

'Doesn't tarnish,' Michael said. 'Very stable. Safe.'

Foster nodded. 'Which is why you have gold teeth. Non-toxic.'

'Beautiful,' Rebecca contributed. 'Desirable.'

(*I'm talking about gold, here, nothing else.*)

She pictured the reel of thread, gleaming softly in her hand. But what could it actually do?

What am I supposed to sew together with this stuff?

'We have a time,' Michael said. 'We have a position.' He indicated the wall of the parlour represented by the blip on the key wards. 'The compass will be giving us a direction, so that implies a second location that has to be reached.'

'And?'

'To find the location we need both direction and distance. The threads measure the distance.'

Rebecca mulled it over. 'Why two, though?'

'Axis points,' Connor said. Rebecca realised he had been silent for a long time.

'Axis points?'

Michael nodded. 'Space is three dimensional, Rebecca.'

Well, I know that, she thought. Just because he's a sculptor and I'm a graphic artist. 'Yes, but –'

'One measurement is the distance across the floor. The other is the distance up. Or down.'

Ah. Right.

'Which is which?'

'Horizontal followed by vertical,' Foster said confidently. 'In the door and up the stairs.'

'I beg your pardon?'

'The way you read a map grid reference,' Connor told her. 'In the door – horizontal – and up the stairs – vertical.'

'Yeah, yeah, okay.'

'But which gives us the first measurement?' Michael asked, and then corrected himself. 'It doesn't matter. It's not a large room. We try both.'

And it proved obvious.

In the absence of any other bearing they followed the compass needle pointing north. The gold thread, unwound from its spool, stretched across the floorboards and expired exactly where it touched the skirting board of the opposite wall.

They removed the lower mirror above that point, lifting it off its nail and propping it against its neighbour, and the candle thread measured its thirty-five centimetres up the wall to a point where the wood panelling – rather heinously painted over in this room and now distinctly grubby from age – appeared to have been patched over beneath the paint, leaving a ridge.

Michael carefully ran the tip of his penknife around the ridge, cracking the dry paint, and a few moments later he had prised away a piece of card and the paint with it to reveal a patch of paper beneath. And under the paper was a keyhole.

To nobody's surprise, the key fitted, and turned.

The door, disguised to match the panelled walls, had also been painted over. As Michael pushed, first the paint cracked and broke around the edge and then the mirrors began to vibrate.

He stopped, and they set to work unhooking the dozen or so mirrors from their places and leaning them up against the wall on the far side of the room. As they came down, their ghosts remained as cleaner rectangles separated by a grid of grime where the frames hadn't quite met. And as the wall was laid bare, the broken paint revealed the size of the door they had uncovered – full width but lower than the other doors in the cottage.

All of them would need to duck to get through this.

Clear of the mirrors, the door scraped open. Rebecca slipped in front of Foster in order to see.

The room had no windows. Daylight from the parlour showed it to be very small, with bare stone walls and a bare stone floor. But it wasn't empty. And it wasn't utterly without light.

Two wooden frames, like simple lecterns or music stands, faced each other across the floor. Each was topped by a bracket which supported a mirror angled at forty-five degrees facing downwards, and had at its foot a second mirror, only a few inches off the floor, angled upwards. On the two stands there were in all four mirrors.

Rebecca noticed that Foster was smiling again.

They trooped into the room, each in turn bending to avoid the lintel. Michael went immediately to the far side, only four feet away. Rebecca saw him carefully skirt the second frame, and peer at the stone wall, running his fingers over the surface.

Foster joined him.

'There,' Michael said.

'Where?' Rebecca asked quickly, crossing the floor. 'What?'

Michael turned round. 'Here.' He took her hand and guided her fingertips to the right place. Rebecca, acutely aware of his skin touching hers, drove herself to concentrate on the smooth stone, and felt a tiny break in the texture. She took her fingers away to see. There was a hole, hardly more than a pin prick, far too small to see through even had she lined her eye up to it.

Foster had now found an equivalent hole on the parlour side. Each hole aligned perfectly with one of the higher mirrors.

'But why?' Rebecca asked. 'What is this?'

Annoyingly, it was Foster who answered her. 'This, I believe, is a Victorian's arrangement for deflecting a light beam. Instead of passing straight through the room horizontally, the light coming in through this hole hits the first mirror, is sent down vertically until it meets the lower mirror, which sends it horizontally across the room to the third mirror, where it bounces upwards, hits the last mirror, and is finally permitted to exit through the hole it was aiming for originally. Very neat, really.'

'But why?'

'Why indeed!'

'Because this way,' Michael said, 'they could maintain the balance between our two worlds without exposing either to great risk, and without turning their backs forever on the possibility of travelling between.'

He straightened up from where he had been examining the mirror. 'In other words, they closed the door without locking it.

Chapter Forty

'IMAGINE this.'

Michael drew a rough shape on a clean page in Rebecca's sketchbook which, once he had added some crosshatching, took on the form of a lump of stone. A monolith. Then he drew a thin horizontal line up to the side of the monolith and, jumping the stone with his pencil, drew it continuing out of the back.

'A single stone,' he explained, 'and a single beam of light, very narrow, very focused, passing straight through.'

He drew a second line at right-angles to the first, implying an intersection somewhere near the centre of the stone.

'And now, a second light beam, like this.'

He lifted his hand and let them see his drawing.

'Passenger did leave records after all. I came upon this last night.' They had each taken a volume back to the hostel. 'This is the Iron Age solution.'

It seemed the problem had arisen centuries before the Romans arrived. Ashendon had been a source of weirdness of all kinds until the Celtic people in the vicinity located the spring, as it were, and put an end to the disturbances by plonking an enormous rock on the trouble spot: the contraption – the 'wyld' that worked its way into the village name.

'Why did they drill a hole through it?' Rebecca asked.

'I don't believe they did. The light beam burned its own way through. Both light beams.' Michael leaned back. 'And it worked astonishingly well, right up until the eighteenth century, when the Age of Enlightenment encouraged over-confident, ill-educated country landowners to dabble in matters beyond their knowledge. The local magnate who laid claim to this hill as part of his estate found a stone with a hole through it and was curious enough to have it lifted and removed to his private museum, leaving the gap open again.'

'Two holes,' Rebecca corrected him. 'Two holes in it.'

'No. One.'

Michael looked at her steadily. Foster made a sharp little

movement, and then leaned back in his chair and began to smile.

Michael said, 'The second beam of light was invisible to him. The hole in the stone that it caused was also invisible to anyone in this world.'

There were two worlds.

Well, we know that, Rebecca thought. Or at least for the last three months we've been behaving as though we know it.

Michael continued. 'This spot on the hill, this specific area which the Celts occupied with a monolith, is shared space, space that exists in both worlds. By putting the stone down there in our world, they had put it down in the parallel world also. It existed in two separate places at the same time – in two dimensions.'

'Quantum entanglement,' Geoffrey Foster said.

Rebecca ignored him. 'And the light beams?'

'One from our world passing straight through, leaving a hole visible to us. In the other world, another beam also passing straight through and leaving a hole of its own, but visible only in the other world.'

'And the two intersecting at ninety degrees,' Foster put in, sounding smug. 'Orthogonality.'

'But once the stone had been removed, the shared space became exposed again. People lost things, and more disturbingly gained things. Imagination ran riot. Unfortunately nobody linked the disturbances with the disappearance of the stone, but at least they did call for help.

'An Oxford academic travelled to Derbyshire to investigate, and over a number of years he and his associates narrowed down their area of research until they too found what the tribe had found... The source of magic, for the Celts; the source of paranormal phenomena for the early Victorian scientists. But they didn't want to repeat the earlier solution by simply filling up that shared area of space. They looked for a more sophisticated answer.'

'Why?'

Michael said, simply, 'Because they wanted to travel. Sometimes a creature that wandered into the space found itself in another world. And sometimes a creature from another world ended up here. Where do you suppose the notion of dragons came from? Or unicorns? Gryphons? Cockatrices?'

'But only sometimes?' Connor asked.

'The way is open for only a few moments in each of our days. Or rather, nights.'

Two twenty-five in the morning.

'At other times the space is harmless. But for those few seconds…'

'And so?' Rebecca asked. 'What was this sophisticated solution?'

Michael leaned forward again and pulled the sketchbook towards him. 'This.' He drew a series of straight lines forming the classic diagram of a transparent cube. Then, as before, he drew in the two lines that represented the light beams, and this time everyone could see the beams intersecting in the centre of the cube.

'They built a room around the space. That way it could be kept locked so that nothing could accidentally stumble into it at the wrong time.'

'And,' Rebecca said, feeling her way, 'if anything came in from Fai– from the other world, it would be safely contained in the room.'

Michael shook his head. 'No need for it to be. The room existed in the other place as well. The walls were built inside the shared space. They had the same dual existence as the monolith.'

A room, built of stone, in the middle of a forest, or a desert, or a plain…

Or a factory? What was to say this other world was not as modern, as developed, as their own?

'Then they built a house around the room to disguise it and to keep it secure.'

Geoffrey Foster added, 'And the light burned its way through, as before.'

'Of course.'

'But intersecting in solid stone is one thing. Intersecting in open air, that's quite another.'

'Why?' Rebecca asked again.

I swear once this is over I'll never ask a question again!

'Because light consists of photons,' the estate agent explained.

'Particles which collide and bounce off one another as if they were solid objects. The stone would have contained them. The space couldn't. Light particles from each world would be flying around chaotically inside the space. They'd never get separated out. Some of them would inevitably leak into the wrong world.'

'So they diverted the beam,' Connor said.

'Of course. With mirrors. Nineteenth-century mirrors, made with nineteenth-century materials and technology, which inevitably began to fail after a hundred years or so once the silvering started to degenerate.'

'Oh.' Rebecca pictured the wall of mirrors in the parlour and their speckled, darkening surfaces where the silver behind the glass had oxidised. The mirrors on the stands were suffering in the same way. 'So some of the light beam is being deflected,' she said, 'but some of it ...'

'...escapes and collides. Yes,' Michael said.

'So all we need to do is replace the mirrors,' Rebecca concluded in triumph.

Apparently not.

Nothing is ever simple, Rebecca thought.

Even modern, twenty-first-century mirror technology has its shelf-life, she was told. The only secure, truly long-term solution was to use prisms.

'Prisms? And where on earth do we get four prisms?'

There was a short – actually surprisingly short – pause, and then Connor said, 'Binoculars?'

Chapter Forty-One

I NEED a nap.

No I don't, I need a proper sleep.

Rebecca looked out of the passenger window at the hedgerows and stone walls gliding by. The BMW was quiet and smooth, not at all like the rented hatchback.

She was slightly horrified to find herself in Geoffrey Foster's car and was doing her best to avoid conversation. This might be a churlish response to his offer to drive her back to the hostel since Michael did not want to leave Ashendon, but if so, tough. She had said Thank-you.

Michael had also offered, but as it was clear that he intended to drop her and come straight back to the cottage she had not felt able to refuse Foster's invitation. He hadn't been completely oily, and had actually been quite helpful over the business with the key... In fact, very helpful. How long would it have taken any of them to guess that the design of the wards represented the layout of the cottage rooms?

He was still irritating though, like a piece of grit in one's shoe that's there even after you've taken the shoe off and shaken it. It would have been much more enjoyable if he hadn't found them here, even if it had added several days to their search.

What does his family think he's doing? Or maybe he isn't married.

Rebecca considered the leery half-smile he wore so much of the time, and the traces of booze on his breath.

No, he probably isn't.

I wonder how old he is. Forty-ish? Younger than Michael, then, even though he looks much older.

Rebecca frowned. Michael. Now there was a much bigger problem than how to keep Geoffrey Foster at arm's length. Just what was Michael intending to do tonight? He had something planned, she was certain, something more than the simple – *hah!* – worry about the gap being successfully secured, and she had a horrible notion that she knew what it was.

He was thinking all the time, she knew. You could say something to him, ask him a question, and watch his attention slowly turn to you as if from a great distance. It was as though he were hauling his mind away from what it would prefer to be involved with in order to deal with your paltry, finicky little problem.

He always did it with good grace, though. He was never sharp or sarcastic, never irritable. Just the dark eyes narrowed as if he were seeing something you couldn't, and then sometimes that slow, half-smile.

What was it with men and half-smiles? But Michael's was so different from Foster's – kind and a little rueful. *I'm sorry*, it seemed to say, *Don't worry, it isn't your fault.* It made Rebecca's insides churn.

I need a nap.

To go to bed at eleven o'clock and then get up two hours later to save the world was not on. Whatever the others elected to do, Rebecca intended to eat lunch, take a bracing walk, and go to bed at four o'clock so that when she got up at midnight she would have had eight hours' sleep and would feel rested and ready.

That was the theory. In all probability she would feel like death, totally jet-lagged, but at least she would have a chance of getting in shape by two-thirty.

Two twenty-five, rather.

She realised she had absolutely no idea what was going to happen. It was nearly midday now. By midday tomorrow – what? Annihilation? Or looking for a nice pub for lunch?

She would have to turn her head soon or her neck would get stiff. She shifted discretely and began to look forward through the windscreen, hoping her change of position wouldn't be interpreted as a readiness to be sociable. She recognised the turning to the hostel.

Less than five minutes to go.

And I do know what Michael's planning. I do know what he wants to do. And I have got – have got – to be alert.

*   *   *

MY, how they resented him! Don't put yourself out, sweetheart, I'm just the chauffeur.

Not that he took offence. It was amusing in a way, like gate-crashing a party of twenty-somethings to find out what passed among them for a good time. Sociology. Or rather, anthropology – the observation of the behavioural traits of another species. Children had always seemed like another species to Geoffrey, or at least since he had ceased to be one, and at – what was she? Eighteen? Nineteen? Twenty? – Rebecca seemed hardly past childhood to him. In some respects she seemed younger than the boy, with his nervy, suspicious stare.

And Michael, the Leader of the Pack, what about him? Forty-four and he didn't look thirty, and there was something not quite...

Well. Something, anyway.

And all of them with that odd hair, not just dark but truly black. Most unusual for white-skinned people. And the looks. You could start an inferiority complex, hanging around with these three, rubbing shoulders with perfection all day – you could start to think you were the odd one. And they had no idea, none of them. The boy showed no tell-tale habits – never flicked his hair back, or preened – nor the girl, with her scraped, bare face and spiky crop. Nor Michael, of course, cool to the point of refrigeration.

But there they were. He had studied the human race a bit, he had learned to read who cared about what and how much they would pay. These three were just out of the picture, somehow – off the graph. Lucky he didn't have to sell a house to one of them! Definitely three of a kind...

Or were they? Or were they in fact four?

Where did Celia Scanlon fit in? Same bloodlines, no doubt about that – she had the same straight, slim build, the same symmetry to her features, the same black, black hair. But she cared how she looked and how! Fashion princess if ever there was one. Yet she too gave the impression there was more, under the surface, coasting silently without making a ripple but waiting, like a pike in deep, dark water.

He had been taken by surprise when she approached, having

spotted him talking with them at the house, but pleased to be presented with an ally. Of course she believed him to be her creature while he was most definitely his own man, thank you, and biding his time.

They would have a shock tonight, the dears, when she turned up. Michael intended to make whatever repairs were necessary to this – leak – and then seal it up tight. Well, not with Celia and himself on the team. Criminal! Imagine the potential of such a source of power, what could be done with it. What impossibilities could be made possible. The nearest thing imaginable to pure magic.

Actually the girl had the right idea. A quiet afternoon, I think, and no alcohol – definitely no alcohol. Bright-eyed and bushy-tailed is what we need to be tonight, Geoff. Pull this off and we could be made.

He swung the car round in front of the hostel. 'Here we are! I'll come for you around half past midnight.'

So much for the ingénue; now for the sophisticate.

HE was a fool, of course. Didn't know it, wouldn't believe it, but that didn't alter the case.

He has no idea. No idea at all.

Did he really think he could tame the meeting of the worlds? That an alternate universe could be mined or tapped or harnessed in some way to make mere money? His simplistic, self-seeking, pedestrian motives had been transparent to her from the first five minutes in his company.

Well. She had learned long ago that you can rely on the never-ceasing greed of small-minded men. He'd be so centred, with his tunnel vision and his dreams of riches, that he wouldn't notice what was happening until it was too late. He'd likely freeze anyway, that type was never the sort for action.

Celia had had enough experience of men like Foster to predict his response to physical threat: a rabbit caught in the headlights, transfixed and shivering, staring as ruin bore down upon him.

He wouldn't stop her. Nothing would stop her. One hundred and one years she had been waiting and planning. What did this

Michael think he was going to do to seal the gap? Play with his toys and knit a padlock?

What had his daddy told him? And his grandpa? 'It's all down to you, precious. Save the world and live happily ever after in the luxury you deserve.'

Celia became aware that the tendons in her neck were taut, and the muscles in her arms and thighs. She relaxed them, breathing deep.

Not much longer. In a few hours all four of them would feel very differently, oh yes, all of them, from the stupid estate agent to the school boy in his sorry, dirty plimsolls.

Over a century of waiting and now only a few more hours.

REBECCA had had the right idea, but the prospect of trying to sleep in the next room to her, with the light streaming in through the flimsy curtains and the hot air and the creaky bunks, had been more than he could face. Instead he left Michael in the cottage and wandered out to the gardens.

There was a series of walled areas beyond the courtyard which seemed to escape most of the visitors, and Connor drifted through the rows of vegetables and cold frames before finding himself in a square of mown grass with rose trees around the edge and a spreading magnolia in the centre. It was very quiet and the grass was dry. He lay on his back in the shade with his knees bent up, and closed his eyes.

Sleep for a bit, eat later.

And then, what?

Connor tried to think about tomorrow but it was impossible. Tonight was a chasm, a gulf dividing Now from Then, and the fact that the minutes would march on, the hours would be used up just as they always are, seemed incredible. Tomorrow could not be contemplated while there was still tonight.

How was it going to work? Was it going to work at all? What would happen at two twenty-five?

Connor pictured the four of them – it seemed inevitable now that the estate agent would be there – gathered in the parlour, staring through the doorway, waiting for the miraculous to happen.

Did he believe it would? It seemed so implausible, so fantasy-fiction. A gateway into Fairyland. Or according to Foster, a way to increase the capacity of computers by a million times.

Connor pictured the estate agent, with his patronising air and his carefully chosen clothes. If this happened tonight, if it actually came to pass, he was going to be peeing in those smart trousers.

Then he thought about Rebecca, so single-minded and so blinkered. She probably didn't believe it was going to happen either, but at least if it did she wouldn't wet herself. Would she care, though? Or would it be a case of good riddance to bad rubbish?

No, not that. She didn't deserve that.

He tried to think about it, to imagine her response.

Pragmatic. She'll be the one sorting it all out afterwards. Good luck to her!

And Michael. Connor turned onto his stomach and buried his face in his folded arms. He didn't want to think about Michael, but he was there anyway, despite his shut eyes.

I'm sorry, Michael.

MICHAEL finished the call and pocketed his phone. There hadn't been much to say, really. He was sure now that his father knew.

I wish I knew how this is going to work.

Impossible not to try to guess. Impossible not to sit on the floor and place one's palm against the plaster, feeling the gentle dip, searching to feel something more.

What will I have to do? What will I be able to do?

What about Rebecca and Connor?

Rebecca will tough it out. It might take her a while – I hope not. But she'll survive. Connor …

Damn. He'd be fooling himself if he thought Connor would survive this intact. Better if he'd never joined them. But he had been needed, and at the time it seemed a kindness to bring him into the fold.

Some fold. Some shepherd.

Michael sighed. Can't be helped. All that he could do now was to wait and see.

Chapter Forty-Two

THE moon was only a sliver, and if Ashendon House had floodlights they were not turned on. With the headlamps off it was inky black.

Geoffrey Foster had parked at the front of the house and Rebecca's feet crunched as she made her way carefully along the gravel path to the cottage, following the ellipse of light from Foster's torch. She was being reminded of something …

Bonfire Night. Bonfire Nights when she was a little girl and they had a home-built fire in the farm yard and fireworks that her father lit one by one. Later, after her mother died, she was taken to public displays, where she stood with the other children behind a chain link fence and watched combinations and arrangements of fireworks set off simultaneously – more elaborate, more spectacular, yet oddly never as exciting as the rockets and roman candles they had enjoyed at home.

But that was the connection, finding her way from the kitchen door to the farmyard with anticipation fluttering in her stomach, while her father made final preparations and her mother washed up after supper. Despite its being summer there was the same slightly smoky scent in the night air, and Rebecca almost missed having a sparkler to hold.

As they approached the cottage a faint light was visible through the curtains. She wondered whether either of the boys had thought to sleep or whether they had just stayed up, staving off tiredness, riding on adrenalin. Rebecca felt pretty good – not exactly crackling with energy, but alert enough. Mostly she was anxious.

Michael opened the door and Rebecca went through to the sitting room, assuming Foster would follow her.

Two oil lamps had been found for the sitting room and the parlour, the light softer than electric bulbs and leaving the corners in shadow. Michael had also unearthed some candles, plain white ones in a box, and set up several in holders or jars ready to be lit if needed.

There were litre bottles of water on the table. Michael nodded towards them. 'No power,' he said, 'so no coffee.'

Rebecca threw a swift look at Foster ducking through the doorway.

I bet he'd prefer gin to coffee anyway, she thought. He'd been a bit slow. Perhaps he'd forgotten to lock the car.

Next to the water bottles were the objects they had spent the last months collecting: the candle, with its secret now revealed; the key; the telescope and the reel of thread, still withholding half their tasks; the facsimile of the manuscript; the modern plastic compass on its red nylon cord, steadily pointing north. Now Foster unwrapped the clock and stood it next to the candle, ready for the moment when the time on its face would coincide with the time on their watches.

An hour to go. They had allowed themselves a comfortable margin. This was not an occasion to miss because of a tyre blow-out on the way.

Rebecca wandered into the sitting room and stood looking at but not reading the spines of the books on the shelves. Her mind was restless. Had it been her decision, she would have driven to the nearest camping shop this morning, bought two pairs of binoculars, and replaced the failing mirrors then and there, in broad daylight. Then she would have locked the room, re-hung the mirrors on the parlour wall, and dusted her hands.

But the decision had not been hers, and she had been outnumbered and out-voted by the men. Under the circumstances it was hard not to think of it as a gender thing. Connor, she supposed, had the excitement you might expect of a sixteen-year-old boy. He probably watched Star Trek and read Isaac Asimov. The prospect of coming close to a parallel universe must be irresistible.

And Foster had his crazed notion of exploiting that universe for monetary gain, but this was so far beyond her conception that she simply ignored it. If he really knew what to do, let him try. She didn't have any spare capacity to worry about his affairs because she was being eaten up with worry over Michael.

He meant to go through. She was sure of it. She had been suspecting this for so long now she could not remember when it had first occurred to her. He was mad, of course, but determined, Rebecca believed, and stopping him was going to stretch her to the limit.

That she had to stop him, or at least try, was unarguable – it was another dimension, for heaven's sake! Totally unknown and potentially deadly. The fact that one person from that dimension had once come here and managed to survive hardly made it safe. Going through the gap was lunacy and she would do her damnedest to prevent him. But it wasn't going to be easy and he wasn't going to like her for it.

The excuse – because naturally they had an excuse – was that the second beam of light needed to be seen in order for them to be sure they were arranging the prisms correctly. Well. That might be true or it might not, but it sounded thin to Rebecca.

Anyway, here she was, with an hour – no, fifty minutes now – to kill...no, not kill, to spare... before the link would be formed, the space would become shared, and she would look into Fairyland...

She sighed and rubbed her face, and time crawled on.

SHORTLY after two an electronic alarm sounded, making everyone jump. Michael cancelled it and slipped his phone back in his pocket. 'Sorry. Just in case we weren't paying attention.'

As if.

Rebecca had tried reading but found herself arriving at the foot of a page with no idea what it had been about. Michael appeared to be reading too, but with how much success was anybody's guess. Connor, of course, was writing. She'd have loved to have seen what. Perhaps she would pluck up the courage to ask him tomorrow, when all this was over. The tension must be getting to him – he looked flushed and his face was taut.

And Geoffrey Foster, could you believe it, had a lap-top open.

Now people were stretching and yawning and standing up to shake themselves out. Even if you are rested, two in the morning is still two in the morning. Rebecca drank some water and wished she had a sandwich or a bar of nut chocolate. Breakfast was the other side of the wall and seemed very far away.

Nobody was inclined to speak. At a quarter past two they congregated in the parlour, Michael in the open doorway of the shared-space room.

Rebecca wriggled past Connor – whatever happened she must stay close to Michael. Her stomach felt unsettled and her hands were shaking very slightly, which was disconcerting. She flexed her fingers, made fists and released them, and shook her arms like an athlete warming up for the long jump.

Stay alert, Rebecca, and don't screw this up.

At twenty past Foster said, 'It was two twenty-five exactly, was it? Not a minute either side?'

He's nervous too, Rebecca thought, with a degree of satisfaction. Not so easy now, is it?

'Two twenty-five,' Michael said.

So difficult to keep breathing, so easy to hold one's breath. Impossible not to try to count seconds, and impossible not to try to imagine what was going to happen. Scraps of stories, snatches of Hollywood special effects came to her mind, auditioned, and were rejected.

So hard to believe, truly believe that the fabric of the universe was about to be ripped apart in this room in this cottage, with the four of them standing there to see it. Far easier to imagine an anticlimax, with nothing to see but perhaps a chink on the wall as alien light entered.

Or perhaps not even that. Surely five minutes had passed by now? According to Rebecca's watch, it was two twenty-seven and nothing had happened at all. Michael was frowning, and Rebecca saw Connor glance at him.

Two twenty-eight. Geoffrey Foster cleared his throat. 'Perhaps there's a discrepancy between Victorian clockwork and quartz technology.'

Michael looked at him, still frowning, and Rebecca felt she could almost see his train of thought: how accurate could mid-nineteenth-century timekeeping have been? Was it unrealistic of them to expect the time to be correct to the minute?

And then Connor said, suddenly, 'Before railways, people used their own local time. Greenwich Mean Time resulted from an attempt to keep the trains running properly.'

And Rebecca said, even as the thought struck her, 'We're not on Greenwich Mean Time. We're on British Summer Time.'

'Good grief!' Foster exclaimed and then laughed. Michael rubbed his face. Rebecca saw Connor's hands twitch, and then clench.

She said, unnecessarily, 'We're an hour too early.'

I could have had another hour in bed.

Tension collapsed. As they left the parlour Rebecca saw the estate agent glance down the hall towards the front of the cottage, probably longing to escape their company.

By all means push off, she thought. No one here wants you.

Another hour. *How am I going to stay awake?*

Chapter Forty-Three

IT was weird to be lining up for a second time, and harder than ever to believe they would witness anything unusual, as if the mistake over the time had deflated them. That nothing would take place now seemed much more probable, much easier to envisage.

Time shuffled on, and Rebecca tried not to look at her watch. Three fifteen; three twenty; three twenty-two...

Connor broke the silence. 'This is wrong. We have to close the door.' He shoved Rebecca forward over the threshold. 'There's too much light – loads of it. There should only be the single beam.'

Of course. Rebecca shivered at the stupidity of their mistake and moved deeper into the room, close behind Michael. Connor shut the door behind them – there was a handle on the inside, Rebecca was relieved to notice – and darkness enveloped them. The clock was outside, and it was impossible to see her watch. How many minutes, now? Two? Three?

One?

And then it was happening. The blank wall opposite was no longer blank. A pinhole of brilliant light appeared, entering the room as a delicate thread and touching the wall behind them. Instinctively they shifted, spreading apart, two either side of the beam – Rebecca and Michael further in, Connor and Foster nearer to the door.

Light from an alternate reality. Light from an invisible world.

Everyone was breathing faster. A thought struck Rebecca. 'Does this mean we're in Faerie now? Can they see us?

Foster spluttered.

'Not unless the light beams intersect,' Michael said. Then he added, 'I think.'

He was on one knee next to the farther stand, unhooking the top mirror while Connor, Rebecca saw, did the same at the nearer stand. Had they rehearsed this? As the mirrors were removed the light beam – *our* light beam, Rebecca reminded herself – passed uninterrupted across the room and there was a blast, like a silent explosion, as it crossed the alien beam. Rebecca's eyes shut tight on reflex, the inside of her eyelids red from the brilliance outside. The air was filled with a crackling sound, like growth gone mad, and a rhythm was beating in her head.

Then it was dark again. Rebecca opened her eyes and saw that the boys had placed the prisms on the stands and the light was once more conducted downwards.

'Okay?'

'Okay.'

Rebecca licked her lips and tried to breathe more slowly.

Get a grip. And be ready.

She flexed her hands, and then glanced briefly at Foster and saw him lick his lips too. He looked both fascinated and petrified, like a rabbit caught in headlights. Whatever he had been intending, Rebecca strongly doubted he would carry it through.

This time she screwed up her eyes in advance, and when the flash arrived she kept them open a crack. Looking directly at the light was too much. Directing her gaze instead at the far corner, Rebecca tried to tune in to the shapes in her peripheral vision where the light was brightest – writhing, snaking forms in chaotic movement, shoots that burgeoned and spread, rustling and entwining, nothing clear, nothing you could get hold of, but somehow... The light wavered, like sunlight through swaying branches, and a shadow was thrown across the floor as a silhouette passed almost close enough to touch...

But the second set of prisms were in place and the flash subsided. Quietness, except for everyone panting a bit. The two threads of light moved around each other.   And then the door opened bringing light from the oil lamp flooding into the room, and reality flew away.

There was a woman standing in the doorway. So shocked was Rebecca, and so disorientated, that for a second she thought she must have come from the other world. The injection of light through the open door crashed into the alien light in the shared space, and the shapes Rebecca had almost but not quite seen were now shimmering all around her. Someone – Michael? – shouted something, but there was confusion and everything was happening at once.

Hazily in the strange light, Rebecca saw the crisp clothes and the make up – dark, smoky eye shadow and deep carmine lipstick – and recognised her, although she could not place her. Someone like this couldn't possibly be from Faerie. So who?...

'Ah,' Foster said, and Rebecca heard the lack of surprise in his voice.

The bastard! He knew about this. What was he up to?

And what was she holding?

Rebecca, born and raised in the United Kingdom, stared at the object in the woman's hand and couldn't place it. It was black and softly shining, clearly hard-surfaced and angular. It looked as though it were probably heavy.

It looks a bit like a gun, she thought.

The woman was holding it like a gun, too, with the mouth pointing towards them, all of them, standing grouped before her bathed in coils of dazzling light, and Rebecca thought, stupidly, in words that she almost said aloud: It is a gun. That's what a gun looks like in real life.

She supposed this was still Real Life. The light was hurting the backs of her eyes, the botanical rustling was all around and a peculiar, sub-sonic throb seemed to have started up in her body.

Where's Michael?

But the woman was speaking, saying something in a dry, sarcastic tone that Rebecca felt she needed to hear but could not make sense of. Something about theft, and inheritance, and betrayal. What betrayal? And Foster was talking too, his voice pitched too high.

If there was a gun – if that was a gun – then it would be sensible to panic, wouldn't it? But the vines were all about her and the light was thrumming, and Michael – Michael was moving towards the centre of the room.

Rebecca lunged, and at the same moment there was an explosion that seemed to be inside her head, and she thought she might have screamed, but her hand had found Michael's arm and her fingers twisted in the cotton fabric of his sleeve, clutching tight when he tugged. She clenched her teeth and yanked backwards, and Michael, off balance and taken by surprise, came backwards with her.

Something heavy clattered on the stone floor, and there was the sound of scuffling, and then Foster's voice, out of breath, saying, 'Come out! *Now!*'

And then the vines had gone. The room was dark again, with only a patch of soft light from the oil lamp in the parlour spilling onto the stone floor. The shapes were fled, and the throbbing had ceased. It felt cooler.

Rebecca, still clutching Michael's shirt, stumbled towards the door and into the parlour. Her foot kicked something heavy as she went, and she forgot to duck and cracked her forehead against the low lintel.

She whimpered and raised her free hand to rub the place. When she lowered it again she found Geoffrey Foster was standing with his arms clamped tightly around the strange woman, pinning her arms to her sides, his face tight with effort and alarm.

The woman's was screwed up into a mask of hatred so vicious it was chilling.

Michael said, quietly, 'You could let go now, I think.'

'YOU could let go now, I think.'

'Oh.' Rebecca relaxed her fingers, releasing their grip on Michael's shirt. She had broken a fingernail, and it hurt.

'What…' She pulled herself together. 'Who is this?' She rubbed her bruised forehead again, the pain not helping.

Foster grunted. 'She's a lunatic.' He sounded very put out. 'Perhaps one of you could call the police? I'm afraid my hands are full.'

Alright, alright.

Rebecca rummaged for her phone and keyed in 999. She was feeling a bit sick, and that wasn't helping either. 'I don't know what to say.'

Michael lifted the phone from her hand.

'There has been an incident at Ashendon House. An intruder. She was armed but isn't any more.'

Armed. There had been a gun. *She had us – me – at gunpoint.* Rebecca shook herself.

Geoffrey Foster must have knocked her arm up and got the

gun from her. Wow. Okay, so she was an old woman, but even so...

Rebecca looked at the estate agent and unfortunately met his eyes. He looked surprised for half a second, and then smiled.

Oh no.

Michael handed her phone back, and Rebecca saw the expression in his eyes.

I caused this. I stopped him from going. But I had to.

Think about it later.

'Where's Connor?'

Michael looked at her, and across the room Foster also stared.

'What?' she asked.

Foster said, 'You didn't see?'

'See what?' Something cold wormed its way into her stomach. *'What?'*

Michael's voice was tired. 'Connor's gone, Rebecca. He went through the gap.'

Chapter Forty-Four

IT was living with the guilt that was the hardest thing. It was tough enough for her. She thought she could see it crushing Michael.

He had intended to go. He admitted it as daylight crept into the cottage. He would have succeeded had Rebecca not clawed him back, and might have managed it even then had it not been for Celia Scanlon – might have torn himself free from Rebecca's clutch, knocked the top prism out of alignment and leapt through the light, trusting Connor to reset it in position. The woman's arrival, throwing open the door and distracting everyone's attention, should have helped, not hindered him. But Rebecca knew he had hesitated, anxious for their safety in his absence, and that moment of indecision had defeated him.

She felt guilty about that too, although he did not reproach her. In fact he was considerate of her feelings at all times, but the flatness, the dead calm remained, and Rebecca was left trying to justify her actions to herself.

It *had* been the right thing to do. If someone is threatening to jump off a bridge, you don't just stand by and watch. And stepping into another dimension, an invisible world about which you knew literally nothing, was that not almost like suicide?

So she had stopped Michael from going, and Connor had gone instead.

How had she not seen that coming? How had not Michael?

It plagued her now, how silent the boy had been the last few days, how withdrawn and contained. Not that he had ever been chatty, even in New York when they had seemed to reach a tentative sort of friendship. He kept himself so private, how could they have guessed?

How awful had his home life been? When had he decided to go? It was tempting to think it had been a choice made on the spur of the moment, perhaps after guessing Michael's intention, perhaps to escape from the mad woman's gun, but Rebecca couldn't believe it. Connor had laid his own plans, and neither of them had paid enough attention to guess.

And in the meantime, Geoffrey Foster's plans had come to nothing at all. After all those weeks of feeling threatened by his involvement, in the end they had reason to be grateful to him.

Gratitude tinged with anger. He had not been surprised to see Celia Scanlon in the doorway because he had left the front door on the latch for her. The nerve of the man! Still, it seemed he had had no idea of her real intentions, and certainly hadn't expected her to be toting a firearm. He'd thought she might be useful if it came to a legal challenge to the inheritance and had been deceived by her from the start.

Not too surprising, given that she was one quarter Faerie and female at that – well able to spin rings around a simple, greedy, big-headed bloke like him. It was noticeable that Celia Scanlon alone of them all had been sufficiently smart to allow for the change of hour.

What a mess. The one good thing was that nobody, neither the police nor any solicitor Celia might get hold of, would give credence to a word of what she told them about parallel universes, alien blood and time portals.

They would think she was away with the fairies.

The police had removed her and her gun, retrieved from the hidden room by Rebecca herself before they arrived. That was what Rebecca had stubbed her toe against.

With Michael in shock and Foster a nervous wreck clamped around the mad woman, it had been left to her to organise them, and somewhat to her surprise – and satisfaction – she had made a decent job of it. The room had been closed up and locked and she had got Michael to help her rehang the mirrors. The cracks were just visible in the narrow gaps between the frames, but you'd have to look closely to see them. Their hard-won collection – the candle, the clock, the key, the manuscript, the thread and the compass – Rebecca swept into a drawer.

The telescope she pocketed, without quite knowing why. What had been its second function? Would it all have been different if they had looked through it at something first? But what?

Forget it. No more questions.

Then the police had arrived and taken Celia, deranged as she was, into custody, and they had each made statements, though the interviewing officer must have had to work quite hard to get Michael's. Rebecca found herself emphasising Foster's intervention, describing how he had attacked the woman while her attention was elsewhere, and later discovered him stealing glances at her that contained far too much admiration for comfort.

I think he's starting to fancy me, she thought. Please, no.

And finally, after what felt like days, they had fallen asleep in the cottage, Michael on the couch, Foster in an armchair with his feet on the table, and Rebecca, of course, given the bed.

She slept like the dead.

'DON'T worry,' Michael said. 'I'll be here when you get back.'

With that she would have to do. It was better than nothing.

He meant, of course, when she came back for the trial. Each of them would be required to give evidence against the intruder, during which, Rebecca realised glumly, they would need to commit perjury several times over.

Well, there would be a few months before it came to that, given the speed of the judicial system. At least for that length of time he would not try to find his way to Faerie. She knew he would not expose the world to the risk of leaving the gap open. Until he designed a mechanism that would enable him to cover or displace a prism temporarily, allowing him time to step through but knowing that it would right itself shortly afterwards, he could not try.

He must know Rebecca would not help him, even though she was not entirely sure herself any more. Connor was on the other side now. Perhaps it would be better if Michael did go through – at least there would then be two of them.

If they could find each other, of course.

Big if.

Foster had gone back to London, subdued, and prepared at least for the present to hang up his schemes for world domination in the computer industry.

Good riddance.
I hope he hasn't got my phone number.
Michael was staying on in the cottage. He would get the water and electricity reconnected and begin working his way through the library, where his great-grandfather – her great-great-great-grandfather – had written his perceptions of the race with whom he had lived his life. and perhaps had written memories of his own world as well.

He drove Rebecca to the station. A day had gone by and the deadness had passed, although there was a quiet melancholy about him still. 'Don't worry,' he told her, and Rebecca wanted very much to hug him.

But she didn't. He didn't invite it, and she couldn't take it.

Instead she received a brief, chaste kiss on the cheek, and walked through the barrier onto the platform.

There were workings on the line outside Derby and the train was late getting into St Pancras.

SHE felt as if she had been away for a year.

Actually, no, she felt as if she were a different person who had never lived here at all. Climbing the stairs to her flat, Rebecca couldn't imagine herself at her drawing board, or cooking on the little gas ring, or riding the underground to the V and A.

She switched on the kettle and took off her shoes. Edie had a visitor, thank goodness, so she was spared the ordeal of explaining, at least for the present.

Exactly how much am I going to tell her?

There had been a bundle of mail for her on the hall console, and now she flipped through the envelopes and found one with a Guildford postmark. She opened it, read the letter, and then read it again.

It was from Cummings and Bakewell. They had liked her portfolio and wished to meet her to discuss a commission to illustrate an edition of Aesop's fables – ten full-page colour plates, and black-and-white line illustrations as chapter headings.

The dream job.

Rebecca stood and looked out of the window at Edie's garden

where the ivy on the wall was growing as strongly as ever.

She thought about Michael, back in the cottage, researching his history. And Connor who knew where, doing who knew what. They were very special, she realised – unlike anyone else she had ever met. Human, but somehow... other.

As was she, she supposed. Logical to presume so, anyway. And her mother, of course, the opera singer who married a farm boy.

She thought about a woman with long black hair and a perfectly symmetrical face, and how she would have seemed to a quiet country farmer. He must have been knocked out when she married him, Rebecca thought, unable to believe his luck.

And then she had died. His fault too, in a way. Not many haystacks to fall on you in the city.

And that left herself, the illegitimate daughter, who rejected all his efforts to keep her safe and ran away to London.

The kettle had boiled. Rebecca began to walk towards the tiny kitchen but as she passed her single armchair she dropped into it instead and fished out her phone.

She dialled home.

Epilogue

ONCE upon a time there was a prince…

No, not a prince.

Once upon a time there was a changeling child…

No.

Once upon a time there was a half-breed, a mulatto, a boy of mixed blood who would never fit.

But he was both cursed and blessed, and when adulthood was drawing close he had good fortune bestowed on him in the shape of a messenger and a key and a magic door into a world invisible, where he might find a sense of belonging.

So he listened to the message, and he turned the key, and when the magic door opened he crossed the threshold.

And now, Connor thought, we'll see…

AUTHOR'S NOTE

THIS is my first novel; I hope very much that you like it.

The idea for the story arrived while I was drawing at the Victoria and Albert Museum, and in case anyone is interested, yes, most – though not all – of the key objects in the museum are real and there, and most – though not all – of the locations in the story are real too, although sadly the Hunting Tapestries, after many years in their gloomy gallery, have now been rehung with much better lighting but rather less atmosphere.

Most of the key dates are genuine too, although I have moved events a little here and there. It was astonishing to discover, as I researched, how much fell into place just as I needed it to.

The genealogy chart of Uriel Passenger's descendents contains far too many plot spoilers to be included here, but it can be found on my website, www.a-world-invisible.com, along with a host of other background information and links to some of the websites that were useful to me while I was researching for this book.

Joanna O'Neill

SCIENCE OR MAGIC?

The Hard Truth About Fact

At sixteen I finished studying science and mathematics at school and pursued literature and art instead. Then at 26 I married an engineer – all physics and Calculus. Imagine my surprise when he told me that although he spent his days working with radio waves, no-one actually knew for certain what they were.

"We can't see them or touch them," he said. "We can't even prove they exist. All we can say is that something is happening which seems to behave like this. Then we design transmitters and receivers on that basis. It's like magic, really, but it's working so far."

This did not fit my conception of a scientist. Science, after all, deals with facts, doesn't it?

My sons at fourteen were told by their chemistry teacher, "All that stuff you learned before this year? – Forget it, it's not true. This is how it really is." Two years later, about to start the sixth form, they were told by the same teacher, "That stuff you learned two years ago? – Forget it. *This* is how it really is." And later he said, "All this stuff you're learning now? When you get to university they'll tell you how it *really, really* is."

(And at university? You've guessed!)

Scientific thinking depends upon pragmatic models which emerge from hypotheses based on observations. Theories evolving from hypotheses which appear to work are often assigned the grand title "Law" – hence Newton's Laws of Motion – and it would be fair to say that a scientific Law is about as fundamentally true as any other man-made law. The model works while it predicts how physical phenomena will occur in future situations *until we find a situation it fails to predict.*

Science teachers, when using models to describe and predict physical phenomena, unfortunately often omit to tell their pupils that these are in fact models and not the Absolute Truth; or perhaps they deliberately do this in order not to confuse their innocent charges' immature brains.

So, in this way a student learns that electrons, using the Niels Bohr model, are some sort of negatively-charged lumps of matter which orbit an atomic nucleus in the same way that we understand a planet to orbit a star (and more about that later). Next, they are taught that an electron can be persuaded to part company with its atomic nucleus parent and move elsewhere, so that we can produce electric current and also so that 'shared' ownership will result in chemical reactions.

As a student progresses towards university, he or she might become aware that this simple planetary model for the electron is not entirely supported by quantum physics.

The next step is the dual-nature description of the electron, in which it sometimes appears to behave like a wave. This gives rise to the obvious question "Is it a particle or a wave?". Sometimes the answer is "Both", sometimes the answer is "Well, at times it behaves as a particle and at other times it behaves as a wave."

A better answer, rarely supplied, would be "The 'electron' is a model which enables us to predict physical phenomena. Unfortunately the model is both inexact and muddy. The particle description is simple and works well for some phenomena, but the wave description is better for certain calculations."

I guess you do need to be mindful of the maturity of your pupils before you lay that one on them.

As if this murky existence for an electron is not bad enough, a student may then find that the stationary electron must now be considered to exist everywhere in the universe *at the same time*. Not bad for a little lump of matter we cannot even see.

Personal point of view interferes too. Returning to the planetary orbit question, how correct was Galileo in asserting that the Earth orbits the Sun?

To an observer on Earth that statement is patently absurd as we see every day that the Sun rotates around the Earth. The only problem is that when using the Earth as the frame of reference, describing the motion of the Sun mathematically is pretty messy and describing the motion of the other planets is a nightmare. The maths becomes far easier if the Sun is taken as the frame of reference.

So Galileo might have been well advised to assert, "Of course the Sun rotates around the Earth, but I have a pretty neat mathematical shortcut which can quickly compute the position of the other planets. *Of course we all know this is only mathematics!"*

(And by the way, neither the Sun nor anything else is actually stationary in the galactic frame of reference.)

So where does magic fit in?

The Shorter Oxford English Dictionary (5th edition) defines 'magic' as: *"The supposed art of influencing the course of events and of producing extraordinary physical phenomena"* or *"An inexplicable and remarkable influence producing surprising results".*

That's the point just after the current model gets left behind, isn't it? As Arthur C Clarke is credited for having said, "Any sufficiently advanced technology is indistinguishable from magic".

My husband maintains that when engineers are asked to produce something unheard of which is in defiance of current knowledge and experience, most will say, "That's impossible". The more creative ones will say, "We don't know how to do that". But the creative and optimistic engineer will say, "We don't know how to do that *yet*."

What you don't know how to do (yet) often looks like magic when done by someone who does. From the 17th until the early 20th century, 'horse whisperers' were able to calm and train dangerous horses apparently by whispering the "Horseman's Word" into their ears. Well, I'm a horse whisperer, and I know that the Word had nothing to do with it.

For sure the horsemen were using eye contact and body language that the horse instinctively understands to persuade horses that they were capable, trustworthy leaders, which is what I do now. The only difference is that they protected their livelihood by whispering into the horses' ears first and telling everyone it was magic, whereas I explain what I'm doing and teach the owners to do the same.

Once you know how the trick is done, it's easy, whether understanding horse psychology or watching the Ace of Spades vanish. Point of view is paramount. It might be magical to us that a salmon can find its way back to its birth place to breed and a swallow doesn't get lost over the Atlantic, but to the salmon and the swallow it's easy-peasy. How can a dog detect that an epileptic fit is soon to happen? The dog would probably say, "Why, can't everyone?". And how could Connor pick up these visions? Same answer – the ability is just part of him because of his ancestry.

And finally, the quantum bit...

I took liberties here, but quantum computing and quantum entanglement are strange concepts and bear being messed with.

Quantum computing

Conventional computers evaluate arithmetic operations typically one after another, and current encryption systems often rely heavily on the fact that the huge number of possible combinations needing calculation would defeat even the most powerful computers working on the task for a lifetime. A "quantum computer" is proposed to have the ability to work as if it were in many possible states simultaneously and therefore able to evaluate all possible combinations in a tiny fraction of the time a conventional computer would take.

Quantum entanglement

This is the term for a strange (to say the least) phenomenon which would permit pairs of quantum particles (electrons etc.) to become "entangled". Remember this is a model, not reality! One result of this entanglement could perhaps be that teleportation becomes achievable if one quantum system takes on the state of another quantum system with which it becomes entangled. (It should be said that most experts believe that objects would not be able to move between the systems...yet.)

So that's it. In making this story I have taken snippets that I barely understand from here, other snippets from there, and mixed them up with a whole lot of What If. In my opinion, in fiction this is allowed. Do I believe in magic? No, but I sure believe in there being more things in this heaven and this earth than are dreamed of in philosophy.

Joanna O'Neill
2010

LaVergne, TN USA
27 January 2011
214216LV00005B/122/P